Paraíso Lost

Jack Polo

Black Rose Writing | Texas

ISBN: 978-1-68433-593-0
PUBLISHED BY BLACK ROSE WRITING
www.blackrosewriting.com

Printed in the United States of America
Suggested Retail Price (SRP) $19.95

Paraíso Lost is printed in Palatino Linotype

To Leslie & Hillary, the best of us all

"And thus I clothe my naked villainy .. and seem a saint, when most I play the devil."
-Wm. Shakespeare, Richard III

Paraíso Lost

Paraíso Lost

1

"Yo," Jamal said on the phone. "We still in business?"

"Which business? Selling or sleuthing?"

"Either or both."

"Last time Singer & Wade, Real Estate had a showing was three weeks ago, remember? With the Whilhorns from Kansas?"

"More like greenhorns," Jamal said. "The wife says, 'Why a home like this in Topeka would be lucky to sell for $200,000. How can you ask four million dollars for it?"

"And you said, 'Because we wanted to price it below the market.'" *Heh-heh.*

Jamal laughed and said, "She grabbed her husband and did the world's fastest U-turn out of there."

"Yep. And that's our real estate business. And since nobody's been shot or knifed in town, our private investigations are even slower."

"Mebbe we too good at stopping crime," Wade said.

Wade's a *summa cum laude* grad from Emory, so he can speak excellent English. And Spanish, French and a passable German. I do the Italian. As he tells people, "We be the Berlitz of detectives."

"Well," I said, "we almost had a job."

"Almost?"

"A guy came in and said he'd heard about us and wanted to hire us."

"Only wanted?" Wade said. "Meaning he didn't?"

"Hey, this is *my* story."

"Okay."

"So, then he asked what our rates were."

"For real estate or investigations?"

"Investigations."

"And?"

"And I told him."

"And?"

"He said, 'Your rates seem high.'"

"Only at the start," I said.

"Meaning what?" he said.

"We deliver."

"Is it negotiable?" he said.

"Yes, I can raise it."

"That's absurd," he said.

"Getting pissed," Wade interrupted.

"Seemed like it. But I didn't comment since it's hard to discuss absurdity without being stupid."

"What if I don't like the results?" he asks me.

"You can hire us again," I told him.

"If you fail, why should I hire you again?"

"Depends on how badly you want results."

"I *expect* results, that's why I would hire you. So, if you don't find her, then I shouldn't have to pay."

"I assume by *her* you mean a wife or girlfriend?"

"Neither."

"A daughter, then?"

"Isn't that's all that's left?"

"Unless you've lost a female pet."

"If you are trying to be funny, you aren't succeeding."

"I'm here all week, and let's have a hand for the band." I waited a moment, then said, "I would like to help you out, if possible. So why don't we start with the basics." I stuck my hand out for a shake, "Mister....?"

He didn't want to shake. Instead he said, "I think if you don't find her, I shouldn't have to pay."

"Then we can't work together."

"Why?"

"Because if someone doesn't want to be found, they won't be."

"Not even by you guys?"

I gave him my most dramatic sigh. "Not even by us."

"Dat be true," Wade said.

"I think he actually sneered at me and left," I continued. "And he slammed the door behind him."

"Man, you always know how to handle people," Wade said.

"I am a silver-tongued devil," I said.

I saw a shadowy form appear at the glass of the office door, and the man opened it and walked back into my office.

"But he'll be back."

"Doubt it."

"No, I have a feeling," I said, "he'll be back. Bet you a lunch on it."

"You're on," Wade said, and hung up.

The man sat back down in the same deck chair that he'd sat in before and looked at me.

"If I could tell you where she is, would you reduce your fees by half?"

"If you could tell me where she is, then our fees would double, maybe even triple."

"What?"

"If that were the case, you wouldn't need an investigation team; you'd need a family counselor."

"That's pretty harsh."

"Sleuthin' ain't pretty."

I drew our standard contract from my desk drawer and signed it. "Shall I fill in your name, mister...?"

"I want to think about it."

"Think about your name?"

"No, and I don't understand why you're so flippant about a serious issue."

"You're right, mister..."

"Finneran," he said. "Peter Finneran."

"Well, we're making progress then, Mr. Finneran," I said, and filled in his name and pushed the contract to him. I didn't want to try another handshake. I don't handle rejection well.

"This isn't correct," he said.

"What isn't?"

"The name."

"I'm sorry, you did say your name was Peter Finneran."

"Yes, but that's not who you would be working for."

"So, this is a mystery about a mystery?" I waited for him to say something, but he was suddenly very interested in the contract. "Are you going to tell me who we *might* be working for?"

"If and when it's appropriate."

"Okay."

Mr. Finneran stood up. "And even if it's a pass, I've enjoyed discussing Keynesian Economics with you."

"Is that what we were doing?"

"Yes, one component of it anyway." Then he drew himself to his full height and took a deep breath, as if he needed all of it to devastate me with his conclusion: "That of inflexible pricing."

If he had then said "Ha!" I wouldn't have been surprised. Instead he just stared at me, so I said, "Oh. I thought we were doing James Taylor's version."

"Excuse me."

"From his Song, *You Make It Easy.*"

I sang it for him, "I'll provide the satisfy, you provide the need."

He didn't wait for another chorus, shook his head and clomped and that is the appropriate word because he walked with a damn heavy step, out of my office. And he slammed the door. Again.

He'd probably gotten mad because I'd switched the words around.

Sure as hell couldn't have been my singing.

2

The best love songs I read some place are writ in blood from a broken heart.

So, when twenty minutes later Peter Finneran returned, or I think more accurately, was *pushed* back into my office by a very expensively dressed, coiffed and manicured woman and an equally impressive man, I had that forlorn feeling that like those *Lady Day* lyrics, "*Good morning, Heartache*," a whole mess of blues had just walked into my life.

Both the wife and the man waited for me to say something.

I just smiled and waited.

"Peter," the woman said.

"Uh," Finneran began, "this is.."

"Oh, for Christ's sake," the woman said.

She looked at me and smiled. And she had a great smile. Obsidian eyes. And stunning white teeth, no doubt enhanced by an expensive dentist.

"Hello," she said, with only the slightest of accents, extending her hand. "I am Oksanna Dillard."

"Matt Singer," I said and stood up and shook, "but you already know that."

She nodded and the man extended his hand. "Charles Dillard." Charles' smile was just as winning, but his handshake was much stronger. He combined the grip with two steely blue eyes that looked right at you, no blinking. Obviously, a captain of industry was Mr. Dillard.

"Nice to meet you both." I gestured to the two seats in front of my desk. I thought about getting a third one for Finneran, but screw him. You don't want to shake my hand, get your own goddamned chair.

They sat and Finneran looked around and I'm sure thought about asking for a chair but probably was too proud and just leaned against the wall.

Oksanna pulled my contract from her purse and slid it across to me. I looked at it quickly and saw that they'd filled it out completely. Then Charles handed over a check. I looked at that much slower, just to be sure.

"This is more than our usual advance."

"We expect more than usual results," Finneran couldn't help himself from saying.

"Peter," Mrs. Dillard said. Then she looked at me and smiled again. "Sorry, but Peter is very protective of us."

"Which we appreciate," Charles said.

I used to feel the same way for a pet dog but didn't tell the Dillards that; discretion being the better part of any beginning relationship; especially until the check clears.

Then I looked at the check again.

"The Dillard Bio-Genetics Foundation?"

"Yes," Charles said immediately. "I own it."

Dillard Bio-Genetics was cutting edge technology, pushing-the-envelope research and in the neighborhood of several hundred million dollars; which is a very good neighborhood.

"Has a scientist gone missing?" I said.

From the looks on their faces, I knew I was having a *Wile E. Coyote* moment: I'd run out there (or I'd run my mouth off) and was hanging in space before the anvil fell, which would have been a second behind my fall.

"What did I tell you?" Finneran said.

"Sorry," I said. "When Mister Finneran came in here, he was somewhat oblique; and now we're being hired by Dillard Bio-Genetics, a company, actually a huge company, instead of a person, so I'm just looking for clues here."

Oksanna nodded, either to confirm what I'd said, or that maybe they should have listened to Finneran. "We got a telephone call from our daughter Charlene a couple of days ago."

"Okay, and I'm only guessing here, but this was an important call?"

"Absolutely. It was the first time she'd called us in over nine months."

"I'm not sure if you folks understand what I do."

"What are you talking about?" she said.

"I'm assuming Charlene lives with her step-father or step-mother and.."

"*SEE!*" Finneran shouted, "I told you he was stupid."

"And volatile, too," I said. "So cool your jets, Finneran."

That got a snap-to-attention reaction from Finneran. And a deep furrowing of the eyebrows from Charles. I don't like to get pissed off in front of clients; especially ones like the Dillards, but stupid?

"What am I missing here?" I said.

"Charlene is our daughter," Oksanna said. "Our only child. We love her so much."

"Sorry, but the flow of information here seems to be restricted. And I'm not sure why. So, let's start with the basics. How old is Charlene?"

"Seventeen," Charles said. "This past August. On the first."

"Seventeen!" I almost jumped out of my chair, but fortunately was leaning back too far to make that effective. "And you haven't seen her in thirteen months?"

"Charlene doesn't live at home," Charles said, probably still in denial.

"Your daughter's run away."

"Oh, God," Oksanna said and gasped suddenly, a deep, sharp inhaling through her fine, narrow nose. Her black eyes gleamed even brighter now as she fought to hold back the glistening tears.

Way to go, Singer.

I opened a lower desk drawer and handed her a box of tissues. Like Jamal had said, sleuthing ain't pretty. And it is amazing how many people that hire Singer & Wade Investigations end up crying. Not that we work at causing them pain, it just comes with the turf.

Some clients for Singer & Wade Real Estate cry too. But those are tears of joy.

"Thank you," Oksanna said. She dabbed at her eyes, but not quite quick enough to stop the tears that overflowed and ran down her cheeks. "Yes, Charlene's .. she's run away." She turned to her husband, "We have to face it, Charles. Thirteen months, almost fourteen."

She turned back to me, "We need to find her before it's too late."

That was definitely a WTF statement. Your only daughter leaves home, or was abducted or worse, and more than a year later you're thinking *now* it might be too late?

"Now, just so I'm not totally out to lunch here, I'm assuming you looked for her before. Yes?"

"Of course, we looked," Charles snapped.

"But we .. *you* had to keep it private," Oksanna said. "So, the damn board wouldn't know we had problems."

"This isn't the time," Charles said.

"It's never the god damn time."

"Mister and Missus Dillard," Finneran said, "we're here about Charlene." Amazing, maybe Finneran *was* more than a fee-gouging asshole.

"So, what did Charlene say when she called?" I said, trying to get us back on point. And on the case.

"I couldn't believe it was her at first," Oksanna said. "We cried for a few moments and then when I asked her if she was okay and what did we do, she said we hadn't done anything. But that she wanted to come home and then .. and then..."

This time, no box of tissues was going to stem the flow of tears. Her head dropped into her hands and she sobbed and sobbed. Charles put a protective arm around his wife's shoulders and just waited.

I waited and looked at Finneran, whose sour expression made me think that somehow, he thought this was *my* fault.

After a few final harsh sobs, his wife quieted down, and Charles spoke: "We thought we heard Charlene cry out."

"I *did* hear her," Mrs. Dillard said and exhaled, long and deep and sad.

"And then nothing," Charles continued. "The line had gone dead."

"Naturally," Finneran jumped in, no doubt still trying to show me how unnecessary I really was, "we had the call to Mrs. Dillard's cell phone traced..." Finneran suddenly stopped as if he'd revealed secrets that we mere common private eyes shouldn't know.

"I am not without influence," Charles said. "Apparently, the call was bounced from several relay stations so it could be from anywhere."

"And, therefore, untraceable," Finneran said.

"Not so. We'll get on that. I'll need anything and everything you can give me, including, of course, photos."

Mrs. Dillard reached into her purse and came out with a manila envelope. She opened it and slid a packet of photos into her hand. I was hoping she would just hand them to me, but they were obviously too precious to her.

"Here's the best one of her," she said and slid a color photograph to me.

"Beautiful," I said. And I wasn't exaggerating. Charlene could be a teen movie star: Shiny blond hair that went below her shoulders, Icelandic blue eyes and a racy smile accented by a set of fellatial lips. And I'm sure some Hollywood producer would be charting that course for her if Charlene was around. She had an innocent, but somehow secretly lustful look that would set the producer's sexual seismographic needles wildly arcing off the charts: Eros Earthquake. All he had to do was forget she had just turned old enough to drive and that besides being against the law was also against any canon of decency. But, hey, that's show biz. And carnal thoughts are what drives Hollywood and what puts asses in the seats, gets Blu-ray and CDs purchased, and makes videos go viral.

"That was maybe a month before .. before she left," Oksanna said quietly. "We got her a new car for her birthday, a baby blue BMW 325, just like she wanted. But .. but it's never been driven."

"Not by her anyways," Charles said. "I start it up, take it around the block a few times, you know, to keep the battery charged, and so the tires don't go flat."

I nodded my approval. I wasn't sure why–whether it was that I approved his automotive acumen or that he sounded like a father who cared. And who, no doubt, lived on the quiet hope that his daughter would return and when she did, her little Bimmer would be ready to go.

Oksanna was clearly upset, so I eased the packet of photos from her and glanced through them. Charlene loved the camera. And the camera was equally smitten. The girl could not take a bad shot. Some of the photos looked professionally done; others were clearly family or selfies. But every one of them showed her to perfection.

Runaway was my first thought. Abduction and sexual predator were next. Charlene would be spotted anywhere she went. Because everywhere you went, they went too–the predators, secretly silently, appraising.

Bus depots tended to be one of their favorite lairs–when young girls and boys arrive in the land of sunshine and Hollywood dreams, looking for a new start, never suspecting they were getting a finish–being dropped into a dark cycle of depravity, abuse, and, sometimes, death.

And those would be your average looking young bait. Nothing like Charlene.But then I couldn't see Charlene at a bus depot.

I hadn't seen the Dillard's home either, but mansion clearly came to mind.

So why leave it?

The usual suspects: Mommy. Daddy. A boyfriend.

I took the easy route. For now. Once we got into the case, suspects One, and certainly number Two would be on our radar.

"Charlene have a boyfriend?"

Oksanna looked at her husband.

"There was a boy," Charles said, "Hunter Milroy. His father is on our board. He and Charlene knew each other since they were just kids."

"I don't think they were .." Oksanna hesitated, "...well, you know, *boyfriend* and *girlfriend*."

"They weren't sexually active. As far as you know."

Charles started to exhibit fatherly rage, but Oksanna just shook her head.

"Does a parent really ever know?" she said.

"We'll find out," I said.

Wah-wah. Alarms went off in Charles' head.

"Wait, you can't just go accusing Hunter like that."

"Mister Dillard, you need to decide what's more important here: Finding Charlene or keeping your fellow board members happy."

"Don't you dare accuse me of putting my business first."

"Excellent, just the answer I was hoping for. Which means, we'll ask Hunter as many questions as it takes to find the truth. And if we must ask his father, we'll do that too."

I could tell Charles wasn't thrilled with that answer, but he knew better than to protest now; especially since he'd already declared his true colors. At least the colors he'd raised in protest. Who knows, maybe under the true-blue flag of patriarchal valor, he was secretly a black-hearted pedophile who'd abused his only child.

I didn't like going down those roads, but children don't hit the road and leave home without a reason.

We spent the next hour or so going through all of the information that the Dillards could give me–what she was wearing the last time they saw her–not that anyone could reasonably expect her to still have those clothes, but you never know, maybe those were here favorite jeans–friends, classmates, teachers, neighbors, coaches–Charlene was ranked second in California in épée, third in sabre–and anyone else I thought might give us a starting point.

"I'll need all of the data your friends in high places was able to get."

Charles hesitated a moment, then nodded his agreement.

"The Dillards will give you their utmost cooperation," Finneran said. "I will call Detective Browner and set up the transfer."

"Detective Browner from BHPD?"

Finneran frowned. Apparently, he didn't approve of my knowing *his* sources.

I didn't know Detective Browner, but since the Dillards lived in Holmby Hills, having a contact in the Beverly Hills Police Department wasn't even sleuthing 101: Holmby Hills was part of their turf.

"I prefer you not contact him until I've cleared the way, "Finneran said.

"Absolutely."

But I was only giving Finneran a half day for said clearance duties.

"Can you find her?" Oksanna said.

"If she's findable, we'll do it." I gave her my most sincere look, which in this case was true: I did intend to find Charlene. But good intentions, as we know, pave that certain road to a fiery destination.

3

"This is some trip," Wade said. "How the hell you get from Holmby Hills to *Paraíso Del Mar?*"

"You know that place on Sea Star Lane?"

"Only seven homes on that street, so by *that* place, you must mean the compound."

"Emory College faculty members, rejoice! Jamal Wade's deductive powers are still intact."

"So's my size thirteen foot," Wade said.

"There you go again with those black men mythical size innuendoes again."

"Ain't no innuendo, jack, that's a fact."

"Anyway, the Dillards own the compound."

"Whoa, so this is a double deal."

"What do you mean?"

"Singer & Wade Investigations needs to do great on this job so maybe someday Singer & Wade Real Estate can sell that place. Got to be worth forty-five million."

"Hadn't thought of that."

"Mebbe you best be thinkin' 'bout changin' dey name to Wade & Singer, way I'm thinkin' so far ahead of you."

"Wade & Singer? Wade & Singer? Nope, doesn't have that nice word flow. You know, like Beauty & the Beast."

"They ever stay at the compound?" he said.

"Supposedly whenever the crush of living down the street from Aaron Spelling's former mansion and the highest income neighborhood in America gets to be too much, they come down here."

"Lots of old money in them thar Hills," Wade said, putting on a fake western drawl. "Back in the day, all of Sinatra's Rat Pack, Bogart and Bacall, Jean Harlow and even Elvis lived there."

"That was a terrible accent. And I know you Googled that."

"We Emory graduates, 'specially us *summa cum lauds*, prefer the empirical method of study."

"A woman?"

"And they say the California state university system has gone down. You get high marks for that."

"So..?"

"So a few years ago I was seeing an *au pair* who took care of some oil sheik's children."

"I don't remember any *au pair*."

"I gotta tell you every woman I see?"

"No, I have to work some time."

Wade and women–the two words just always seem to be connected; and not just because they start with a W.

"Most *au pairs* aren't much older than the children," I said.

"She was old enough."

"So, she gave you Holmby Hills' history along with..." I didn't finish.

"We schooled each other on various subjects." Wade said. "Now, speaking of working, we're supposed be on a case. In fact, the first paying job we have in months and you're wasting time speculating on my sexual prowess."

"Why would I need to speculate when you're right there testifying about it."

I opened the file on the Dillards.

"I contacted Detective Browner," I said.

"Before Finneran, I'm guessing," Wade said.

"Good guess. We wait for Finneran to decide when a good time for us to get the information is, we'll never find Charlene."

"Browner any help?"

"Pretty minor. Their trace couldn't go too far since it had to be under the radar."

"They get anything?"

"They triangulated that the call could have come from just over the Cahuenga Pass in the Valley and to downtown L.A."

"That's a big triangle," Wade said. "Might as well be the moon."

"I'd take the moon."

"What?"

"You can see the moon, can't see all that territory in the triangle."

"I bet that joke was big in fourth grade."

"I think it was junior high."

Wade shook his head slightly, his dreads shifting back and forth, "I'll make a couple of calls down to Parker Center, see if Famous Ramos has anything."

Detective Juan Ramos was a dedicated, hard core LAPD detective Wade and I knew from years back. He'd gotten the nickname from a pimp he'd busted who'd said, "Ramos, man, you gonna be famous. You busted Big Tiny! Yeah, Famous Ramos, you be just like that cookie man."

"Except I don't crumble," said Ramos as he handcuffed Big Tiny.

"Famous is SIS, wouldn't someone from Juvies be better?"

"Maybe, but somehow, my gut's saying this is going to be a special investigation, more than a juvenile runaway."

"Okay. I've already called Tommie Shea Shoh."

"And," Wade said and shifted into his best Ray Charles sibilant voice, "if Tommie Shea Shoh..."

"One of these days you're going to do that in front of her and Tommie's going to kick your behind."

"She may be six feet, but I think I can take her," Wade said. "Maybe even two out of three."

"Tommie never needs to resort to violence. She'll just destroy you electronically."

Tommie is six feet of stunning Eurasian female whose angular cheekbones below enormous black eyes used to beckon at you from *Vogue, Mademoiselle, Harper's* and another half-dozen European magazines devoted to high *couture*. Sometime during those days, she met an eastern European billionaire with ties, it was said, to the

Rossiyskaya Mafiya, and illegal arms trading and drug running, and had a child with him. No one's ever uncovered the truth. Partly because it's really none of anyone's business; and partly, but mostly, because Tommie is flat-out the best electronics surveillance expert I've ever met. I think between the modeling and the child she secretly did a brief stint at NSA.

"Duly noted," Wade said. "Although she might think it's cute." Wade shifted in his chair and just looked at me.

"What?" I said.

"The check."

"What check?"

And then I got it. The advance we'd received from the Dillards.

"You're expecting to be paid on this job?"

"No. I just gits my monies from de massah becuz of mah good buck looks." He waited a moment. "An' sometimes so's I don't hafta let de white womens see mah ebony body."

"I'll give you your check," I said, "*only* if you stop with that Uncle Tom foolery."

"Oh," Wade said, "mastah Singa done made a word play. Us darkies jus' gone haf to tries harder to stay in de game."

I removed the check from a desk drawer and handed it to Wade.

"No problem," Wade said as he was about to pocket the check and then looked at the amount. "This is *half?*"

"They gave us a huge advance."

"Meaning they expect it to be more complicated and take a while."

"Not according to Oksanna. She wants her baby home *now!*"

"So, why'd they wait so long to get serious about finding her?"

"I think that's the real mystery in this case."

"You said the wife was upset and called the husband out."

"She was definitely unhappy."

"A father's too worried about what his board members think to try and find his daughter? What kind of father's that?"

"A rich one. And despite of what Fitzgerald said, they *are* very different than you and me."

"But this is his flesh and blood, he's supposed to love her for Christ's sake."

"A father's love isn't always guaranteed," I said.

"Don't let your pops hear you say that," Wade said. "He'll pop you one."

"And then tell me how sorry he was, but that it was for my own good."

4

"I would never say that," my father said an hour or so later after Wade and I had met him for dinner at Kincaid's and outlined the case to him. "If I had to pop you one, you had it coming. There's no altruism in a smack, it's pretty much straight out aggression." He smiled and took a long hit from his vodka and tonic. "But then, since I never hit you even once in your life, it's all a moot point."

"I never gave you a reason to hit me."

My father laughed. "You really think that?"

"Sure."

"So, wiping out the side of the Mercedes when you were being so nice to me and taking it up to the Shell station to fill it up, that wasn't a time?"

Crap, I'd forgotten about that.

Or blotted it from my memory.

"That was an accident." This time I took a drink and debated whether to press my point. "But you did smack me once."

"I did not."

"You did. And I had it coming."

"Oooh," Wade said, "this I gotta hear. Matt Singer confessing."

"It was when I told Mom to..."

"I remember," my dad said, cutting me off. "And you *did* deserve it."

He looked at Wade. "Matt kept ignoring his Mother's requests to do his chores or something like that and she told him if he didn't he couldn't go to some dance."

"No, it was Rod Chamber's birthday party." Wade looked at me funny. I shrugged. "It was *the* party of fifth grade. Locals still talk about it."

"So, when the time came and Matt couldn't go, he told his mother to fuck off."

Wade grimaced, and then told my dad, "I hope you decked him."

"No, it was worse than that," I said.

And the moment hung there while they tried to figure out what could be worse than getting knocked on your ass by your father.

"You slapped me in the face." And I involuntarily put my hand to my cheek. "And the humiliation hurt a million times more than the pain."

My father's eyes blinked a few times. I don't think he was teary, but I think he was slightly ashamed.

Way to go Singer.

"But that's okay," I said. "I was a jerk. And a slap across the chops for giving lip was appropriate."

"Maybe." My father knocked back the rest of his drink. "Sorry, Matt."

Wade put his massive arm around my dad's shoulders. "Nothing to be sorry about, Mario. You made Matt the man he is today." Then Wade leaned in like he was saying something confidential but made sure he said it loud enough so I could hear, "Actually, a couple more shots would've have made him even better. Taken out some of that attitude."

"You really think her father..." my dad hesitated, not that he's squeamish about sexual matters; in fact, women still find him highly attractive; even at age 72.

But a father's sexual advances on his daughter was, "*Un crimine contro la famigila. Un tabù diabolico.*" 'A crime against the family. An evil taboo."

And then, just to make sure we were crystal clear on it: "*Un uomo gradice quello, è come un cane pazzo che dovrebbe essere colpo.*" 'A man like that is like a mad dog that should be shot.'

"We don't have anything yet," I said. "But a kid living in the epicenter of luxury needs an extraordinary reason to make her think that being out on the street is better than a twenty-eight thousand-foot mansion."

"That's how big their house is?" my dad said. "Jesus, she could have hidden in one of the back bedrooms and they'd have never found her."

The barkeep came by and asked us if we'd like another round.

"Not me," Wade said, "I have to get home and get my beauty sleep. Got to look my best for the people we gone be harassing tomorrow."

"What's that mean?" my dad said.

"We're interviewing neighbors of the Dillards," I said.

"You think they'll answer the door?" my dad said. "And that's even before they get a look at you two." He smiled and finished his drink, set it on the bar with a loud clink.

"We be relying on the element of surprise," Wade said. "But we won't be too surprised if no one opens the door. We're mostly doing it to check out the turf and see what twenty-eight thousand square feet looks like."

You realize," my dad said, "my house would fit into theirs ten times! Why the hell's anybody build a house that big?"

"Same reason you got three girlfriends, Mario Singer," Wade said. "If you can get away with it, why not?"

"Speaking of your house," I said, "we still on for tomorrow?"

"Yes. They're scheduled to come around ten. It'll take them a couple of hours to tent it, so my guess is they'll start fumigating after lunch."

"We'll be up in the rich folks' neck of the woods," I said, "and you've got a key, so just let yourself in."

"I probably won't be there until late afternoon." He gave us one of his sly grins, so I knew he was waiting to drop a bomb on us. "Got a lunch date."

Wade smiled. He knew my dad's tricks too.

"You mean three ain't enough?" Wade said.

"I think my bench is strong enough," my dad said, "but whenever a super star becomes available, you'd be a fool to not try and get them into your lineup."

I paid for our drinks. "So, how'd you meet this one? An internet dating site?"

My dad looked at me like as much as he'd tried, I was truly a disappointment to him.

"You ever see some of the women on those sites? You know the photos they put up are probably from a decade earlier and even then, they didn't look so hot."

"C'mon, Dad, I've seen some of them and they look pretty good."

"Yeah, but you're looking at women in their thirties and forties. I'm starting at the half-century mark."

"And even then, you're giving away almost two decades," Wade said, smiling. We both like to give my dad shit. Not because he deserves it, but because he loves to fire back. Keeps him alert. Not that much ever got past him, no matter what his age.

"You're right," I said. "So, what the hell age do you put?"

"I don't put any age because I don't need to go on some freakin' internet loser website and read how some fiery redhead who loves walks on the beach in the moonlight' is looking for her true Romeo to spend a lifetime of thrills together. I'm not that far gone yet."

"So, where did you meet Ms...?"

"Carmen. Carmen Rosales. And it was a business meeting."

"Yeah, monkey business," said Wade.

"Okay, pops, we're waiting."

"Carmen was the rep for the termite company." He shrugged and gave us another of his smiles.

"So, she was there talking about gassing the little chewers and you stepped on the gas and somehow managed to wrangle a date."

"I didn't wrangle anything. It was *Senorita* Rosales' idea."

We headed for the exit.

"So little Miss Rosales is what? A rookie sales rep and was so grateful you gave her an order that she acquiesced and said okay to lunch? Pops, you're slipping."

"And you've once again underestimated your father." He held the door for Wade and me. "Carmen isn't just a rep; she owns the company. Has eight trucks, thirty-two employees."

"You're the one that said rep. Didn't he Wade?"

"He did. But then I think your father was just trying to be slick."

"You don't try to be slick," my dad said. "You're either slick or you're not."

"Well, being Eye-talian," I said, "you're already a little oily anyway."

"Mind your manners, *son.*"

"Let's see," said Wade, "eight trucks, thirty-two employees, I'm guessing not *Senorita*, but *Senora* Rosales."

My dad looked at Wade and you could tell he was slightly uncomfortable. Because he knew what was coming next.

"So, Carmen either got the business from *Senor* Rosales through a divorce or as the surviving spouse."

"How the hell'd you figure that out?" my dad said.

"We Emory graduates is truly brainiacs."

I saw Wade turn away to hide his big grin. So, I knew there was something more to what he'd just said.

"And also bullshit artists," I said. "You've already met her."

Wade turned up both palms in a gesture of surrender.

"She came by your house to give you an estimate."

"You had me going there for a moment," my dad said.

"A moment's pretty good. You being the *Don Juan* of *Paraiso Del Mar.*"

"And damn tough to get much past," my dad said.

"Even at his advanced shelf-life. Both real and internet variety," I said.

My dad made a fist and shook it like Jackie Gleason used to threaten Alice: *One of these days. POW!* And meant it about as much.

"So?" my dad said to Wade, "what do you think?"

Wade smiled and said, "*Senora* Rosales is *muy hermoso.*"

"What did you expect?" my dad said.

5

"I wasn't counting on seeing red," I said.

"Rose-red for Rosales," Wade said. He pointed at a gleaming white termite company truck parked next to the curb. On its doors, painted in a cursive Coca-Cola logo style, with rose letters, outlined in soft blue was: *Rosales Exterminators*.

My dad's house was covered in a red termite tent. I drove past it on our way to Holmby Hills because I told my dad I'd check on it for him while he stayed at my place.

"I don't ever remember seeing those before," I said. "And I sure the hell would have noticed."

"That's because the lovely *Senora* Rosales is new in town. I think her company just started doing work here."

"Why's that?"

"Who did your termite work, you remember?"

I thought for a moment. "Mulveny's Termite. Hell, that was five, six years ago."

"Right. Back then and up until a couple of months ago, if you needed termite work, Mulveny's is who you got. Because Greg Mulveny was an old friend of our dear departed mayor..."

"Reed Lockhart."

"Exactly. So, when Reed passed, so did his old boy network of favors and deals."

Reed hadn't just passed.

He'd been shot by his best friend of forty years, Chief Ben Black.

And then he'd died a second time when he burned to death in a single car accident that Black had staged as a cover-up.

The discovery of that cover-up had come from Singer & Wade Investigations.

It had ended violently and badly when the Chief and I had struggled over his .38 and he'd been shot in the femoral artery of his right thigh. That was the official press release. The truth was Ben and I had struggled over his .38 and somehow the gun had fired and shot him in the part of his body he was most proud of: His dick. Ben was so well-endowed, he swung like a pendulum, hence his nickname of Big Ben.

He bled to death in the mayor's house in the same spot where Reed had died.

Closure could be poetic.

"So back to the termites," Wade said. "I'd say things have really opened up for new tradesmen or trades*women* like Mrs. Rosales."

"Who is making a killing, termite-wise and money-wise," I said as I turned on to Spinnaker Street and pointed out another home halfway up the block also tented in red.

"I'm not so sure about the money part," Wade said. "Her rates were about fifteen percent lower than what I remember Mulveny's being."

"Fifteen percent's probably the vig that Mulveny was paying Lockhart to be the preferred vendor for all of his real estate clients. "

Wade looked at me before he spoke. "You think Leah knows about all the shit her dad was into?"

"I don't know. Hard to tell. She's pretty much left all of that to her attorneys."

Leah Lockhart, living proof that all those Beach Boys songs about the perfect girls of summer were still true nearly a half-century later. Leah had long blond hair, huge sparkling blue eyes, and a lithe, athletic figure with hidden assets. She also had financial assets of seventy, eighty million dollars that she'd inherited from her father.

About a year ago, Leah and I went to dinner.

A few days later we went to bed and have been together since that night.

But there are some secrets between us.

Secrets that I can never share.

About her father Reed.

About the years before she was born.

About the affair he'd had with a beautiful Spanish woman, Mayleen Santiago and gotten her pregnant.

And wasn't going to marry her.

And that Mayleen's brother Miguel had beat the shit out of Reed for it.

And that Ben Black had killed Miguel in retaliation.

And that he and Reed had buried Miguel's body.

And that the discovery of the bones four decades later when the foundations for a new building had been excavated had set in motion a wave of trouble that hit our little beach town like a *tsunami*–including the assassination of the mayor and the accidental shooting of the chief of police.

And that Mayleen had given birth to and raised Reed's Son, Ritchie.

Which meant Leah had a secret half-brother.

"What Leah knows isn't anything close to the truth," I said.

"Sometimes," Wade said, "it's a good thing to not know *every* thing."

"Especially when it comes to something like her father's mania for power."

I made the last turn out of town and headed east for the freeway.

"You ever gonna tell her about Ritchie?" Wade said.

"Not my place to do that." I blipped the accelerator on the *Snake,* my Porsche-eating, Carroll Shelby tricked out Ford. Yeah, I know, retarded adolescence. But damn, having more than five hundred horses under the hood–actually a herd of Mustangs, couldn't be beat when you were in a hurry. Or when you wanted to prove to some metrosexual asshole that he had spent about eighty thousand more than necessary for speed, comfort, and a damn great set of wheels.

"So, what happens if she finds out?" Wade said,

"And then finds out that I knew about it?"

"Yes."

"I guess we'll deal with that if or when it happens. What the hell would you do?"

"Growing up with your family's hard enough. Every family's got their secrets, their battles. But to suddenly find out your father, who you worshipped–and for Leah, her father damn near walked on water–to find out that he not only screwed around on your mother but sired a child too, that could blow you away. I don't know how you deal with that."

"Especially since her father's gone, so she can't talk to him about it."

6

"So, you want to talk to the father first, or the mother?" Wade asked an hour later as we pulled onto the long circular driveway of the Dillard's mansion.

"I think we talk to the tour guide first. Damn, look at the size of this place."

"It looks a little like Tara from *Gone With The Wind.*"

Wade was right. I'd never seen so much white house, except the one in D.C.

"Hell, maybe Miz Scarlett done be openin' de door," Wade said in a slow Uncle Remus drawl.

"You do Butterfly McQueen and I'll shoot you."

"Lawd, lawd, de massah done git angry again at us po' coloreds," he said and got out of the car. He stood there and swiveled his head left, then right to take in the enormous long front of the mansion. "Four columns," he said. "Pretty impressive. And I know it's two stories, but that roof looks higher than any building code."

"How do you know about Holmby Hills building codes?"

"The *au pair* spoke to me of other things."

"Koo-koo-ka-choo."

"What?"

"It was the walrus from Lewis Carroll's *The Walrus and The Carpenter*, who spoke of other things and it was the walrus, from the Beatles, that did the koo-koo-ka-choo."

Wade looked me like I had lost my mind.

At least he didn't say, "...and the walrus was Paul."

"What do you think?" I said quickly to change the subject. "Knock or ring?"

In the center of a twelve-foot high front door painted matte black was a massive lion's head door knocker in shiny brass without a fingerprint on it.

"You think they'd hear that in this place?" Wade said. "Even if it is a damn big knocker?"

I shook my head and pushed the doorbell. From somewhere deep inside the house, the SC fight Song chimed musically.

"Doctor Dillard is a Trojan?" Wade said. "Why doesn't that surprise me?" Wade made a face like liver bile had scalded his throat. "God, I hate that song."

"Really?"

"Well...no, actually I do like it. *When* it's played at the Coliseum for a football game. Then it's great. But in somebody's foyer? No."

The front door swung open and a Spanish woman smiled at us.

"*Si?*" she asked Softly.

A very pretty Spanish woman.

Which is the testosterone-fueled, Pavlovian trigger for Wade to switch personalities in a heartbeat—instantly transforming from a grump who's against too much college spirit into a smooth-talking Prince Charming.

"*Hola, senorita,*" he said in impeccable, Castellan -accented Spanish. "*Perdónenos para molestarle.*"

"Oh, no," she said in impeccable English, "you are not disturbing me at all. You are Mister Singer" she said to me and held out her hand, which was soft, slender and yet quite firm. "And you," she definitely smiled at Wade, "can only be Mister Wade."

Wade took her hand in both of his, turned on the 1,000-watt smile and said, "At your service..?"

"Maria. Herrera." She opened the door wider and stepped aside. "Please."

"Herrera," Wade said, showing off, "comes from the Spanish *herrería*. Meaning the place where ironwork is made."

"Oh," Maria laughed, "impressive. Yes, my great grandfather was a blacksmith in the Villa of Pedraza." She softly shut the door behind us.

"Pedraza?" Wade said, "that's somewhere in...Leon, right?"

"*Sí, sí!*" Maria was genuinely impressed. "It is in the province of Segovia, in Castile, which is next to Leon, Spain. You have spent time there, Mister Wade?"

"Please, call me Jamal."

When Wade's in this mind-set, I just stand back and watch the show.

"*Tristemente*, no, I have never been. But it is a journey I hope to make one day."

"Oh, but you must. There are so many beautiful things to see in Pedraza"

"And *from* Pedraza too."

Okay, enough was enough.

"The Dillards are expecting us," I said.

Wade shot daggers at me, but I pretended not to see.

Maria smiled politely and turned to escort us down the hallway.

"*Tristemente?*" I said quietly.

"Means sadly. Which is an apt description for you and the spark of romance."

"*Au revoir Tristement?*"

"That's French, but nice try."

"It was also a movie, although that was called *Bonjour Tristesse*."

"Stop," Wade said, although a little too loud because Maria turned and looked at us, not sure what was going on behind her.

"Ah, Matt and Jamal," said Oksanna, coming up to us from a side hall.

She shook my hand and then shook Wade's. He didn't take her hand in both of his. This was either to show Maria she was special, or that while Oksanna was extremely attractive, she was also married, so hands off (or at least both hands).

Maria left us, but not before she gave Wade a wonderful smile, and we sat down in a huge room that had floor-to-ceiling French doors that opened out to a lush garden bursting with a myriad of flowers in full bloom.

"Can I have Maria get you something to drink?" Oksanna asked.

We both declined.

"Is your husband here?" I said.

"No. Unfortunately, Charles got called to the office. Some trouble with a research project."

"When will he be back?"

Oksanna shifted, clearly not comfortable with this line of questioning. "I don't know really. Sometimes he's only gone for an hour or two; sometimes he doesn't come home until midnight."

"Would it be okay if we visited him at his office?" Wade said.

"Why would you have to do that?"

"Gathering information in the beginning stages of a case is always critical," I said. "And it's important that we talk to both parents in a case like this. "

"I can call him and see if he has time," Oksanna said. "But when it comes to the Foundation, nothing else seems to matter." She looked at us, the sub-text of her statement hanging in the silence, but she rallied quickly. "But I'm sure he'd make an exception if this helps find Charlene."

"Excellent. We'll see him later then," Wade said.

"We've looked through the search materials by your former people," I said, "and, well, frankly, they aren't worth much."

"Pretty minimal," Wade added.

"I wasn't happy with them either," Oksanna said. She looked at the door where Maria had gone, then reached under the skirt of the sofa where she was sitting and pulled out a manila folder. "Charles doesn't know about this, I paid for it with my own money." She handed the folder to me. "If you could look at that later?"

"Absolutely."

"Anything in there you can tell us right now?" Wade said.

Oksanna shrugged. "Lots of people *thought* they saw her, or someone like her, but in the end, nothing. It's like she vanished."

"But you did get that call."

"Oh, yes. It was so...oh my God, I was so excited .. and so nervous...and so worried. And then when there was that yelp. And I know Charles doubts it, but I *know* my daughter's voice and she definitely cried out."

"Do you think someone .." I hesitated to finish, but it was necessary. "Perhaps, maybe she slipped, or bumped her foot."

"No. I'm so sick thinking about it, but I think someone *hit her!*"

"Before Charlene left," Wade said, "was there anything going on that, now, maybe you think might have been some trouble? You know, like her boyfriend…"

"Hunter. Hunter Milroy. No, like I said, I'm pretty sure they weren't having sex. But what parent ever really knows?"

"After Charlene was gone for a few days, "I said, "you talked to Hunter and..?"

"We talked to him, his parents, obviously the police. Hunter was genuinely worried, but no help really. He'd seen Charlene four days before she was gone. He would come here, and they would study together in the den."

There was a soft chirping of Wade's cell. He was as surprised as any of us. He checked the caller ID and immediately stood up. "Sorry," he said, "I have to take this." As he went into the hall, Wade glanced at me and I couldn't read his face; except that he looked worried. And Wade *never* looks worried.

Oksanna looked at me as if I had an answer.

I decided to keep questioning.

"No trouble with Hunter, nothing with her friends. From what you've said, she was doing fine at school; so that leaves...home."

Oksanna's face showed another surprise. "Home?"

"Yes. Family problems are usually the catalyst for personal problems."

"Why that's .." Oksanna didn't know what to say. Perhaps no one had ever suggested that there might be trouble in paradise.

"Beyond the traditional mother daughter issues, how were things between you two?"

"Charlene and I got along wonderfully. Sometimes other mothers would ask me what was I doing? Because she and I never argued, I mean, it was wonderful. I felt so lucky, so blessed."

"And Charlene and her father?"

But before Oksanna could answer, Wade came back into the room.

"I hate to interrupt, but something's come up." He looked at me and this time there wasn't any confusion: We had trouble.

Oksanna and I got up. I shook her hand and apologized and followed Wade toward the front door.

"What the hell's going on?" I said.

"Not here," he said.

Maria came to the front door, "Leaving so soon?"

"Yeah," was all Wade said, plowing straight ahead, his mind obviously somewhere else or time traveling to where we were heading; because he missed the doe-eyed look Maria gave his retreating back.

"I'm sure he'll be in touch," I said to Maria quickly.

Wade was already in my car and buckled up by the time I opened my door.

"You mind telling me what's going on?" I said. "We're supposed to be looking for Charlene."

7

"I think they've found her," said Wade as we drove out.

He held out his cell phone.

On the screen was a pretty blond girl that *could* pass for Charlene, except her face was swollen and distorted. But then death does that to you.

"Famous sent this," Wade said, his voice quieter than usual. "Last night I'd emailed him a couple of photos we had of Charlene along with the file, then we talked, and he wasn't too optimistic. The forty-eight hours thing and all. And especially it being fourteen months." Wade slammed the armrest–the *whoomp* echoing through the interior. "And now he calls and sends this."

I looked at the cell phone photo again, "If that is Charlene, how the hell did she die?"

"From childbirth?"

"What?"

"If it's Charlene–and this sure as hell looks like it is, she gave birth to a baby boy last night at Angels Mercy Center."

"Where's Angels Mercy?"

"You ready for this? It's a private care facility over on Whitley. Not twenty minutes away."

I swooped around a silver Explorer.

"Or maybe fifteen."

I made it in about eleven minutes, only running one yellow light that was just turning red. Luckily the only cops we saw were heading in the opposite direction.

Angels Mercy Center was a two-story building from the 1950s that would be described, by the sharp real estate agents as, "Some possible deferred maintenance."

The side parking lot was small and had once required visitors to pay, but now the guard-gate arm was broken, its orange and white striped paint faded and peeling. The lot was just as bad–rutted and filled with pot holes as its uneven asphalt had been shaked and baked over the decades: cooked during the heat and intense sunshine of the hot summers of Los Angeles, and cooled in the short rainy season Angelinos always felt was too long, even though it's usually only a few weeks. Add an annual small earthquake or two and you had a parking lot that could double for a moto-cross racecourse.

There were a few cars in the lot, but two of them caught my attention: a lime green 1970 Plymouth GTX muscle car that looked like it just rolled out of the showroom. And next to it–an LAPD van with a blue stripe.

"There's Famous' ride," I said.

"Yeah, and the long dark ride to the morgue," Wade said, surprisingly down in his mood. A mood I rarely saw in Wade. This case had affected him more than I would have guessed.

I parked close to the building and we got out and headed for the entrance.

Just then the main doors opened, and two city techs came out pushing a gurney that was carrying a somber black body bag. Right behind the techs was a tall, impeccably dressed, young man. He clocked us and maintained his position behind the techs.

"And that pretty boy got to be Famous' new partner," said Wade. He stepped in front of the techs and held up a hand. "Excuse me."

Immediately Pretty Boy stepped up and was in Wade's space.

"Police business. Move out of the way. Now, sir."

"We need to check out the young girl in there."

For a moment, Pretty Boy was off balance: How did *this guy* know there was a young girl in the bag?

Wade kept him off balance.

"I'm going to reach into my pocket, nice and slow, and bring out my cell and show you a picture."

"No, you are not. You are going to move aside. And I mean right now."

The two techs looked at Wade and Pretty, then at each other. Oh, shit.

Wade reached inside for his cell and Pretty went for his inside shoulder holster.

Wrong move, but especially with Wade.

He trapped Pretty's gun hand against his chest with his left hand and locked it down, then brought his cell up to Pretty's face with his right hand–just as Pretty swung with his left and got blocked hard.

"GONZO!"–that was another thing Famous was famous for: He could be freakin' loud. Darth Vader on steroids. His voice hit like a Sonic boom.

"WHAT THE FUCK?" Famous strode up to us and whacked Pretty on the back of his head with a four-knuckle rap. Ouch.

Wade had moved back out of the danger zone.

"Jesus, Sarge, what the hell?" Pretty said.

"You drawing down on two citizens?" Famous said.

"They were impeding police procedure."

"And what exactly was that?"

"They wanted to see inside the bag."

"To which you said...?"

"No. They're not authorized."

"Oh, and you know this how?"

Now Pretty was in free-fall. He opened his mouth to explain, then realized he wasn't sure, so gaped a couple of times like a fish out of water, which he truly was right now.

"Jamal Wade," Famous said and moved his hand towards Pretty, "*Estban* Gonzales. Or Gonzo as I like to call him. Although I should be calling him *mierda*."

"No problem," Wade said, and extended his hand to Gonzo, who took it reluctantly.

"And this is Matt Singer." I bumped fists.

Then Famous shook hands with Wade and me.

"We're going to be needing Doctor Benson," Famous said. He waited a moment and stared at Gonzo. "Like right now."

"What?" Gonzo said and pointed at himself. "Me?"

Famous gestured with his hands out, as in supplication, and Gonzo turned on his heels and stomped back to the hospital.

"Rookies," Wade said.

"Yeah," said Famous.

"Gonzales," I said. "Wasn't your last partner also a Gonzales?"

"Good memory, Matt. Yeah. Antonio. Except he wasn't a Gonzo. He actually knew how to follow orders. He's doing okay. They got him teamed with Stabler out in Van Nuys, give him a little slower pace for his OTJ."

"Thanks for doing this," I said.

"I don't know whether there's any real thanks in it. Wade sent me those photos and a few hours later we get a call from the hospital and well…" He stopped, puffed out his cheeks and let out a long whoosh of air. He nodded at one of the techs, "Open the bag, please."

Things got suddenly quiet and the zipper sounded like a rip in the fabric of time as we waited to see what would emerge from the darkness of that rubberized tomb.

Death doesn't become you. In death you *don't* look like you did in life. Because, moronic as it sounds, you have no life. It's just your husk, your *former* you. And no great lines from Shakespeare or Milton or the Bible came to me when I looked down at the young, but still beautiful girl laying in the body bag.

"Shit," Wade and I almost said it simultaneously.

It *was* Charlene Dillard.

Wade opened the folder with her photos, but he didn't really need to check.

Then Wade did something I'd never seen him do: He caressed her cheek so softly and then looked away at the doorway where Gonzo had gone.

"She was full term?" I asked.

"Yeah," Famous said. "With the gift of youth."

"Okay, it's a freak thing that she dies in childbirth, but why's she going downtown?"

Famous didn't say anything, just gently reached into the bag and slowly turned Charlene's head. "Because they found this." He pointed to a small spot at the back of her neck where her hair had been shaved away. Even I could see the swelling at the occipital bone.

"Somebody hit her?"

"I'll let the doc explain it," Famous said. He turned and we watched as the doctor, probably an intern from his youthful look, walked toward us, Gonzo trailing behind, a puppy with his tail between his legs.

"Norm Benson," he said, shaking my hand and then Wade's.

I looked at his name tag: Chief Resident. I had seriously underestimated Benson's age, or his abilities.

"So, she didn't die in childbirth," Wade said.

"Technically, she did."

"I don't understand," I said.

"She died *in* childbirth, but not *from* childbirth. In other words, she delivered that beautiful baby boy that's in our nursery, but the delivery didn't kill her. She died from a stroke, no doubt exacerbated by the strain of delivery, but already set in motion by the blow to her head."

"Had to be a blow and not a fall?" Wade said. And then quickly added, "I'm just covering all the bases."

Doctor Benson maneuvered Charlene's skull carefully.

"It's hard to fall and hit that precise angle. Not impossible, but difficult. So, I checked further and found damage to the *foramen magnum*, that's the large opening through which the nerve fibers from the brain pass and enter the spinal column. It was really just a matter of time."

"So, the blow to her head could have generated a clot?" I said.

"Precisely," said Benson. "If she could have come here right away, we could have saved her. But without any knowledge, with the effects from the blow, it was just a matter of time."

"So, the rapist could be a killer too?" I said.

8

"You think he'll ever know his father?" Wade said.

We were staring through the nursery glass at a beautiful baby boy.

"Too far down the road to figure that one out," I said.

Famous and Gonzo had left after the van drove off with Charlene's body, then Doctor Benson had taken us into the hospital. Where we got a big surprise.

The inside was immaculate, high tech and easily the match of UCLA Medical Center, Cedars-Sinai, or SC's University Hospital. The lobby's marble floors gleamed despite bearing more than a half-century of traffic. The main admitting desk was behind a clean, sparkling wall of glass (probably bullet-proof), and the family waiting area was quietly decorated with tasteful and very comfortable-looking furniture.

Benson led the way past the admissions desk and nodded at the nurse behind the glass; and as we approached a set of electronically guarded doors, they quietly hissed open and we walked into another immaculate area. On the right was another wall of glass–the nursery, where we'd gone and were now standing.

We watched a nurse pick up the baby and carry him to the changing station.

"He's a specimen," Doctor Benson said. "All vital signs not only good, but robust." He looked at me, "It's like she put all of her young life into making sure he made it."

There was a lot of truth in what he'd said.

Charlene had staggered in last night, her dress covered in blood, carrying a bundle. There weren't very many people in the waiting room, but they all freaked.

"Help me, please, my baby," Charlene said. She fell to her knees, then slowly collapsed to her side, making sure the bundle didn't hit the floor.

Two aides leaped over the counter to help.

"Oh, my God!" shouted one of the aides. "We have an infant!" He started to lift it and realized it was still connected by its umbilical cord to its mother. He held the baby while the other aide administered CPR. Other hospital staff came, they got Charlene into the ER, cut the cord, stabilized mother and infant and tried to figure out what the hell had just happened and called the police.

Two patrolmen had arrived, but there wasn't anything they could do to identify the young mother and were reduced to taking down the scant information and leaving their cards with the usual call us if anything changes statement.

Things were looking good through the night. But in the morning, Charlene died. Benson had examined her, found evidence of foul play, and called downtown. Then this afternoon, Famous had called us.

"How often does a mother die in childbirth nowadays, Doctor?" I said.

"There were two thousand, four hundred and two live births to teens in the County last year. Zero mothers died from having a baby."

"We checked every cab company around here. None of them reported picking up anyone and driving to the hospital or near it."

"Uber, maybe?" the doctor said.

"Nope. So, she goes into labor, how far could she walk?"

"Hard to say, we could never know her determination, which was obviously very strong. But I'd say, maybe three miles tops."

"I'll call Famous," I said.

The nurse had finished changing the baby and held him up to the glass.

"Now that's a beautiful baby," Wade said.

Doctor Benson smiled at the baby, "I wonder why she didn't call 9-1-1?"

"Maybe she didn't have a phone," I said. "Or was afraid to use it."

That must have set Benson to thinking. After a moment he said, "Girl that young, I'm sure you've already considered the fact that, terrible as it sounds, her father might be the father."

"Yes," I said.

"Or that the father might not be old enough to drive," said Wade.

"Detective Ramos said you had contact information for the parents?" Doctor Benson said.

"Yes. We gave it to Famous. That's officially his job."

"Famous?" Doctor Benson said.

"Just a nickname we have for Detective Ramos. Long story."

"Aren't they all?" the Doctor said. "And this one's going to be a stunner."

"Yes. First, he has to tell them that their daughter's dead, perhaps murdered. And that they're now grandparents."

9

"The loss of a child will be more devastating than the joy from the arrival of a grandchild," my dad said.

And he said it without a moment's hesitation and with the immutable gravity as if he'd just explained gravity: This is a law.

"I guess," I said.

We were having a late lunch at The Source, one of the newer restaurants in town. Wade and I were going to see the Dillards this evening after they'd had some time to absorb the fatal news.

"No guessing about it," my dad said. "There is no more horrible loss for a parent than to have to bury their child. No matter from what cause or what age." He took a long hit on his beer. "I feel sorry for the Dillards. Their lives will never be the same, no matter how much money they have. And I hate to say it, even if their little grandson's the most terrific kid in the world, there'll always be a melancholy tinge to that relationship."

This was like a sermon from my father. And totally unlike him. At least unlike anything I'd ever known about him and this subject.

"You're rather serious about this."

He looked at me and, god damn, his eyes grew bright. He blinked rapidly and turned away for a moment.

"Dad? What is it?"

"Nothing, nothing."

"You sure?"

He signaled the waiter to bring us two more drinks, then looked at me for a long moment. I wasn't sure what to say.

'Hey, pops, c'mon, this is Matt. Our *sesto senso* works all the time. And mine's sounding klaxon horns. What is it?"

"*Sesto senso eh?* You remember some *lingua Italiana*. Your grandmother would be happy."

"I'm waiting."

My father took a deep hit on his drink and then a deep breath and said, "I .. this is .. I've never told you .. nobody knows about this except your mother of course and me." He shrugged, still not sure how to begin.

This *wasn't* my dad.

He started...and stopped. And started and stopped again.

"Dad, what? Please."

"Your mother was always a lot stronger than me," he said. "And more polite. So, she didn't want to burden anyone with it." He looked away and then back to me. "You had a sister, Matt."

"What?"

No way.

No fucking way.

I didn't hear that.

"Only for three months." He took a deep breath, his words getting shrill as he fought to choke down his tears and pain. "Alison. Alison Leigh."

"Dad, what? I..." I didn't know what to say.

"You were barely four, so there's no way you'd remember. She was so beautiful, little Ali, and she fought so hard. But her little heart, it .. it wasn't formed quite right and she couldn't get enough blood and..."

"Oh, Dad." I wanted to come around the table and put my arm around him, but that didn't seem quite right; especially since I knew he had more to say.

A lot more to say.

"I'm so sorry."

"I'm sorry, too. My little *bambina*. And I'm sorry that we had to lie to you, but your mother felt you were too young and that in time, well, it'd pass."

The waiter came with our drinks and my dad waited until he was gone.

"But it never passes," he said. "Never. When you lose a child, you've joined a Society you never would have imagined becoming part of; a Society you can never leave."

He searched my face for my reaction.

"I know it sounds overly dramatic."

"No, no."

"That's okay, I know it does. I think I felt that way too before I became a member of this cursed group. Because it's beyond your imagination. You only think you feel the heat until you're in Hell."

I didn't know what to say.

My dad gulped down most of his drink. "I'm sorry."

"No, Dad, c'mon. I'm…"

"And I know there's no way to rank death, but losing a child is the worst. I mean, husbands and wives pass, people get remarried."

"You never did."

"Yeah, well, there was only one of your mom. And I'm a little weird anyway." He tried smiling but didn't make it. "I feel for the Dillards," he said. "And I hope to hell that what we suspect, that he might have raped his daughter, I hope that's not true. Because to have done *that* and then she dies too? That kind of guilt? I don't know how a man could go on."

My dad's cell buzzed. He looked at the ID and ruefully smiled at me and said, "Sorry, I've got to take this." He got up, said hello and walked away from the table.

I wasn't an only child?

Shit, I wasn't an only child.

Only for three months.

Well, no, actually, for all of my life. You have a brother or sister, you're no longer alone. Just because they've passed on, they were still part of your life. This time *I* gulped down my drink. Damn, to discover that you have a sister and then to lose her in a heartbeat screwed up my balance. Alison Singer. Nice name.

"You won't believe this," my dad said as he came back to the table. "That was Carmen. Mrs. Rosales."

"And…?"

"They found a dead man inside one of the houses they fumigated."

10

It was the house on Spinnaker.

The other house I'd seen with the red tent as we were driving out of town to the Dillards.

Hard to believe that was only six hours ago.

The red tent was gone when my dad and I drove up, replaced by yellow police tape blocking off the front. Wade was already there, talking to two of the cops assigned to the crime scene.

"There's Carmen," said my dad.

"You go to her; I'll go see Wade and talk to Bartley and Tucker."

I could have said talking to a brick wall. Not in brain power, but body power. Wade's a big man, but so are Alan Bartley and Jim Tucker. They're about 6' 5" and tip the scales over 260, with about 10% body fat.

But as I approached them, Bartley and Tucker looked my way and decided they'd talked enough to the team of Singer & Wade; or at least Wade. Singer, no way.

Some fights are never over.

Bartley and Tucker are good, dedicated officers. Never any disciplinary sheets in their files, never any issues of excessive force or questionable decisions. The fact that after ten years on the job and they're still motorcycle jockeys does say something about their managerial abilities. But, hey, some guys are just made for a job and they were it. And they *loved* being cops.

So, when I quit the force, it was natural for Alan and Jim to never forgive me for not being true blue.

"They can run, but they can't hide," I said, as I watched the two behemoths duck under the yellow tape and go inside the house.

Wade looked at me: what?

"If Remington's in there, he'll send them back out in a heartbeat."

Glenn Remington had become the new Chief in a unanimous decision by the city council. And with good reason. Glenn was a brilliant police officer. He'd made lieutenant in record time. Which mean he was an equally brilliant politician, too. Glenn worked the system better than anybody I knew. Chief Black had been at the top for twenty years by brute force. Glenn would be there for as long as he wanted the job because there wasn't anyone in town that could match his acumen or, when it was necessary, his kick-you-in-the-nuts toughness.

It looked like he had just done the latter because Bartley and Tucker had done a U-turn and moved their asses back under the yellow tape. They passed Wade and me without a glance in our direction and went to stand in the middle of Spinnaker Street to make sure the gawkers kept moving.

"They identify the body yet?" I said.

"Steve Fordham," Wade said. "Real estate agent works, or *worked*, for Johnston Brokers."

"Name doesn't ring a bell. Must be a new agent."

Not that I knew every real estate agent in town, but *The Gold Rush*, the ultra-parochial local newspaper was probably forty percent recycled news and sixty percent advertising. And of that sixty percent, real estate agents represented almost ninety percent. If you bought or sold real estate, even if you didn't have a listing, you got your name out there.

"Maybe he didn't advertise too much," I said.

"Fatal," Wade said. "Can't get share of market without share of mind."

"Wow, two Keynesian economics theorists in two days."

"Nothing Keynesian 'bout that," Wade said. "More like Dolly Parton."

Okay, I walked into that one.

"She was on the Johnny Carson show and he asked her about a low-cut dress that showed off her, uh, considerable assets and she said, 'You got the goods, you put 'em in the window.'"

"You think anyone under twenty would relate to that?"

"Don't care. What twenty-year-old knows anything worth knowing anyway? Facebooking, texting, twittering self-centered d'oh junkies. They're all glands and adrenaline. You remember what you were like at twenty?"

"I choose to forget."

"Exactly my point. Besides Dolly is a classic. And the classics are usually only known to those of higher intelligence."

"What's bugging you today?"

He never answered because we both saw my dad waving at us, so we joined him and Carmen by her company truck.

Everything about Carmen was dark; and not just her mood. Her hair shone like a raven's wing, her eyes were shiny black, and her rich coca complexion was flawless. But when she smiled, her face glowed and those teeth! I could see why my dad had made his move. I thought he was in trouble. Carmen could break your heart.

After the introductions, I asked her, "Anything like this ever happened before?"

"Never," Carmen said. "We take more precautions than any other termite company. Something like this just, it's just not possible. And yet.. *Oh madre de dios,* that poor man."

My dad patted Carmen's shoulder and she reached over with her hand and put it on top of his and squeezed.

"Mrs. Rosales!" We all turned to see Chief Remington coming our way. Glenn had always been a sharp dresser, but lately he looked like he was modeling for GQ. His laminated ID interrupted the beautiful, flowing lines of what had to be a tailor-made suit, set off by a brilliant white shirt and an expensive muted blue tie. "If you have a moment," he said. He looked at me and Wade and my father and efficiently herded us off by saying, "Gentlemen. I need a private word with Mrs. Rosales."

"She going to need a lawyer?" I said.

The Chief didn't necessarily like my interfering, but my experience with the police, despite having once been a cop, wasn't great.

"I'm not qualified to give Mrs. Rosales legal advice," Glenn said.

"So how is this a homicide?" I said.

I saw Wade's head rotate slightly in my direction even though I was looking directly at Chief Remington. I saw the Chief's head move back slightly, as if in recoil.

Throttle down here, Matt.

"I don't recall saying anything about a homicide," the Chief said.

"A homicide?" Carmen said, her voice rising.

"I think we can discuss this quietly down at the station," the Chief said. "Can you be there in a half-hour?"

Carmen nodded her agreement and Remington walked off, talking on his cell.

"I'm calling Spanish Carlos," Carmen said.

Spanish Carlos was a famous attorney who was neither Spanish, nor named Carlos. Demitri Benediktos Christopoulos was Greek, on both sides, as far back as they could trace the family history. He became Spanish Carlos because many years ago he got a Spanish boxing champion off an aggregated assault charge filed by his former crooked business manager who'd cheated the champ out of at least a million dollars.

Demitri staged such a brilliant defense and rationale that the business manager had tears in his eyes and was so remorseful he promised to pay back every penny. Of course, once he was out of the court room, the only thing he paid was his parking validation and drove all night to Mexico.

Didn't matter, Demitri's reputation was launched. A few weeks later, another boxer, this time Mexican, and another victory. Pretty soon if you spoke Spanish and needed an attorney, you called Demitri, only you called him Spanish Carlos.

When Carmen came back to us, my dad said, "I'll drive you down to the station and stay there with you."

Wade and I had our own drive to make, back to Holmby Hills.

11

"A drive like that," Wade said, "we should get something to eat first."

"We don't have time."

"If I promise to be extra neat, mother, can't we eat in the car?"

What? This was *verboten!*

But before I could veto that idea, Wade said, "In-'N-Out. And I'm buying. I mean if you're going to eat in your car, you've got to eat a hamburger from the kings."

"You know we're breaking a rule here."

"I know that. But it could be a once and done. No precedents set."

I was weakening, only because Carmen's call had interrupted my lunch at the Source, and I was hungry. "Okay."

"Hot damn! Alert the media!" Wade headed for my car. "I'm ordering mine Animal Style."

"You're pushing it with extra pickles, extra secret sauce, plus grilled onions." Wade slid into the seat, buckled up. "And I'm having a Neapolitan shake; strawberry, vanilla, and chocolate together. Swirled together, and not blended."

I started the engine. "James Bond martini style."

"That's shaken, not stirred. But, yeah, same idea."

"May as well make it a double. And I don't mean a double-double, although that is what I'm having."

Wade looked at me. "Man, yo English be all fuck'd up."

The burgers, animal style, and the *tri-fecta* Neapolitan shakes, along with another off-the-menu item–Animal style fries, which had secret sauce, onions and cheese heaped on top–were damn good.

"How do you know about all these goodies?"

"I is, after all, a dee-tective," Wade said.

"Oh. I thought maybe you had dated one of the waitresses."

Heh-heh.

Wade laughed, but never answered my question.

We made good time getting back to Holmby Hills, driving fast with the windows open to air out the smell of burgers and fries, and pulled into the Dillard's long driveway again.

I checked my teeth in the rearview mirror.

"Your makeup's fine," Wade said.

"I'm just making sure I don't have animal breath." I pulled a couple of mints from the center console and handed one to Wade.

"Grrrrr," he said, unwrapped it and popped it into this mouth.

I had thought about telling Wade about the news that I had a sister, but I was still processing the information. I thought about my mother all those years and wondered why she felt for she needed to keep it a secret from me.

Why? I suppose to protect me, but when you're that young, even if they'd waited until I was in school, or a teenager, the significance of something like that really doesn't impact you.

You're so self-centered, so concerned with finding *your* way in the world, the weight of it–losing a sibling, losing a child–doesn't fall heavy on your shoulders:

Oh, that's too bad.

A few moments pass, then–

I wonder if I'm going to get that Rawlings glove for my birthday.

Wade has a younger sister: Andriel, who joined the Army the day after the Twin Towers went down; which was right after she'd just finished her residency at Johns Hopkins. Andriel had a military bearing long before she put on Army khaki. Her first tour was as a MEDEVAC doctor, saving lives, usually under heavy enemy fire, and getting our men and women to the nearest U.S. forward operating base for Provincial Reconstruction Team Kunduz in north-central Afghanistan.

So, when she became one of the youngest soldiers to make Major, it wasn't that much of a surprise. Wade says she's up for Lieutenant Colonel and will be wearing silver oak leaves soon.

And Wade worries about his sister every day.

I have a sister who didn't exist in my life until a few hours ago.

And now we had to talk to the Dillards who had lost their only child and gained a grandson from a father they don't know.

"Some shit, huh?" Wade said, almost as if he was reading my mind.

When Maria opened the door, it was obvious she'd been crying. Her eyes were puffy, and she sniffed as she closed the door quietly behind us.

"Está tan triste," Maria said, "una tragedia."

"Yes," Wade said. "Entonces joven, así que hermoso."

She was so young, so beautiful–that part I got.

"You were close to Charlene?" I said.

"Oh, yes, yes." Maria said, and the tears blossomed in her eyes and spilled out.

She quickly dabbed them away, almost embarrassed at being so vulnerable.

"I was the au pair, but, really, Charlene and I we were .. friends. She said I was her best friend." She looked down the hall where I knew the Dillards were waiting. "We had to keep that our little secret; because, Senor Dillard is...he is very business about so many things."

The door opened and Maria gave a little gasp and Wade and I both moved in front of her, I guess instinctively shielding her from Charles' piercing gaze. He looked at us for a moment and then waved us back toward him. It was a wave that seemed devoid of any authority. It was more a hopeless resignation of defeat.

Without looking behind me I palmed my card out to Maria. "Call me," I said Sotto voce. "So, we can talk. In private."

I waited a moment and when nothing happened, I thought that Maria might be too sad or frightened or maybe had something to hide, but then I felt her soft fingers brush my palm and she had the card. "Si," she whispered.

Oksanna was a wreck. She was collapsed on the sofa at the far end of a room that had to be thirty feet long; but even from that distance I could see her face was puffy, red and totally devastated.

Charles sat down by his wife, took her hand in his. Maybe he wasn't *all* business.

"I'm so sorry," Wade said.

"Yes," I said. "There can be no more devastating news for a parent and...we can only imagine, but really have no way of comprehending. And sorry..." I stopped because I was rambling and really didn't have any way of dealing with this.

"Thank you," Charles said quietly. Oksanna nodded in agreement.

Nobody knew what to say for a few moments.

Finally, Oksanna, said in a voice that was cracked and hoarse, "Your friend, Detective Ramos...he...he was very kind. He said that Charlene was very brave, very strong..."

"He said we could be extremely proud of her," Charles finished for his wife. "That she was and would have been a wonderful mother."

And then Charles sobbed, harsh and hard. He clasped his hands together and squeezed them so hard I'm sure he could have crushed steel, a man fighting to control himself. "A mother .. and she is...was...*a child!*" And then Charles lost control and his head dropped and his chest heaved as these deep, rasping cries were wrenched from his soul.

I thought of Shakespeare's two warring fathers - Montague and Capulet–realizing, too late, that their feud had cost them the one thing they loved in life more than themselves or their money or power.

I thought of my father. And my mother. And the silent, enduring pain they had endured over their loss of Ali, a magical gift that had appeared and vanished so quickly and yet had left a memory for a lifetime.

I thought this was a case *too hard* for us; certainly, for me.

"Maybe we should come back in a couple of days," Wade said; again, intuitive for both the Dillards and me.

They didn't say anything. Oksanna turned and folded her husband into her arms and held him. She closed her eyes, not bothering to hide her tears.

Wade and I left without another word.

Not even to Maria who waited for us near the front entrance.

"Tomorrow," she whispered. "We will talk then."

12

Wade and I didn't have much to say on the ride back home.

Not until we were taking the off-ramp to drop down to the coast highway and slip into town along the ocean did he finally speak.

"I don't see us going down the incest road with Charles," he said. "I could be wrong, and he could be an Oscar-winning actor, but that's not how a guilty father acts."

"I agree. That's a father overwhelmed with grief, not guilt."

I pulled up in front of Wade's house. "You think we need to bring in Duncan on this?" he said.

"Duncan?"

"Yeah, in case the paperwork on getting their grandson released to them takes longer than it should. You know, them being grandparents, no knowledge of the father. Shit like that, little guy could be two years old before he sees Nana and Papa."

"You don't think Dillard has attorneys who can handle that?"

"Sure. But they ain't Duncan."

"Nobody's Duncan except Duncan."

Duncan Fitzgerald is easily the best lawyer I've ever met, read about, or heard folk tales about. Years back when I'd quit the force, Chief Black had made my life shit for over a year. The word was out and so I got tickets for moving violations, equipment violations and trumped-up parking tickets. Then I did a favor for a client, off the books, who returned the favor by introducing me to Duncan. I explained everything to him and a week later he called and said, "Your tickets are dismissed. And there should be no more contrived problems with Chief Black and the *Paraíso Del Mar* Police Department."

A guy who can police the Chief? That's a man you don't forget.

"Okay," I said. "I'll call Duncan."

Wade tapped his fist on the window frame twice in goodbye and walked to his house.

I pulled away and my phone rang. I hit the Blue Tooth and said, "Hey, Dad."

"How'd it go?" he said, his voice soft, reserved.

"It didn't."

"What's that mean?"

"Too emotional. It just wasn't the right time to talk about it. Any of it."

My dad didn't say anything for a moment, and I checked the phone to make sure we hadn't been disconnected.

"Their lives will never be the same," he said finally. "And no matter what, no way in hell it could have been their fault, they will always blame themselves."

I knew he wasn't just talking about the Dillards.

"You can't blame yourself for…"

Wow, I had a moment where I couldn't say her name.

"For Ali. I mean…"

"Right. But I do. We *both* did, your mother and me. It happened on our watch."

Shit. I was about to launch into all the reasons it wasn't his fault–a congenital heart defect, the laws of nature, and maybe a half-dozen other points when I realized my reaction was pointless. Who was I to tell my dad how to feel? What the hell did I know about any of it?

"I'm so, so sorry, dad."

I turned a corner and realized I was only a couple of blocks from his house.

"You doing anything right now? You want to get a drink? Something to eat?"

He hesitated a moment, then said, "Uh…Carmen's here."

"Oh. Right. How's she doing? Any news?"

"We didn't go to the station. One call from Spanish Carlos shut that down. So then we came here and she was on her cell pretty much all the time since you and Wade left; talking to Antonio and Billy, those were the two guys who did the fumigation; then to Spanish Carlos and I don't know, maybe ten other people, with several more calls to Carlos and then she just kind of ran out of steam. So, she had a glass of wine and the next thing I know she's asleep on the sofa. She's been out for at least an hour."

That explained why he was talking so quietly.

"Okay," I said. "Hopefully by tomorrow we'll have some answers."

Then from out of nowhere my dad said, "I sure hope dying isn't like dreaming."

"What're you talking about?"

"You know, when you're dreaming, you're kind of free-floating and events come at you so fast, even when it's a slow, detailed dream that it feels *so real*? I'm hoping dying isn't like that. If it is, they can keep it. Give me straight oblivion."

"I don't think you get a choice, Pops."

"I know and that's the bitch of it. "

"What's with all this morbid talk lately? You feeling okay?"

"I felt any better they'd arrest me."

"So…?"

"I don't know, really. All this crap, innocent young girls dying, maybe murdered. This guy, Fordham, in the house they're fumigating. That doesn't sound like an accident to me."

"Have you heard something?"

"Not really. But listening to Carmen talking to her crew, to Carlos, the precautions and safety measures they take, for something like this to happen, has to be a suicide or somebody offed him."

"That's got to be a terrible way to take your life."

"Worse than drowning."

"Hard to believe his body's automatic reflexes wouldn't take over. You can't breathe and, I mean, if you're riding your board and you get crushed by a wave, you're zooming for the surface with everything you've got. A guy inhaling that shit, I would think he couldn't stop from running out into the air."

"Unless he took something to zone him out, so he was pretty much out of it when he went into the house."

"He went *into* the house *after* they put up the tent?"

"Antonio told Carmen that one of the clamps didn't look right. Like somebody had fastened it, but not exactly the way they do it. Rosales Exterminators has a Procedures Manual. And a couple of the clamps weren't by the book."

"Really? They could tell that for sure?"

"Carmen's husband, Ricardo, who died from a heart attack four years ago in case you were wondering, had been a drill sergeant in the Army. So, there's only one way of doing things: Ricardo's way."

"Shit," I said. "If the clamps were on, how'd Fordham get them back in place?"

"Right. He can't do if from the inside."

"Dad, this is a homicide."

13

"Ain't no one hired us to investigate any local murder," Wade said about a half hour later when I'd called him an explained what my dad had said.

"No, but since when has that stopped us?"

"Typical, "Wade said, switching off his accent, which meant I knew he was now serious. "A couple of days ago I was asking about work and now we've got to find two killers. And only of them includes a fee." There was some noise through the receiver, probably shifting to his other ear and some metallic sounds.

"What're you doing?"

"I'm heating up some pasta *fagioli,* probably not up to the Singer standards, but not bad for your southern cousins."

Wade has always laughed at the absurdity of Tarantino's *True Romance* where Dennis Hopper's character insulted Christopher Walken's Sicilian *Mafioso* thug by saying his relatives had been invaded and raped by just about every country in and around the Mediterranean, particularly Africans, and therefore Sicilians had some *melanzane,* or eggplant, in their DNA. But he still never walked away from the opportunity to give me a jolt about it.

But then I never let a shot off the starboard bow go unanswered.

"What's your tomato to water and pasta ratio?" I had no idea what the hell the answer was, but I'm sure he didn't know either.

"Whatever's good enough for *Pietro's Ristorante is* good enough for me."

"It's takeout? And you were letting me believe it was homemade."

"Since when can I make or let you believe anything? So, you hungry?"

"I'm starved. I'll pick up a *caprese* salad and an *anti-pasto* and come over. You need a wine?"

"Always need wine. I've got a bottle, but my guess is two homicides, two bottles."

"That's not a guess. That's a fact."

"Okay. And step on it. My wrista she's ah gettin' tired."

"Only thing your wrist is getting tired of is abusing your meager manhood."

"I know many fine women who would disabuse you of that phallic fallacy."

"God, I think I like Uncle Remus better than this."

Heh-heh.

Wade was having a good time at my expense. Once again.

14

"Why are you fighting me on this?" Wade said.

"I'm not fighting, just trying to make sure we aren't jumping to conclusions, making the case fit what we've got instead of fitting the clues to the case."

We had gone through one bottle of wine, the pasta *fagioli*, the salad and *anti-pasto*, plus a couple of frozen waffles that Wade had toasted and served with warmed maple syrup. Not bad with a good pinot noir. During that time, we'd decided to wait until we'd talked to Famous and the Dillards before putting on our full court press crime solving personas. We'd gone a couple of rounds on the exterminator extermination; that being just one of the dumbass names we came up with; no doubt the second bottle of wine having something to do with that.

"Okay, suspects," Wade said. "Marvin and June Hertzman, owners of the house. They're selling because Marv got a new job up in Palo Alto. Moving to Silicon Valley. No reason they'd want to off Fordham."

"Unless he gave them a low-ball offer on their house."

"I thought we were being serious."

"Sorry. Cross off the Hertzmans. None of the Rosales crew even knew Fordham, so they're out."

"And if they had taken him out? They'd have closed the clamps correctly."

Wade poured the last of the second bottle of wine into both our glasses. "Think we need reinforcements?"

"I'm good. I want to appear somewhat intelligent tomorrow."

"That be difficult even under the best of circumstances."

"Thank you, Jamal Einstein."

"I be thinkin' it be Jamal Holmes."

"So, *I'm* Watson?"

"Somebody got to be."

"I think we've lost our focus," I said. "Or at least I have."

"Okay," Wade said and drained his glass. He stood up and gathered the wine bottles and his glass.

And out of the blue I said, "I have a sister."

Wade looked at me for a moment, then quietly put the bottles and his glass back on the table and sat down. "Somehow I don't think you mean a *sistah*."

"No."

And then I told him what my dad had said about Ali. And it was harder than I'd imagined because I choked up right in the middle of it.

And since Wade didn't say anything during my telling; and was quiet for another minute after I'd finished, I knew this was as stunning to him as to me.

Finally, he said. "Shit, Matt, that's heavy. I don't think there's anything worse than a parent having to bury a child. And that doesn't change, no matter the age."

"That's pretty much what my dad said."

Wade nodded.

"I had an uncle, Ezekiel. The Biblical meaning is–'strength of God.' And that damn sure was Uncle EZ. Lived through all that segregation shit down in Alabama, man was the Rock of Gibralter. EZ married Ruth and they had a son Aaron. They were very Biblical, my relatives. And Uncle EZ lived to be ninety-six. Auntie Ruth died when she was seventy something and my uncle was pretty broken up. But when Aaron died at age seventy-two, I never saw a man so devastated as my Uncle EZ."

It was my turn to be quiet.

"And Matt, Uncle EZ was one of the toughest men I've ever known. Not just physically, but in his ability to weather trouble, to keep moving forward, never complaining. But when Aaron passed, all I can remember is my uncle weeping, saying 'My baby boy's gone, my baby boy.' And Aaron was seventy-two!"

"We are always our parents' children. And even when the children end up caring for their parents in the last days of their lives, we are still the little kids."

Wade nodded.

"Our lives are the sum of our memories," he said. "So, when you lose a child, there are no more deposits to be made in our memory banks. You're robbed of the future. And the child is robbed of everything."

Wade looked at the two empty bottles. I could tell he was thinking if we needed a third.

"So how you doin'?" he said.

"I'm still processing," I said. "The news is mind-blowing. And I feel so bad for my father. And my mother. And, of course, little Ali. But what's strange is I feel sad for myself, too. Because—just like you said—never having a life together with a baby sister who was taken way too early. A sister that until a few days ago I never knew I had."

15

"I knew we would have grandchildren," Oksanna said.

And for the first time, I noticed the slightest burr of an accent in her speech. Probably because she was devastated by the events and whatever protective coloring she'd taken on to camouflage her past had slipped away.

"Just not like this," she said. "So sudden, so tainted with...sadness."

Wade and I were having coffee with Mrs. Dillard the next morning, sitting in their amazing high-tech kitchen, looking out to a lush patio and garden. Charles was with his teams of attorneys assembling all the legal machinery he would need to get custody of Charlene's baby boy.

"And yet, also" she continued, "...joy." She started to drink her coffee but put the cup back down. "My emotions, they are so...mixed."

"That's understandable," I said. "Two very powerful events."

"And so opposite," Oksanna said. "In Vyazma, where I was born, we had a saying, *Happiness never travels alone*. When I was younger, I didn't understand it. And now I am sorry that I *do* understand it."

Tears formed in her eyes, but she dabbed them away with a beautiful silk handkerchief.

"Vyazma?" Wade said. "Russian?"

He'd noticed the accent too.

Oksanna nodded. "Yes. It is a small town near the river of the same name which is in the Smolensk Oblast." She saw that Wade's cup was half-gone and refilled it. She looked at me, but I shook my head no. "During the War, Vyazma became a battlefield between the Red Army and the *Wehrmacht* during the Battle of Moscow. So not much happiness traveled our way. My grandfather told me that the population was reduced from over sixty thousand to seven hundred and sixteen." She shrugged. "I have read books and much research of this; and it's true. Somehow my grandfather and his wife, Oksanna, whom I am named after, got out of the country. Vyazma is on the main railroad line to Moscow and eventually they were able to come to America."

She stopped talking and shook her head so slightly.

"Do you feel up to answering some questions?" I asked.

"If it helps find Charlene's killer? Absolutely."

We spent another hour going through every possible line of questioning with Oksanna and at the end, really didn't know much more than when we'd started.

We *did* confirm that the only thing Charles was guilty of was being an absentee father. He was always out promoting and growing the Institute so that Charlene rarely saw him. When she did, their relationship was excellent. Charlene was her father's daughter. She adored him. Of course, we were still going to question Charles, but he didn't seem like a suspect.

"What about your buddy Finneran?" Wade said as we got back into my car.

"Discussing something other than money? You think he's up to it?"

"Maybe I'll do that one," Wade said. He pushed the button and his window slid down and he took a deep breath of the rich, rarified air of Holmby Hills.

It didn't smell like money, just more trouble on the wind.

16

"Well, look what just blew in," Famous said.

He was sitting alone at his favorite booth, the last one on the right, next to the kitchen, at Chin Lee's Seaport restaurant. The booth was a huge semi-circle designed to hold six people, but Famous always had it to himself. The owner, Ralph Song, who was Korean, didn't hold it for Famous, but if Famous walked in and someone was at the booth, Ralph would tell them their dinner was on the house and would they mind moving to another booth?

"I could never figure out," Wade said as he slid into the booth first and I followed, "where's the seaport part? I mean how far we from the ocean?"

"Well, it's on San Pedro Street," Famous said. "And that's a seaport." Famous took a sip of his Tsingtao beer and looked at us. "Hell, Ralph is Korean, his wife is Jewish and I'm sure every one of his chefs is Mexican. So there ya go. Welcome to America."

"Where's Pretty?" Wade said.

"Jesus," Famous said. "I need a break. Damn rookie asks more questions than a year of *Jeopardy*. He's up getting his quota around the hospital. Seeing if anybody saw anything, knows the girl and I'm sure fifteen other questions I'd never think of."

Ralph came over, all smiles and handed us menus.

"Would you like beers?"

Wade and I said yes, and Ralph waved his arm without looking behind him and two seconds later a waiter appeared with our beers on a tray. He deftly popped the caps and placed them in front of us.

"The usual?" Ralph asked Famous.

"You guys are hungry, right?" Famous said. And without waiting for an answer told Ralph, "Bring us four orders."

Ralph looked a little puzzled.

"My partn..." Famous stopped, started over. "My associate might join us."

Ralph smiled and headed back to the kitchen.

"You're looking out for him anyway," I said.

"Mebbe. But having the order already here means he can't ask, 'What's good?'"

We all clicked bottles on that.

"So...?" Wade said.

"So, I hate this freakin' case."

Famous had a daughter, Meagan, who was Charlene's age, so I knew this one hit close to home.

And almost on cue, he said:

"This kid, this *victim*, she's the same age as my Meagan. Jesus, something happened to Meagan ..." He didn't finish his sentence. He didn't have to. He took another long swallow of his Tsingtao. "How the hell's somebody *not* look for your kid for all that time?"

"I think they did," I said. "Just did it on the low."

"Right!" Famous snapped. "Like some fucking PIs, could do a better job than us. Not you guys of course..."

"Of course," I interjected.

But I don't think he heard me and was glaring off into space.

I couldn't remember the last time I'd seen him so pissed off, so close to really showing his true emotions instead of his cop persona. But when you start thinking along the lines of, "there but or...could've been me" you're vulnerable and open.

"How'd your meeting with the Dillards go?" Famous said.

"We spent some time with the wife," Wade said. "She's wiped out. The husband is too. Only he buries his pain by working."

"You guys got anything else?" Famous said.

"We're going back, talk to the neighbors," I said.

"And the *au pair*, who was tight with Charlene," Wade said. "Maybe even have her smooth things over with the neighbors. Kind of introduce us."

Wade looked at me and I nodded. Great idea.

"Where's Pretty looking?" I said. Famous didn't say anything, waiting for me to explain why. "Well, unless you found a car or she took a taxi or hitched a ride, she could only have walked so far."

Famous thought about that for a moment. He nodded like I'd scored a point. He held up a finger and pulled his cell phone, hit a number. "Yo, Gonzo! No, I don't know. Just listen. I want you to go back and talk to Doctor Benson...I'm about to tell you what about. Ask him how far he thinks Charlene could have walked...*Damn it!* Gonzo, do not ask another question until I am finished"

Famous looked at the phone.

"You there? Oh, you aren't saying anything." Famous rolled his eyes at us. He took a deep breath, I think so he could get all his instructions in rapid-fire before Gonzo's automatic questioning kicked back in, no matter the instructions. "Ask Benson how far she could have walked, her condition, see if they have her clothes...yes, her clothes."

I guess three was Gonzo's limit.

"We want to see if her clothes give us any clues. Like were the shoes run down, any particular kind of soil, shit like that....Yes, if they have the clothes take them to the station and get them to Forensics...Yes, *Esteban*, you can ask Doctor Benson anything else you'd like. Goodbye."

Wade and I could only smile.

Give Gonzo a few years and he might turn into a good detective. Obviously, he had something on the ball to get partnered with Famous at a fairly young age.

But living through his development might be murder.

17

"Is there foul play here?"

The woman asking the question was in her late fifties and looked like she ran marathons (she had long ropy legs and wrinkled loose skin).

Wade and I had decided that my idea of canvassing the area that Charlene could have walked had merit. Not Sleuthing Hall of Fame stuff, but definitely smart; and we weren't going to wait for Gonzo to do it first.

"Have you seen her?" Wade said.

The woman made an exaggerated point of studying Charlene's photo then handed it back. "Nope, Sorry."

"Thanks," Wade said and took back the photo.

"Wait a minute," she said. "Is that the girl on the news?"

Shit. There must have been a leak down at the Department.

"What news?" I said.

"On TV. You can't have missed it, it's on every channel. Young girl that was a runaway, died in childbirth. Her parents are *gazillionaires*."

As we walked to the next house up the hill. And I mean *up. La Presa* Drive was steep and winding, Wade checked his cell phone. "There it is." He scrolled through several pages and cleared the screen. Then he dialed and said, "Famous, hey..." And then I'm sure he was listening to a tirade, some of which I could hear when Wade held the phone away from his ear, the words 'Fuck' .. 'Asshole' .. and 'Rookie' burst from the phone. Wade put the phone back and said, "Okay, sorry, man." And hung up.

"Gonzo gives as many answers as questions?" I said.

"Apparently somebody at Mercy knows one of the reporters for ABC and they were down there when Gonzo was talking to Benson."

"Famous sounded ballistic."

"Gonzo might take one in the Gorgonzolas," Wade said.

Just as we started up the path to a very nice Spanish style home, the front door opened, and a man and a woman stepped out. They had that sleek look of money, botox and conceit. The woman's attitude seemed to go with her fiery red hair. She looked at us like we were dog waste and she was going to be sure to step around it.

"Excuse me," she snapped.

Wade didn't move.

"What do you think you're doing?" And without turning around she said, "Richard!"

Richard looked like he worked out. His charcoal Armani suit was slightly tight in all the right places. He stepped in front of the woman.

Wade was immobile.

"Perhaps you can help us," I said, moving to take up the rest of the path so the only way around us was on the neatly trimmed lawn. And judging from those stiletto heels, the woman wasn't doing that.

"We are late," she said. "And we aren't in the buying mode."

"We aren't selling anything, ma'am."

She flinched. Ah, the power of words.

"Ma'am? You think I'm a ma'am? How dare you?"

"I call all women over eighteen years old ma'am. No offense meant."

"Who the hell are you guys?" Richard said.

Wade pulled the photo of Charlene. "Have you ever seen this girl?"

"No," the woman said. She gestured with her hand, like okay, we're done.

Wade held the photo right in her face. "Take a real look this time. This is somebody's daughter!" Wade said it with menace. And there is Wade's size.

The woman looked at the photo for a few moments. "She's very pretty. But no, I haven't seen her. But to be honest, I very rarely notice other women."

Fuck you, bitch.

This is a seventeen-year-old child-mother.

"Not even to check their foreheads to see if they've been botoxed?"

Her hand involuntarily went to her face, along with a short gasp of indignation, but Wade and I had already turned and headed back for the street.

"Why do I think there's another name besides ma'am for her?" Wade said.

"Rhymes with itch?"

"Or a term in baseball for a short hit by the plate"

We spent about two hours being poorly equipped mountaineers hiking up that damn street, knocking on doors, getting rebuffed, or in street terms, dissed. We also got reported because as Wade and I were just getting into the Snake, a patrol car cruised by. The cop riding shotgun slid down his window and gave us his baddest look.

"Afternoon," I said, and hit the remote on the Snake.

"You guys know a Monique and Richard Draper?" Shotgun asked us. I guess he wasn't too interested in the answer since he hadn't bothered to get out of the car.

"We suppo'sed to?" Wade said, laying on the cornpone.

"Well, they called into the station, said they'd been harassed by two men, one black, one Caucasian, who were impersonating private investigators."

"Impersonating? Nope, that's not us," I said. I opened the door and got into the car. Keep moving is my motto. I looked at Wade. He apparently didn't believe in that motto since he was standing by the fender staring at the cops.

Then Shotgun opened his door.

Oh, shit.

"Where were you two gentlemen headed?"

"Back to the beach," I said, my head out the window.

"Why you need to know that?" Wade said. He doesn't like cops. This case had upset him. And it had been a long shitty day.

I got out of the car. So did the cop that was driving.

"What's going on?" the driver said. His right hand moved down toward his gun.

"Nothing," I said and moved toward Wade.

"Un-uh," he said to me and held out his hand to ward me off. He hadn't taken his eyes off Shotgun.

"You have a problem answering questions?" Shotgun said.

"Not if they're appropriate," Wade said, still not taking his eyes off Shotgun, still not blinking either.

This could get volatile in a heartbeat.

"Either of you officers know Famous?" I said.

A blip in both cops' concentration.

"Why?" said the driver.

"Damn it, Matt," Wade said and turned for my car.

I could feel him glaring at me. I knew he thought I'd taken the chicken shit way out by mentioning Famous. But we weren't here to prove who was or had the biggest dick. And not just because we were private ones.

"We're working on a case together," I said.

Weak, Singer, fucking pussy ass weak.

And you're going to catch a load of shit when Famous finds out you and Wade have been horning in on official police work.

"Bullshit," the Driver said. "Famous don't hire out." He stepped closer, but his hand had moved away from his gun. "So, why're you here? Besides hassling the Drapers?"

"We didn't hassle anybody. Now I'm going to take a photo out of my jacket okay. Just a photo."

Shotgun and Diver looked at each other for a split second as if: What's with this bozo? Then Driver said, "Okay. Why are we looking at a photo?"

"Because that's what we're up here doing. Showing this photo around to see if anyone recognizes her."

I held out Charlene's picture. They both looked at it, then at me.

"This is that girl," Shotgun said. And I knew he didn't mean Marlo Thomas. "The one died having the baby."

"Or so they're telling the news," Driver said. That's why he was the driver, he was the smarter cop.

"Yes," I said. "We're working for her parents, looking for clues."

"Why all the way up here?" Shotgun said. "This isn't the scene of the crime."

"That's why we're checking," I said. "To make sure."

18

It was a long and quiet ride back to the beach.

A very quiet ride.

Wade didn't say shit. He was clearly angry that I'd used Famous's name in the stant-off.

"Look," I said as I made the turn down to Pacific Coast Highway. It was a dark night, no moon reflecting on the ocean, no phosphorous white glow of the waves as they hit the beach. "on a different day, a different case, yeah, I'd have stonewalled them too. But this isn't hat day or that case. Think about it."

And I guess he did think about it.

Because he didn't say anything, just slid down his window and let the ocean breeze fill the car.

And finally, he said, "Ahhh...fuck! You're right." He looked at me. "I'm not sure what the hell's eating at me, but I am god damned pissed. I'm looking for trouble when there's none there. And if I can't find it, I'm going to manufacture it."

"It's a shitty world, Jamal. Girl that young, that beautiful? Die like that? And she was smart, all that going for her and she just tosses it."

"And then gets knocked up, gets knocked around hard enough to eventually have a stroke, but still has the backbone to get herself to the hospital and make sure her baby's safe." Wade shook his head, his dreads barely moving. "Girl like that? Would have been nice to see how she turned out. My guess is she'd have made something of herself, contributed, ya know?"

"I know."

I gave the Snake a little gas and we hit the long curve into town doing about seventy.

"You better slow down," Wade said. "You don't want the cops on your ass."

"For my sake or yours?"

Heh-heh.

I slowed down as we drew close to the two road signs that identify *Paraíso Del Mar.* The first is the official city limits sign: white letters on a green background; not too many chips in the paint from where teenagers shot it with BB guns, or sometimes a .22. The other sign is simple black script lettering on a white background: *"Paradise By The Sea."*

I pulled up in front of Wade's house and he got out, "I'll call Famous, give him a heads up," he said.

"Yeah. Tell him which houses we knocked on, maybe save him some time."

"You think he's going to take our word for it?

"If not, then he's got to take Gonzo's."

"And those gone be a lot of words."

Wade gave me the peace sign and headed for his house.

I checked my messages. Several that could wait, two that couldn't.

"Hey," my dad answered. "You guys were gone all day."

"Gone but not forgotten, except for some folk. How's Carmen?"

"Upset, worried."

"I'm sure Remington will clear her pretty quickly. Nothing points her way."

"It's not that. She's worried whether anyone in town will ever hire her again."

"A little notoriety never hurt anyone. And sometimes it even helps." I turned down my street. "Carmen still there?"

"No. She was going to have dinner with Spanish Carlos. Did you eat yet?"

"No, you want to go to Kincaid's?"

"I'm thinking Something simple. What about the Copper Pot?"

"Okay. I've got to call Leah."

"Sure, ask her to come along."

"Okay." I pushed the remote button on the visor for my garage door. "Hey, Dad? I...uh, I told Wade about...Ali."

There was a long silence.

"How'd he take it?"

"We didn't talk that much about it. I'm still trying to get *my* head around it."

"Yeah, I know."

I pulled into the garage, turned off the engine.

"I think Wade's the only one I'm going to tell. For now."

"What about Leah?"

"I'll play that by ear."

"You guys okay?"

"Perfect. I just...well, like I said, I want to think about how I feel about it before I get any input."

"Whatever works for you. And you want to talk about it, I'm here."

"Okay, let me call Leah and I'll get back to you."

I clicked off and was about to dial Leah when the phone rang.

"Tommie. What's up?"

"Now you know me," she said, with a tone in her voice I don't usually hear. Mostly because Tommie never lacks for confidence, but she sounded a little off her game.

"I know you very well," I said. "And...?"

"And this one was a bitch. It took me all kinds of triangulation, calling in some high- level favors and, as always, some damn luck." Then her voice brightened. "So, here's what I've got.

"Thanks."

"Don't be thanking me just yet."

"Oh? 'cause what you got ain't that great?"

"I could still bitch-slap you."

"Flirt."

She laughed. And Tommie Shea Shoh has one of the most infectious laughs I've ever heard; so, I had to laugh too.

"Okay, based on all that techno shit I said before and other computer geek shit, the call came within a quarter-mile area up in..."

"The Hollywood Hills," I said.

"Now how the hell you know that? You guessing?"

"Somewhat. But we came at it the other way. We asked the doctor how far she could have walked in her condition and used that as a start. But we were looking at a two-mile wide area."

"I'm down with that."

My phone chimed.

"That's me," she said. "I've just emailed you the streets to check. Somewhere in that grid is the location of the call."

I opened the email from my phone: *La Presa* was one of the streets, so we'd been close. *Castilian, Oporto* and *Los Tilos* were the others. I checked them out on Goggle Maps and not only were these streets steep, they corkscrewed around and doubled back. We certainly weren't going to be wearing our high-heeled sneakers tomorrow.

"As usual, thanks. And as usual, I'm impressed."

"You're welcome. Good thing is there aren't that many houses up there. Bad thing is..."

"It's damn hilly."

She laughed again.

19

"You seemed so serious tonight," Leah said.

We were lying in the middle of her enormous bed looking at the enormous moon through the French doors that were open to her balcony and the ocean beyond them.

'You mean besides Steve Fordham being found dead in a house being termited, and a 17-year-old runaway girl dying in childbirth? Those aren't serious?"

She'd shifted off my shoulder and was looking directly at me. "It seems like this time there's something more, something heavier," she said.

Moment of truth Singer.

Hey Leah, guess what? You and I aren't only children. I have a sister, Ali, who died in infancy. You have a half-brother, Ritchie, who's worth a couple of million thanks to your dad's insurance policy.

"I'm just tired."

Why tell the truth when a lie will do just as well? Coward's way out, but I just wasn't up to familial matters.

I looked at her. Damn she was beautiful.

"And to tell the truth."

What? Really, now?

"Charlene's death has hit both Wade and me harder than we thought."

Yes, and the truth won't set you free, but it will change the subject.

"Do you want to talk about it?"

"Not yet."

I swung my legs to the edge of the bed, slipped into my boxers.

"You're leaving?"

"Yeah, I don't think I'm going to get much sleep tonight and no sense keeping you awake."

"Oh, I don't mind when you're *up*." And she laughed.

I laughed too. What man wouldn't, given a compliment like that from a woman like that?

"I know, and that's the good and the bad."

"I like it when you're bad," and she growled, laughing and reached for me. And managed to get her hands on the waistband of my Levis and .. she was right, we didn't get much sleep. At least right away. And then it was the sleep of the vanquished.

So, when Wade called me on my cell at 8:30, I was groggy as hell.

"As the teens say- WTF?"

"Where are you?" Wade said.

"Overslept."

"D'oh. My question was...No, never mind, you at Leah's."

"Give me twenty minutes and ..."

"Twenty minutes? No wonder Leah be frustrated."

I looked at Leah, she smiled, still half-asleep.

"That's one thing she's not."

"Oh, now you braggin'."

"Twenty minutes, I'll pick you up."

"No. I'm driving."

Wade driving was kind of like Wade in everything else in life: Whoa. And while we were going through the worst stretches of road–the 405 North then up La Cienega through all that craziness near the Beverly Center and then the damn streets up in the Hollywood Hills—and at the very worst time–rush hour–he zipped his BMW in and around and sometimes it looked like right through traffic, we made good time.

We decided to start alphabetically, so *Castilian* was our first street.

"Damn, this is narrow," he said as we wound our way up. On the left, the houses looked like they might fall off the hill. A nasty steep embankment that went straight up hugged the other side of the street. "That's *Maravilla* up there," Wade said.

"And I forgot the pitons and carabineers."

"Just so long as you didn't remember *lederhosen*."

Wade pushed the doorbell. We waited. He pushed the doorbell again and I knocked on the door. Nothing. "One more time," I said and whacked the door hard. We turned to go, when from within we heard, "I'm coming, Jesus."

"Had a girlfriend said same thing," Wade said.

The door was flung open and a heavyset woman, clearly pissed off, glared at us. "The goddamn doorbell does work!"

"I rang it three times."

She looked at me, then at Wade. "Oh, well, I was back in the library."

"Do you have a moment? "

"Let me get my checkbook. Lorenzo and I always support the local police."

"We're not here for charity," Wade said. He held out Charlene's photo. "This young girl, have you…?"

She snatched the picture before Wade could finish. Hard to surprise Wade, but this woman did that. We looked at each other: Wow.

"I don't know. She looks familiar."

"Familiar like you've seen her around or just one of those faces?"

"When I say familiar, I mean, yeah, I've probably seen her before. If you're not cops, who are you?"

I held out my license. She peered at it closely.

"Private eyes? No shit?"

"No. Shit."

"Wow, wait until I tell Lorenzo. He's gonna be pissed he wasn't here."

"So, this girl?"

"I think somewhere around here in the hills, ya know? I dunno, maybe down by the church?"

"The Hollywood Methodist Church?" That was the only church I knew of around there.

"No, that's down on Highland. I mean around here," she waved her hands to indicate the general neighborhood. "They call it a church, but it's more a cult if you ask me." She narrowed her eyes, thinking. "I think it was her, or someone looks a lot like her."

We thanked her and moved up the street.

Wade Googled any churches in the area. "Uh-oh."

"What? You found Something?"

"No," he said and pointed back behind us.

"Gonzo," I said. "And looks like a couple of teams." I turned back and picked up the pace. "Anything on a church?"

"Diddly. And I don't mean the late Bo." He stopped in front of the next house. "I'm thinking maybe we give Gonzo this street and go over to *Castilian*."

"Okay, but not via *Maravilla*."

"No, Sir Edmund. I'm gonna get the car, why don't you knock on this door anyway."

"Aye, aye, sir."

This house was totally different from its neighbor. It was ultra-modern, lots of glass, a mossy green lawn without any trees, just a series of low bushy plants. I rang the bell, knocked, did that several more times and was back standing in the driveway when Wade pulled up. I looked back at Gonzo and the boys as I got in the car, but they were already at the next house, so it didn't look like they'd been any luckier than us.

"Lots of people work up here," Wade said and drove quickly up the hill.

"Or maybe they just like their privacy."

We turned a corner, "Yo," said Wade, "that woman likes her looks. And so do I."

A very striking and very tall blond woman was walking up to a black Jaguar.

"Looks like she's headed to the gym," Wade said. The woman was in a curve-hugging work-out suit cut way up on the thighs. "She looking better as we get closer," Wade said.

The woman had the door to the Jag opened and was about to slip inside when Wade bipped his horn–just once, so short a note it almost didn't seem like he'd done it. But the woman had noticed and looked up.

"Excuse me," Wade said, leaning out his window, his dreads swaying slightly in the breeze. "Can you help us, please?"

The blond looked at Wade, then his shiny BMW, maybe me, and decided since she was right at her car, she was safe. Ha, if she only knew.

Wade stopped and held Charlene's photo up. "We're private investigators."

"No shit," I hissed, "and Jamal would like to investigate your privates."

Wade whacked his hand back, but I'd anticipated it and had moved close to the window. His hand whumped the seat loudly.

"This young girl," Wade said and got out of the car. "She's .. uh, would you mind looking at her photo? Perhaps you might remember seeing her?"

He moved to the woman, slowly, the photo held out almost like a peace offering. She closed the car door, feeling secure no doubt, and took the photo. She gasped. "Oh, no."

"You know her?" Wade said.

She looked at him and shook her head. "No, no. But I think..."

She stopped and looked down the hill, again in the same direction that the first woman had looked. "This is that girl from the news, right?"

"Yes," Wade said, his words barely audible.

"Such a tragedy. But .. I don't recall actually seeing her. I mean we've only lived here six, seven months, but she does look familiar. I don't know, maybe she was part of the church."

I had gotten out of the car by then and had closed the gap.

"There's a church around here?" I said. "We haven't seen it."

"Me either," she said. "But, Harriet, she's two houses up; said there was a church that was in the neighborhood."

"What kind of church?" I said.

"I don't know. Mystic or something."

"Scientology?" Wade said.

"No, I'm pretty sure about that."

"Why's that?" I said.

"Because when I see them walking around, and they're all like her," she pointed at Charlene's picture, "very beautiful. But very sheltered or shy because they never look at you or your car when you pass, nothing. And that's sure not any Scientologist I've ever met."

20

We didn't meet any Scientologists either.

Nor Zoroasters, or members of the *Baha'i* Faith or even a single Jedi devotee. Our religious search was pretty much agnostic.

Or as Wade said, "This church be like a UFO. People claim they saw it, but no one can prove it."

We spent several hours climbing the hilly streets, knocking on doors, showing Charlene's picture to the few people that were home or answered their doors, and ended up with zero. Several people thought they'd seen Charlene or someone like her or maybe thought that way because they'd seen her on TV, but no one could say even with a half-assed degree of certainty that they'd seen Charlene. Same for the church. A few people denied the possibility of a church up there. They'd never seen any extra people on Sundays–no profusion of cars clogging the already tiny streets, no one walking dressed up, no one, as one stoner dude well into his sixties said, "No one singing."

"Singing?" I said.

"Hey, man, people go to church, they sing. I ain't heard any chorus up here; and sound carries."

"That dude may not have heard any singing," Wade said as we headed back to his car to go home, "but he's definitely hearing voices."

"Marching to a different drummer," I said. "How red were his eyes?"

"Those were eyes? Looked like bullet holes."

We stopped and had empanadas at Gardel's on Melrose, a 2004 bottle of *Finca La Anita*, and finished with Vanilla bean ice cream with swirls of *Dulce De Leche* and a couple of espressos.

"Only thing missing was a tango," Wade said as he started up the car.

"And maybe Madonna on the stereo, singing *Don't Cry for me, Argentina*."

Wade didn't pull out but tapped keys on his cell.

"No shit," he said, looking at the screen.

"What?"

"That stoner's house? How much you think it's worth?"

"You're doing real estate?"

"It's on my lunch hour. So, guess."

"A million six."

"Three point nine." He held up the screen so I could see.

"Gil Crutchfield. What the hell does he do that he can afford that kind of house?"

"Maybe he's a dealer."

"I don't think so. He uses too much of his own product."

I checked my watch and hit a preset number on my phone. Wade looked at me: Who you calling?

"Zak," I said as our computer genius answered. Wade gave me a thumbs up while I listened to Zak's adrenaline-fueled, hyper speed talk as he went through just Some of the esoteric programs he was working on—most of which I said, "Wow" or "Cool" and one time, "No shit?"

Zak had been a surfer who could shred waves with the best, but his secret passion was computer sciences. Tommie was the best computer wizard in southern California, but Zak's territory was planet earth. He'd designed some incredible software programs back when Ben Black was the chief of our little town. Programs that got noticed by other law enforcement agencies and eventually Zak went back to teach at M.I.T. But we all know he does covert work for NSA or Homeland or one of the initialed government agencies.

"Yo, Zak," I said, finally having to stop the flow of information. "We need to find a church that doesn't exist. At least to normal folk."

While Wade negotiated through traffic, I filled Zak in on our problems, the case and other facts. He said he got it, no problem and rang off.

"Maybe tonight, but the latest tomorrow," I said.

"Zak ever remind you of Sherman?" Wade said. "You know, from *Rocky & His Friends?*"

"Wow, that's going way back," I said.

"Matt Singer, punster."

"He's more like Peabody," I said. "Always has a way of sorting through the data to come up with the answer."

"Peabody was a dog," Wade said.

"And Zak used to be a surfer dawg."

"Ain't no heh-heh for that one."

"Ain't no laughs period. Damn, we're striking out."

Wade cut left past a big SUV into a turn lane, then swooped around in front of the vehicle and got a horn blast.

"The Babe held the strikeout record for a long time, 1,330. But what do we remember him for? Those 714 blasts."

"You think we're going to hit a home run on this one?"

"Like the Bambino said, 'every strike brings me that much closer to the next home run.'"

21

Wade made the run home to *Paraíso Del Mar* in good time considering it was rush hour and the start of the weekend, so everyone was on their worst behavior.

Including Wade, who cut off several slower drivers and blew through traffic lights that were red as we reached the center of the intersection. But by the time we made it down to Venice Blvd, he gave up and just went with the flow.

We used the time to review the case from every possible angle and still ended up with more questions than answers.

Some of the questions came from Famous who called and asked us what we'd learned, if anything.

"Whole lot of NOHs," I said, meaning No One Home. "And same for D-SATs", which meant that for those few people who did answer the door, Didn't See A Thing. Wade calls them I-ASSs, for I Ain't Seen Shit.

"Yeah," said Famous. "That was pretty much what Gonzo and the boys got."

He didn't mention anyone thinking they saw Charlene or someone who looked like her; or anything about the church, so I didn't either. We weren't out to screw Famous. If we found anything, he'd be the first one we'd call, but this had gotten personal for Wade and me.

Wade turned down my street, "No, drop me by City Hall," I said. "I want to talk to Bartkowski, see if he has anything on Fordham."

"Helping out your pops, huh?"

"And Carmen. My dad said she's pretty messed up about this."

"Think she knows something she's not telling?"

"Don't know. Don't think so but Bartkowski might have some answers."

Wade pulled around the back of City Hall.

"I'll drive tomorrow," I said.

"Amen," Wade said and rolled out through the parking lot.

I went inside and down the hall. Hal Bartkowski had been promoted to city coroner when his boss Gerry Kelly, one of Chief Black's cronies suddenly quit the job and moved to Palm Beach, Florida.

Hal looked up as I knocked on his door and went inside without waiting to be admitted. "Matt! What's up?"

As good as Hal is at his job, he's that bad at social skills and confidence. I'd heard that even when he automatically replaced Kelly, he thought for sure it was only temporary and had sent out resumes.

"Nothing," I said and sat down in one of the chairs in front of his desk. "Some shit about Fordham."

"You're working that case?"

"Not officially. But the owner of Rosales Exterminators, Carmen? She's a friend of the family."

"Then I can't tell you anything."

"Why, it's not a murder, it's an accident, right?"

That momentary hesitation and the sudden fluttering of Hal's eyes told me that our suspicions were right.

"Okay," I said. "But just let me get some facts right, okay?"

Hal checked his wristwatch. "I'm out of here in eight minutes."

"Methylene bromide's some serious shit."

"Yes. Even minor contact with it on your skin gives you neurological issues."

"Like?"

"Ataxia, memory difficulties, sometimes dizziness. Minor, but still not good."

"So, inhaling it can fuck you up permanently."

"Right. But that isn't what Fordham inhaled." Hal smiled, the cat with the canary.

"So it was sulfurye-fluoride," I said.

I had researched everything termite after I'd talked to my dad. But if it went beyond this, I was screwed.

"I have nothing more to say."

"Bullshit. You love talking about this stuff. The scientific anomalies, the conclusive facts. C'mon. Besides remember, you hadn't told me about Miguel Santiago's blow to the head we'd have never connected him to Chief Black."

Hal thought about that for a moment or two, his head nodding. I was blowing smoke up his kimono, but it was true. Hal's work on those long-buried bones had started the Chief's downfall.

Ah, shit," he said and pulled a file folder from a drawer. "This doesn't go out of this room."

I pantomimed sealing my lips and throwing away the key.

"Okay, first, his body stank to high hell."

"I would think so."

"No, sulfurye fluoride has no odor, has no color. What stinks is they include chloropicrin, which does stink, so when humans come in contact with it, they'll react and get away from it."

"Okay." I wasn't sure what to say because I didn't want Hal to stop. Fat chance of that.

"Fordham's brain was swollen ten to fifteen percent. His lungs had filled with fluid, his kidneys were congested. He was seriously messed-up. It was a horrible way to die."

"Assuming he died from the termite gas."

That stopped Hal. Shit.

"I'm just spit-ballin' here."

"Who's been talking?"

"I'm just throwing out ideas. I'm sure you heard about the clamps."

"What clamps?"

"On the tent?"

Shit, he hadn't heard, so maybe we could go *quid pro quo* .

"Okay, I'll divulge some news to *you*. Rosales Exterminators are very precise in their work. And not just because the fumes are dangerous. They have one way of doing things and one way only. So, when they went to remove the tent, before they went inside to check and instead of dead termites found a dead body, a couple of the workers noticed several of the clamps on the tent by the back door weren't fixed properly."

"Somebody changed them?"

"Unless you think Steve clamped them up from the inside and then offed himself."

"Oh, hell yes!" Hal slapped his desk. "We've got a murder case."

I think I'd just made his day. Or maybe his month.

"So?" I said.

Hal checked the door, as if he thought someone might come in and discover this insider trading of forensic evidence. "Damn, I kept thinking this looked off, but I kept telling myself I was just looking for some excitement."

"What?"

"According to the MB-289," Hal stopped for a moment and was going to explain what that was, but I cut in:

"Number 289, the crime scene write-up, I remember."

He smiled and nodded: the implication being good boy Singer.

"Fordham was found straight down from a second-floor landing. So, it looked like maybe he had gotten dizzy from the gas and went over the railing."

"Okay."

"The cops just assumed that Fordham, whether he wandered in by mistake or committed suicide, died from the gas. But they never considered homicide."

"Why not?"

"Don't know. Most likely, they just assumed. I mean who'd choose to go that way?"

"And Remington's signed off on this?"

"I haven't heard anything to the contrary, but you know, Glenn plays it pretty close to his chest."

"Which is usually covered by the finest Egyptian cotton."

Hal looked at me a little strangely. Like maybe that was a fact one man shouldn't know about another man.

"Fordham had bruising at the base of his neck. Right here," Hal pointed to the spot on his neck, "his medulla oblongata."

"Which is pretty much always fatal."

"Because the blow causes internal bleeding. And intraparenchymal bleeding that occurs within the medulla oblongata causes damage to cranial nerve X, more commonly known as the vagus nerve, which plays an important role in blood circulation and breathing."

"Whuff. Too much info for my little brain. Give it to me in simpleton terms."

"He could have died from either the blow or the gas."

"And that's where the bitch of this case will be, determining which was first."

Hal looked at me like I'd suddenly removed the dunce cap.

"Yes," he said, "with one you've got an accident…

"And with the other, you've got a murder."

22

"It wasn't a suicide?" my dad said. "You know this for sure?"

"No, but I'm betting on it."

We were having sandwiches at his house instead of going out for dinner and I was telling him what Hal and I had discussed. I did have a moment of anxiety about Hal's warning that whatever we talked about stayed inside his office, but then I hadn't signed a confidentiality statement. And if I couldn't trust my dad, who the hell could I trust?

"Great sandwich," I said, holding up the tasty combo of sliced turkey, mayo and mustard, lettuce, a couple slices of Swiss, sliced Romano tomatoes and grilled red peppers, all stuffed between thick slices of homemade Italian. We were washing it down with icy cold *Pacifico* beers.

"It's the bread," he said. "Your grandmother's special homemade bread. *Nana's pane fatto in casa.*"

"Right," I said. "From her secret recipe."

"Yes, her *receipe segreto*," he said, smiling. He was so proud of that secret recipe.

"You ever going to tell it to me?"

"Maybe in my will." He laughed.

I didn't have the heart to tell him that I already knew the recipe. Ida, his grandmother had passed it down to Flavia, my dad's mom, who had told me. It was wasted clandestine knowledge because I am terrible in the kitchen.

"Of course, you're going to have to learn how to cook first," he said, pretty much reading my mind.

"I'll stick to sleuthing."

"Sounds like you've made some headway for Carmen anyway."

"Hal didn't confirm anything, just expressed some theories."

"Well, Spanish Carlos says Carmen's in the clear."

"So then now Remington and the boys need to find out who killed Steve Fordham."

"And why they killed him," my dad said.

"Find out the why, you usually find out the who." I took a sip of beer. "That's Singer's Rule Sixteen of Super Sleuthing."

"How about your real case?"

"None of the rules apply so far. We're still in the dark about what happened to Charlene."

"But she *was* murdered, right?"

"Can't say one hundred percent until the autopsy comes back, but I'd bet on it. But what I meant was we've got no suspects, we've got no motivation, we've got no nothing. And plenty of that."

"Don't sing it," my dad said.

I ignored that. "For all we know," I said, "it might really have been an accident."

"And nobody knows where she was all those months?"

"A little over fourteen months. So, she didn't get pregnant and run away out of shame. The time frame doesn't work."

"Anything more on the parents?"

"Her father's certainly not a role model, but he's pretty typical of your ambitious captain of industry. So, they're clean. I think tomorrow we'll talk to them after we do some more hill climbing."

That reminded me of Zak. I hadn't received any email notifications or text messages, and for sure no calls. I pulled my cell to call him, and then checked the clock: 9:30, already past midnight for Zak. I slipped the cell into my pocket and went back to my sandwich and beer.

"You like Carmen?" I said.

"Do I like her as a suspect?"

"Quit avoiding the question. Do you like her?"

He took a sip of beer, delaying his answer. Which meant, Yeah, he did.

My cell buzzed.

"Saved by the bell," he said.

"Your lack of an answer *is* an answer, pops."

I checked the ID and said, "Hey, Zak. I was thinking of calling you but figured it was too late."

"Vampires don't sleep you know that," he said, his voice as clear as if he was sitting at the table having a beer with us. "So, I got a lead, but I've got to warn you, it's a bit sticky."

"Sticky how?"

"Dark sticky. Bad sticky. There is a property on road that doesn't exist, just off *Los Tilos* and…"

"What's that mean, doesn't exist?"

"Not part of the official road system of Los Angeles County."

"And…?"

"And from what I can dig out, and I've had to dig deep, but there's a building up there that's got some super high mojo. Like governmental."

"How high the mojo?"

"D.C. and I don't mean comics." He chortled a bit at his own joke. "Although the boys in Washington are pretty damn funny, all the shit they pull."

"So how do I find it?"

Zak stopped talking and I could hear his computer keys clacking like a machine gun. "I've just sent you the geographical coordinates."

"Jesus, what the hell is this place?"

23

"Temple of the Blood of Christ."

That's what the small brass plate said to the side of the door. The name plate was small, but the house and grounds were enormous. More like a compound. Several dogs of various breeds lazed about on the wide lawn and on the front steps. At least three cats also lay in the sunshine, co-existence being pretty easy up here.

I had called Wade after I'd finished talking to Zak and we decided to keep this one to ourselves. At least until we got a chance to look things over first. There was some kind of government connection to the building. And not just because it wasn't officially on the map.

We got on the road before the heavy traffic. Although in L.A. there's always traffic. It's either bad or WFT.

But we made good time and got to *Los Tilos* before 9 am.

Zak had emailed the geographic coordinates. But when our GPS matched up to 35° 8'N, 119° 21'W, there wasn't any road. At least one you could see from the car.

We parked and walked back to the epicenter of the coordinates. And there was an opening off the asphalt, a dirt entrance to something. On the right side of that entrance was the biggest pepper tree I had ever seen. Its enormous branches draped nearly across the road, its green curtain of leaves dense and thick. It was the perfect camouflage. We pushed through the leaves and there, like some low-rent Xandau was a narrow, winding road. And at the top of it, a mansion.

"Arrrgggh," Wade said in his best pirate growl, "this be like looking for treasure." He'd pointed up at the mansion. "X marks the spot."

"Was that Long John Silver or Johnny Depp?"

"Black beard," he pointed to his face. "As in black." Then rubbed his day-old stubble, "and beard."

"Yo-ho-ho," I said.

We walked up the long driveway but didn't see anyone.

"For a Fed building," Wade said, "security's pretty low key."

"Unless that golden retriever suddenly turns vicious," I said. The dog opened an eye, then its head lolled back, and he went back to sleep. So much for our physical threat. I stopped before going up to the door. "Listen."

Wade tilted his head. "Yeah? I don't hear anything."

"Exactly. Hard to believe it's so quiet up here."

"Considering nobody can find it, that's not so surprising."

We stepped around a big fat white cat lying in the middle of the three wide steps leading to the entrance.

"What do you think a place like this goes for?" Wade said.

"If the lot goes as far back and as wide as I think? And based on Crutchfield's price? Thirty or so big ones."

"That's some collection plate, pay for all this."

There wasn't a doorbell, but there was a large brass door knocker in the shape of a Sheppard's staff.

"And don't say, 'Get the flock outta here,'" I said.

"I might say flock, but the next word would be you."

I raised the staff and hit the brass plate twice. It was loud. A few moments drifted by, it was so quiet and peaceful up here you could fall asleep standing up. We heard the handle being turned and the door opened and a serene, beautiful young girl who could have been Charlene's sister smiled at us from inside the hood of a long, white flowing robe made of some expensive looking fabric that nearly touched the ground. She moved slightly with the door and I saw a long slender foot in a thin-soled sandal.

"Good morning," she said, softly, "and God bless you kind gentlemen."

"Good morning," I said. "I'm Matt Singer and this is my partner, Jamal Wade."

Wade smiled and nodded hello. "We're looking for…" I stopped. "I'm sorry, the *Temple of the Blood of Christ*? I've never heard of your church before."

"Oh, of course not," she said. She looked at us for a moment as if we should have grasped that fact long before we came to the door. "We are a very small group serving the Lord." And then she sighed. "Oh, my, where are my manners? I am so sorry," she said, shaking her head and then pulling back her hood, revealing long and thick, shiny blond hair that would have made a Wilhelmina model insecure. "I am Sister Chastity," she said, extending a delicate-looking hand that was solid and firm when it shook mine.

"Sister Chastity? What's your real name?"

"That *is* my real name."

"Do you have any ID?" I said.

"Why would I need ID in my own house?"

"Okay," Wade said. "Do you have anything with your name on it?"

"No. I know this is difficult for you. Brother Jordan always warns us of this, that the…" she gestured out beyond us, but also included us, "…*Others*, people who don't understand, would present trouble. And we are prepared to endure that."

"You don't have any identification?" I said.

"When the Temple found me, I abandoned all connections to the past, including my unclean name."

Okay, time for the direct approach.

"We are looking for this girl …" and I started to show her Charlene's photo, but Sister Chastity gasped and dropped to her knees and threw her arms out in supplication, "Oh, thank you, Lord our Redeemer, thank you for returning my sister. Oh, God, oh, God. Thank you."

She looked up at Wade and me, huge tears welling in her eyes.

"Your sister?" Wade said.

"Yes," she said and stood up.

"I didn't think Charlene had a sister," I said.

"Yes, that's because of the way you think."

"Excuse me?"

"You think that we're not related by blood." She paused and then smiled. "Well, we *are* related by blood. The blood of our Lord and Savior Jesus Christ. Sister Felicity, her *true* name, and all her other sisters here in Christ's blood are related." She looked at Wade, then me. "You said partners? In what?"

"Investigations."

"Is she okay? We haven't seen her for several days and..." she stopped, unsure, then said, "What's happened to Sister Felicity?"

"Is there someone in charge?" Wade said.

"Who wants to know?" A man said that from down the hall, accompanied by the harsh sound of heavy footsteps, two sets of them. And then two burly men appeared.

Without turning back to them, Sister Chastity pointed behind her and said, "Brother Thomas and Brother Jonas."

"I am Brother Thomas," he said and stepped to the right of Sister Chastity. He was also wearing a robe, but it was a light tan in color and didn't hide his camo-colored military boots. So was Brother Jonas, who stepped to her right. A couple of hard ass bookends, judging from their aggressive stances - beefy arms slightly out, fists curled and baleful stares. "And again, who wants to know?"

I felt, rather than saw, Wade shift his body slightly so anyone trying to attack, foolish idea that it was, would have less of a target; although with Wade's size that's still damn big.

"Los Angeles Police," I said.

"You don't look like cops."

"We're undercover."

And before he could say anything, I held out a business card.

Neither of the Brothers reached for it, so Sister Chastity, who could add politeness to her name, took it. "Private Investigations?" she said. "Oh, no, something's happened. Something bad."

Brother Jonas, in a move that was much faster than I would have expected from such a bruiser, snatched my card from her hand, looked at it for a second and then stepped in front of Sister Chastity, his bulk blocking her from our view.

"We are sorry, but we cannot help you."

The door slammed in our faces so hard the Sheppard staff bounced a couple of times.

"I'm thinking the blood part of the Temple mean they don't mind spilling a little of it," Wade said.

"As long as it's not theirs."

"I think we knock again," Wade said.

"The door or heads?"

But then the door opened and a small, dark man with a nose that sliced the air like a scimitar appeared and nodded curtly.

"I am Brother Dominic. How may I assist you?"

Apparently if you were a member here, you wore a robe. Brother Dominic's robe was white like Sister Chastity's but had red piping on its edges.

"We're looking for information on Charlene Dillard."

"Oh, I'm sorry, we don't know anyone by that name," Brother Dominic said.

"Do you know anyone who used to go by that name?" Wade said and stepped in closer to the Brother.

"Clever," Brother Dominic said. "But, '...we are not ignorant of the devil's devices.' 2nd Corinthians, 2:11."

"Yeah, well, there's always Hell to pay," Wade said. He held up Charlene's photo. "This young woman, Charlene, whom you know as Sister Felicity, what can you tell us about her?"

"We never discuss confidential information about anyone who is a member of the Temple."

"Listen, Brother Dominic, Charlene or Sister Felicity, whichever name you want to call her, was a member of this Temple; and as such, you are the last group of people who saw her."

"Last?" Brother Dominic said, "is she missing?"

"Yeah," Wade said. "As in permanently."

Brother Dominic blinked rapidly several times, absorbing this information. Then he bowed his head and while I could see his lips moving, I couldn't hear anything. But it was obvious he was praying.

Wade and I looked at each other: you don't stop anyone in mid-prayer.

"Amen." He looked at Wade, then me. "Can you tell me where she is? She will need to be sanctified and cleansed."

"I think that's up to her parents."

"You mean the ones that abandoned her?"

And then the door closed in our faces.

Again.

24

"This ain't the first time you two stepped in shit," Famous said. He was pissed at us. Very pissed.

Wade and I had decided not to say anything in our defense. Mostly because we really didn't have any: We should have given Famous the information right away and let the police act on it. But we had our own investigation to conduct. And a client who not only expected results but had paid for them. But Famous couldn't really be all-out mad because if we hadn't shown him the *Temple*, they would still be looking for it.

Which is why it wasn't until close to midnight that we finally got inside the Temple with Famous.

"Only as observers," Famous said

That was his cover story in case the Chief demanded an explanation. But it was really his way of doing us a solid in return.

Even with all his connections Famous didn't get the warrant until after 8:00 P.M. Then he had to assemble a team, secure the perimeter, and serve the warrant. Once inside, all Famous and Gonzo got was stony silence and protests of religious prosecution and zero help. Besides Dominic, Thomas and Jonas, there were two other Brothers, Eli and Aaron; each also big as a house.

"Lot of beefy protection, "Wade said.

"Yeah. For what?"

"The Sisters, I'm assuming," Famous said.

All of them virtuously named.

"Hope, Chastity, Serenity, Charity and Faith," Famous repeated for us.

"And they could be sisters," I said.

You would have a hard time at a Hollywood talent agency or central casting, finding five women who looked and acted so much alike. They were all tall, willowy and blond. And extremely young. Chastity was the senior at nineteen, the other Sisters were all eighteen. Or claimed to be.

There was also a young child, Micah, who was two.

"Who's his mother?" Famous said.

"We all are," said Faith. "When a child is born into the Temple, we are all the child's mothers."

"Great," I said. "But who actually carried Micah? And anybody want to hazard a guess as to who's his father?"

"The Sisters are not required to answer that," said Brother Dominic. I was getting the impression that Dominic was the leader.

"Since you're giving all the answers," Famous said, "I'm assuming you're the...what? Minister? Pastor? Rabbi?"

The Sisters rolled their eyes, almost all on cue, at the Rabbi reference. Sister Hope, at least I hoped that's who she was, held a polite hand to her mouth while she smiled. If I'd been closer, I'd bet I'd have heard her say, "Tee-hee."

Before Famous or Wade or I could ask another question, there was some noise from the front of the house and one of the patrolmen came up to Famous, handed him a business card and said something to him *Sotto voce*.

"Just what I need," he said. "An attorney." Famous moved his hand, almost in resignation, and motioned the patrolman to go get the attorney. "A mister *Zaafir Chawla*," Famous said to us.

A tall man wearing a white robe with navy piping entered and nodded to us. "Good evening," he said.

"And who do you represent, Mister *Chawla*?"

"Please, call me Brother Victor."

"Victor for victory," Wade said. "That's what *Chawla* means."

That got a snap head turn and Brother Victor stared for a moment at Wade and then me.

Wade held up his hands, "Sorry, that's about all the Pashto I know."

"I don't know any," said Brother Victor. "I speak Dari."

"If this UN meeting's over," Famous said, stepping into Brother Victor's line of sight, "answer my question: Why are you here?"

"I am the legal counsel for the Temple. And in that capacity, I am hereby advising my Brothers and Sisters to stop answering any questions."

"They haven't answered much of anything," Famous snapped.

"I would be more than happy to help you if I can, sir." He reached into his robe and pulled out what could only be a legal document. He handed it to Famous.

Famous read it, then read it again. His eyes were wide with surprise and indignation. He handed it to me.

I read it and couldn't help saying, "Are you freakin' kidding me?"

"Sir!" Brother Victor snapped. "This is a holy place. You will not profane its sanctity with blasphemy!"

"Actually, that was the condomed version of it. But I understand. My apologies."

Famous acted like he hadn't heard us; or he didn't give a damn.

"The blood of the mother? Seriously?" Famous took the document back, scanned it quickly. "And who's Brother Jordan?"

"Brother Jordan is our Spiritual Master. For lack of a better word, our leader."

"What do you mean," I said, "that the Church is invoking it's right to the blood of the mother'?"

Brother Victor stared right at me and didn't flinch; and he didn't hesitate when he said, "The child of course."

25

"Bloody hell," Wade said when we were in the car heading back to the beach. "That's one fucked up religion."

"I agree."

"I get the connection to the name, *Temple of the Blood of Christ*. But this is taking it a little beyond the pale."

It was an amazingly clear night and the full moon's reflection on the Pacific was like silver rungs of a ladder stretching back to the horizon. The Church claimed that all its members are considered "parents" of any children born to them. Therefore, the child *had* to be raised by the Church. It was a canon of their religion.

"Like I said: Fucked. Up."

"I'm pretty sure the Dillards can stop that, but my guess is it's going to be a bloody battle. In every sense of the word."

Wade looked at the water for a long moment. "We've only been on this case for a couple of days and already we've caught more equine excrement than I can remember."

"Equine excrement?"

"I figure we best be mindin' our language 'round da Sisters."

I turned up Wade's street. "Shit, we didn't eat dinner."

"Somehow I'm not hungry, "Wade said. "So tomorrow we meet Big Brother?"

"Mister Jordan. And not the one from the movies either."

But I was wrong.

Brother Jordan had leading man movie star looks. Maybe it was the blindingly white robe he wore–this one with shiny gold piping, that set off his shiny blond hair and icy blue eyes so light they almost looked white.

"A blond Jesus," I said. I thought I'd said it quietly under my breath as we walked into the room at police headquarters.

"No. Just an ordinary man." He stood and held out his hand. Just before we closed hands, I noticed he had an unusual tattoo in the webbing between his thumb and forefinger: A variation of a Janus face–with Jesus facing to the left, and what looked like Mohammed facing to the right. It was an intricately detailed and no doubt expensive inking.

"Officer...?" he said to me.

"Matt Singer." We shook and his grip was dry, firm and had a strength that hinted of much more power. I looked at the tattoo again as we broke the shake.

"You like it?" he said. "I think of it as the duality of life and religion, of Christianity and Muslim."

"And this is Jamal Wade," was all I said.

Wade and Brother Jordan shook hands.

"They aren't cops," Gonzo said. And got a withering look from Famous.

"Oh?" Brother Jordan said. "Then why are you here?"

"They've been hired by Sister Charity's *former* parents, the Dillards," Brother Dominic answered for us.

"They're still her parents," Wade said. And didn't say it nicely.

"I'm not here to argue past issues," Brother Jordan said. He looked at Famous, "What about my request?"

"Tell me again why you feel you have a right to claim it?"

"This is harassment," said Brother Dominic. "We've already explained this."

"Tell me again," Famous said. "I'm sure Brother Jordan will be even more eloquent."

"'*A faithful witness will not lie.*' Proverbs 14:5."

"You're the father of the child?" Famous said.

"The baby belongs to the church."

"That remains to be seen. But even if that were possible, we'd have to know who you were, *besides* Brother Jordan."

"As I told you, once I was found by the *Temple*, I abandoned all traces of the past." He folded his hands neatly on the table. "I like to think of it as our own 'Witness Protection Program' from Satan."

Famous practically leaped across the table and got right in his face.

"Yeah? Well who's going to protect you from me? I don't know what game you're trying to run here, but right now you're looking at rape, assault and maybe even murder. So cut the holier than thou crap and give us some answers."

Brother Dominic jumped to his feet but was waved back down by Brother Jordan. He waited until Dominic was seated, then looked at Famous. He could have been Gary Cooper staring down a desperado, or Harrison Ford playing one of his many heroic roles. "I have no answers, Detective Ramos, other than the ones I have already given you. And I will give you those answers again. But just because they are not the answers you seek, however misguidedly you seek them, does not mean they are not the truth."

"That's right, keep playing smart ass with me, keep hiding under your cloak of religion; you may find yourself in a cell with some big nasty guy named Gabriel."

This threw Brother Jordan. Threw me, too. I thought Famous would have said, Bubba.

"Gabriel?" Brother Jordan finally asked.

"Yeah," said Famous. "And he's going to be having you blow his trumpet daily."

Brother Dominic slammed his hand on the table, "This is insulting and degrading."

Famous probably thought he'd taken it a little too far I could tell because he did look away for a moment.

"Okay," he said, "let's start with the basics. Will you submit to a DNA test?"

"What will the scope of the test be?" Brother Dominic said.

"What does that mean?"

Brother Jordan answered, "I don't want you to play the lottery and run me through every system you've got."

"Why? You have Something to hide?"

"'*The words of his mouth were smoother than butter, but war was in his heart.*' Psalms 55:21. Everybody has something to hide."

"'*cept for me and my monkey.*' John Lennon, 1968. Stand up. You're under arrest."

"Stop!" yelled Brother Dominic, "Stop."

But Famous didn't stop or wait. He jerked Brother Jordan to his feet and cuffed him and wasn't gentle about it either.

"And here's another memorable quote," Famous said, "You have the right to remain silent."

26

"Talk to me?" Sister Chastity said. "Or interrogate me?"

"We are trying to help Charlene's parents, or Sister Felicity's parents, whichever one you prefer, find out what happened to their daughter."

Wade and I had doubled back to the Temple right after Famous snapped the cuffs on Brother Jordan. We figured Brother Dominic would be busy trying to arrange bail and it was a good time to ask questions without interference.

"Walk with me," Sister Chastity said. She stepped between Wade and me and headed down the long driveway. One of the dogs eased out of his full body recline and trotted after her. Wade and I, fellow dogs, did the same.

"Life is strange, don't you think, Mister Singer?"

"Call me Matt."

"You see, Mister Singer, Sister Felicity seemed the one of us who was the most deeply washed in the blood of our Lord and Savior Jesus Christ." She smiled at me and then included Wade in her radiance. "And she was the one who strayed."

"Strayed?"

"Yes. If she had remained within the sanctity, the safety, of the *Temple*, I don't believe any of the misfortune that came to her would have happened."

"Which misfortune was that? Having the baby? Or getting beaten in the head?"

Sister Chastity stopped as if she'd been jolted with a stun gun. And maybe she had. "What are you talking about?"

"Somebody clobbered her. Right here," I pointed at the base of my skull. "Very vulnerable spot."

"Oh, no that's not true. She fell. She lost her balance going down the stairs and tumbled. But she was fine, just fine."

"Did you see her fall?" Wade said.

"No. It...it happened when we were asleep."

"Everyone in the house was asleep and yet she's up?"

She smiled, again as if we were so dense. "Her pregnancy was difficult. She would get these severe cramps in her legs, Chuck Ponies."

"What?"

"Chuck Ponies, that's what she would call her leg cramps. You know, Charley Horses? But she said they weren't *that* severe, so...Chuck Ponies. "

"And when she fell," I said, "how long was that before she left the Temple?"

"A few hours." Sister Chastity's brows furrowed as she thought about it. "Yes, she fell that night. Brother Jordan explained it to us all at breakfast the next morning when she wasn't there."

"Did he tell you where she'd gone?"

"No. He just said she felt she needed to walk and left."

"She has a nasty fall and yet Brother Jordan just lets her walk out into the night?"

Sister Chastity went silent for a moment, looked out toward the Hollywood hills. "Perhaps the fall was more severe than we thought."

"Or were led to believe," Wade said.

"We are not *led* to believe anything, Mister Wade. We are *not* brainwashed."

"Okay, tell me again because I'm slow. I don't get it. You left your parents, your family, and your friends because you were what? Angry? Lost? Searching for Something? You had problems. But for this? You're prisoners here."

"We are not prisoners."

"You never leave."

"I have no reason to leave. Everything I want, what all of us, Brothers and Sisters want, is here. Our lives, our futures are all right here."

"Could I ask how old you are?" I said.

"Four."

"Never mind."

"No, it's true. It has been four years since my rebirth in the blood of Jesus."

"How old were you before you were reborn?"

"It doesn't matter."

"You don't think that's being brain-washed?" Wade said.

Sister Chastity looked at Wade and *laughed.*

Politely, but still a laugh. Right in his face.

"Brain-washed? Yes, yes, then we all are. And thank God for that. Washed of all the sin and guilt and cleansed of the dark vision that Society, *your* Society, perpetuates."

This was going to be a long haul. This is a young, malleable girl, Singer. Put your damn thinking cap on. There's got to be a way to reach her.

But Wade was ahead of me.

"One of the Lord's main tenants is forgiveness, right?"

Sister Chastity nodded, not sure where this was going.

"And one of his chief instructions is to honor thy father and mother..."

"Exodus 20:12," Sister Chastity said.

"Yes," Wade said, and looked at me for confirmation.

I shrugged. I knew the verses, but not who had said them.

"Therefore, you can help Sister Felicity honor her mother and father one last time by telling us who fathered her child."

"I would, I would. If I knew, but I don't." She looked at Wade and then me. "'A faithful friend is the medicine of life'. Ecclesiasticus 6:16. I would have done and will still do now, anything for Sister Felicity."

We walked up *Los Tilos* with her for a good half-mile, heard an impressive number of Biblical quotes and some vague circuitous answers, but when we returned to the entrance of the Temple, we didn't know anything more than when we'd started. Either Sister Chastity was the youngest spy craft master alive, or like her name, truly chaste.

27

"This guy's a goddamn choir boy," Famous said as Wade and I walked back into the station. "We've been grilling him nonstop and look at him, like he's just stepped out of the shower."

It was true. We looked at Brother Jordan on the monitor that showed the videotaping of his interrogation and he looked composed, serene, even.

"Detective Gonzalez," he said to Gonzo, "you look tired. Why punish yourself by pursuing this futile course? Just to prove you're one of the boys? That you, indeed, are worthy of that shield, even for one so young?"

"Listening to your crap doesn't make me tired," Gonzo said. "Just bored."

"Perhaps. But the blood of Christ courses through me as a mighty river and I will never weary in His cause."

Famous went back into the room and Brother Jordan nodded to him as if he welcomed an additional adversary; that just him against Gonzo wasn't fair.

"And his cause means that you rape teenage girls?" Famous said.

"I did not rape Sister Felicity."

"She just turned seventeen, you pervert. Seventeen. That's rape."

"Our Society does not recognize your feudalistic, repressive laws."

"Yeah? Well, your Society only exists at the mercy of the American Society. And you broke the law of that Society."

Brother Jordan smiled at Famous like he still had a few more cards to play. "Ah, but of course, I understand your anger. You have a personal stake in this."

"What the hell are you talking about?"

"Brother Jordan! Don't," warned Brother Dominic.

Brother Jordan waved him off with a sharp flick of his hand. "Your personal stake, Detective Ramos. Your daughter Meagan. I believe she and Sister Felicity are the same age."

I thought Famous was going to come across the desk and send Brother Jordan to meet his maker right there. But he controlled himself and burned a hole into Brother Jordan's eyes, then pivoted and went out of the room fast.

"Damn," Wade said. "Where the hell did he get that?"

"I'd say Dominic. And I'd also say that's a threat."

"Not smart to do that to a cop. Especially *that* cop."

Wade was right. *That* cop,

Famous struck fast and hard.

By the time Wade and I were back at the beach, Famous's actions were all over the news.

"Look at this," my dad said, when we stopped by to pick him up for dinner.

The TV showed a media frenzy in front of the Temple. Every local station, all four of the major networks, CNN, MSNBC and the other big cable news channels and just about any other media outfit you could think of was bivouacked outside the Temple grounds. The roads and surrounding area were packed with equipment, gear, lights, cameras, and cables snaking everywhere. A small army of reporters, local anchors, pundits, and so-called experts looked to the cameras and spouted shit. Brilliant, well-written shit; but still shit because no one really knew anything yet. But, hey, that's never stopped the news. It's just never had much connection to the truth.

They all pushed up against the yellow crime scene tape. Because that's what the police, thanks to Famous, had declared the Temple. When he walked out and ducked under the tape, they hit him like the proverbial plague, shoving tape cassette recorders, microphones, cell phones, anything they had that would record. It was so much sound, the truest example of cacophony I'd ever heard.

But one reporter did get through; or at least did for the local ABC affiliate.

"Detective Ramos, how many wives or really concubines, does this so-called minister have?"

Ramos kept walking towards his squad car.

"We have no evidence of that, or a comment."

"Why are the police taking these young women and the child into custody?"

"We are moving to protect what we believe are underage minors and one infant."

"Is it true that one of the mothers was raped and murdered?"

Famous made his car, yanked open the door and slammed it shut. Gonzo was behind the wheel, waiting, the engine running. Reporters moved alongside of the vehicle as it slowed parted the sea of humanity, shouting questions.

Through the car windows I saw Famous motion to Gonzo and say something. Then, suddenly, the whoop-whoop-whoop of the siren and the lights blasted the soft California night air; effectively killing any more questions.

A police van lumbered down the driveway, paused while a patrolman lowered the tape, and then drove through, following behind Famous. I thought I saw a blond head through the back window, but then I was probably just imagining it.

A cameraman shot the retreating van, then a long shot of the Temple, the chaotic scene on the steep hill, and then finally to the reporter as she delivered her closing of the "news": "Marcy Bryant in the heart of the city. A heart, broken tonight by a church whose rites of baptism would appear to include sexual crimes."

I clicked off the TV and decided it was time to worry about our own local troubles.

"So, how's the heart of *Paraíso Del Mar?*" I asked.

"What's that line," my dad said, "about screenplays and Hollywood?"

"They're like assholes. Everybody's got one."

"And they all stink," Wade said.

"You've just defined the Steve Fordham story. Absolutely amazing shit. It was a suicide. It was a mob hit—as if there's even that connection here or that Steve would be worth the trouble. His wife did it. A jealous lover did it. Only guy that isn't a suspect is Elvis."

"And he left the building, just not the one on Spinnaker."

"Anybody think it's an accident?" Wade said. "The facts don't support it, but you never know."

"Remington's not even investigating the accidental angle."

"How's Carmen?"

"Upset, but Spanish Carlos said she's in the clear."

"Legally, but not emotionally."

We went to dinner at a small favorite restaurant of ours, *Chef Fritz*, which not only doesn't serve any kind of German food, but doesn't stock a lager, pilsner or *Altbier* or even a *Riesling*. Fritz, whose real name is Francois, serves a distinguished array of *haute cuisine*. He has a menu, but Francois prefers you don't order from it and let him decide what you're in the mood for that night.

Even Francois had a theory about Steve Fordham. "*Cherez la femme.*"

"Look to the woman," Wade said.

"*Qui.* He was fucking the wrong woman."

That theory seemed automatic, given Francois' heritage.

But a couple of hours later when I was having a nightcap at Kincaid's, that theory had gained in popularity.

I was at the bar, talking with Pat Kincaid when a very sexy brunette took the seat next to me.

"Hey, Matt," she said.

"Hello, Lo-Lo." I signaled to Pat to give Lo-Lo a drink, which he was already mixing. "How's the world of real estate?" I said.

Lo-Lo, which I think is some derivation or substitute for Louisa, was one of the hottest real estate agents in town. And not just for the way she looked. Lo-Lo's clients liked money, had a lot of it, and weren't afraid to spend it on themselves; especially when it came to their homes. It was a slow month for Lo-Lo if she didn't have at least one multi-million-dollar listing.

"I'm having a great month." Which probably meant a hundred thousand or so in commissions. She picked up her drink and clicked her glass against mine. "Thank you, Jesus," she said.

"You're welcome. And don't call me Jesus."

She blinked for a second, and then smiled, her grey-blue eyes merry, but not one crinkle line at the corner. Thank you botox.

"So, what's your theory on Can't Afford Him?" she said.

"Can't afford him?"

"Steve Fordham—Can't Afford Him. He bought most of his listings."

"He *was* new to real estate."

"He didn't act like it. I heard he outmaneuvered Sullivan a couple of weeks ago."

William Sullivan had been a top-selling agent in *Paraíso Del Mar* for twenty years. And now his two sons, Marc and Samuel, had carried the family name to new heights.

"Which house?"

I was curious because despite of how loyal your clients tell you they are, their loyalty can be bought.

"289 *Avenida de las estrellas*. The Mullers."

Fuck. Mike Mullers.

My emotions must have raced across my face because Lo-Lo said, "Oh, shit,

Matt. Was he your client?"

"Was."

"I'm sorry."

"No problem. He was probably never really a client, just pretended to be.

Because I can't remember a more duplicitous sonofabitch than him."

Wade and I had negotiated our asses off to get Mike that house. We'd been in a bidding war contest with six other buyers. And we were successful because I knew the sellers had some logistics issues. The husband had gotten hired away by a hotshot Silicon Valley software company. They'd included the down payment for his new house as part of the incentives to sign with them.

It was a sweetheart deal. The only problem was they needed Mike up there like yesterday. And he'd only lived in his house twenty months. So, if he sold his house before the California state two-year minimum, he'd have a huge tax hit.

Wade and I wrote the deal for a hundred thousand over list and said that Matt would lease the property for five months so the seller could delay the sale until they'd passed the two-year limit.

It got Mike the deal.

And for fifty thousand less than the highest bid.

And that lying, ungrateful bastard hadn't even had the balls to call us and say he was selling or to even give us a chance to compete for his business.

Although now that listing was up for grabs again.

"Hell, Matt, you could go after it now," Lo-Lo said. "I mean since little Stevie Wonder's gone."

"Stevie Wonder?"

"That was another of his nicknames. Because you wonder how the hell, he kept getting listings with his crappy track record. Although the way he looked, most of the time all he had to do was show up."

She took a couple of long swallows on her drink and set it down, empty.

I signaled to Pat for another.

"So...Can't Afford Him shows up and...?"

"Right. Sullivans, I heard put the house at four point two. Steve comes in, tells the owner, 'Oh, four point nine? Not a problem, call the movers. I know I can get that price.' Bingo. New listing. Steve's the hero."

Pat delivered her second drink. Lo-Lo took a long swallow. She was either intent on getting drunk fast or had some serious issues.

"And you know, no intelligent agent's going to tell his buyers to make an offer anywhere near that price. I mean even a reasonable offer seems like a low ball when it's that high."

"And no agent wants to seem like a bottom feeder."

"So, they don't do anything."

"Why waste your time?"

"That's the problem. When they're that high, *every* offer's a low ball. So, you come in and the typical buyer always, always wants to *steal* the damn house, so you've got to make a bid that's ridiculously below the realistic market price and not even in the same country as Steve's price."

"C'mon, Lo-Lo, you shy?"

"Hell no. But, still, when you call the listing agent, you feel put out...no, you feel diffident."

"Diffident? Wow."

"Yeah, that's my new word for the day. That's one of my self-improvement strategies: learn a new word a day. Shit I can't believe I freakin' worked it into a conversation and did it legit, too. Woot!" She reached over her shoulder and patted herself on the back. "Go, Lo-Lo."

Lo-Lo wasn't trying to get drunk, she already was.

"It doesn't do anybody any good," she said. "The other agent thinks you can't control your client."

"Even though the other agent *knows* you can't control a client."

Lo-Lo threw back the rest of her drink. I looked at Pat, but he slightly shook his head and moved down the bar.

"So that's why some agents call him 'Can't Afford Him.'" Lo-Lo said. "Because you goddamn *can't* afford him. He takes a listing and the freakin' house sits there and sits there. After a while it sits there and the market–buyers, agents, your neighbors, everybody–they all think, something's wrong with that house. Well, there's nothing wrong with the damn house; except it was priced too high."

Lo-Lo looked at her empty glass and then at mine, which still had a quarter inch of booze left in it. "Shit, I'm getting hammered."

"Can I get you a taxi?"

"A taxi? Damn, you really are in love."

"What?"

"Nothing, nothing."

She stood up suddenly, lost her balance and I caught her by the arm. She looked at me and threw her arms around my neck and kissed me. A big, wet kiss.

I eased out of it. Feeling guilty. Hoping that no one who knew me and knew Leah would feel compelled to report this, but then thought that was pretty stupid.

"Hey, Lo-Lo," Kincaid said, "here's a coffee. On the house."

"What the ..? You think I'm drunk?"

"Not too many sober women kiss Matt."

I gave him the finger.

"Give me your keys, Lo-Lo," Kincaid said.

"What?"

"I love you Lo-Lo," Kincaid said, "but I also love staying in business. And what I love most of all is you being alive." He held out his hand.

Lo-Lo reluctantly fished her keys from her purse. A young waiter came up behind us. When Kincaid had signaled for him, I hadn't seen. Kincaid tossed him Lo-Lo's keys. "Josh will drive you home."

Lo-Lo turned and gave Josh an appraisal and nodded her head in approval.

"Okay, handsome," she said, and hooked her arm in his and went along.

"Wow," I said.

"Yeah," Kincaid said, "she's taking Steve's death pretty hard."

"What?"

"They were hot and heavy. Everyone in town knew that."

I was always behind the curve.

"I thought Steve was married?"

"He is. Or was. Going through a nasty divorce."

"And Lo-Lo's the reason?"

"One of them."

28

Marcella Turner, Joleene McCane, Anne Bingham and Chloe Tibideaux were the other reasons.

At least they were the most recent.

Rumor was the list was much longer but was being squelched; mostly by the other reasons.

Steve Fordham was handsome enough to have been a model, and apparently charming enough to get a long list of women out of their panties and into bed, some of them the very owners who had him list their homes.

"Hell," Wade said, "that might have been why his real estate business was so bad: his loving business was so good."

Wade, Leah and I were having breakfast the next morning at the Koffee Korner Kafe, one of *Paraíso Del Mar*'s best coffee shops, if not its worst offender at being kute in the spelling department.

"His wife kicked him out of the house," Leah said. "Huge screaming match like in some bad movie. Throwing his clothes out the front door, his golf clubs. Gave him a mild concussion too."

"Oh?"

"She threw one of his autographed baseballs at him; hit him flush on the temple."

"Hell, hath no fury," I said.

"And no right arm like Cathy Fordham," Leah said. "Although she's devastated now."

"How long ago did this happen?" I said.

"Six, seven months."

"So, Steve just kept screwing his way to more listings and more women?"

"I don't know," Leah said. "Kinda looks that way." She finished the last bite of her egg-white omelet and dabbed her lips with a napkin. "One of the other rumors is that Steve was sleeping in empty houses for sale."

"Now *that's* a bad divorce. Really?"

It was simple enough. You went through the active listings, see which ones were listed as 'Vacant' in the agent notes section, make sure no one saw you and slipped in after dark.

That was the rumor.

But I'd never known anyone who'd done it.

And not just because it was illegal and violated every rule of real estate ethics.

It was creepy.

"Saves on motels," Wade said. "Home away from home. Or home instead of home."

The other rumor about empty houses was that agents had been known to sneak into them and get a quickie. Saved on motel bills. Didn't leave a credit card trail. And you couldn't stick around afterwards for small talk, which made things easier in case sex was all someone was after. It added a new twist to private showings.

And of course, there were some lovebirds who didn't need the house to be empty, just for the owners to not be home.

You hoped the lovers hadn't slipped under the sheets. But then lust has no boundaries. And if it became a regular tryst, then you'd get careless. And something would be left behind. Or the sheets wouldn't be smoothed and tucked tight.

But if an owner suspected, how the hell could he ask?

"The house have Ring or Blink video security?"

"Nope."

"But what about the lockbox?" I said. "Every time someone opens the lockbox, it's recorded electronically."

"But if there's been a lot of activity on the house, how the hell you going to know?" Leah said.

She held out her phone to me.

It was a lengthy scroll of lockbox entry and exit times.

"Those all yours?"

"They're Seaview's. But for some damn reason I get linked into every one of them because I'm the owner."

Leah had inherited Seaview from her father. It was clearly the most successful real estate firm in town. Big, big bucks. Lo-Lo was an agent. So were the other top fifteen agents and brokers in town. The rule of twenty percent controls eighty percent? At Seaview it was more like only five percent. There weren't that many agents at Seaview, but they did incredible business. They didn't have *all* the listings in town, just the most expensive and best ones.

"And the police went through all of Steve's lockbox usage."

"But there'd be nothing for Spinnaker," I said.

Wade and Leah looked at me for a moment. And I didn't wait to let them figure it out since it doesn't hurt to gain what little advantage I can with those two.

"No record because the house was in escrow, being tented, and they'd taken off the lockbox."

"Right. How'd you know that?"

"Carmen told him," Wade said. "Or his pops."

"Ah, so" I said in my worst bad '50s movies Chinese spy accent. "Two wrongs and I'm still right." But I don't think Leah or Wade got it. Or appreciated it.

"Standard operating procedure for most agents," I said, "once you're in escrow, you remove all access to the house. The owners don't want to be bothered because they think it's a done deal. And as an agent, you want to eliminate any possible risks."

"Top marks," Leah said, and kissed my cheek.

29

I got another kiss on my cheek two hours later.

This one from Maria.

Of course, Wade got one too.

She was glad to see us and hoped that we had good news for the Dillards.

But our news was that we had no news.

Brother Jordan had stonewalled Famous long enough for the legal wheels of the *Temple*, mostly through Brothers Victor and Dominic, and I secretly suspected, some bigger wheels higher up some place, to shut down any information gathering.

"Do you think he's the monster that raped Charlene?" Mrs. Dillard said.

"That's our assumption. We'll know as soon as we get the DNA work back."

Oksanna shuddered. "And if he is? Then he might be able to take Charlene's baby? Our grandson?"

"I have no idea," I said.

"Not a chance," Charles Dillard said. He turned to his right and called down towards a hallway: "Finneran!"

A door opened and a moment later Peter Finneran marched into the room with a thick manila file folder and handed it to me.

"You can look at it later," Charles said. "Those are copies of what my attorneys have filed with the courts. Motion for guardianship. Motion for immediate custody. Motion to suppress any and all claims by that fucking monster Jordan. Those are the most important documents, but there are twenty-seven in all."

I was impressed. The Dillards hadn't acquired all those billions by waiting for things to happen or others to make decisions. They made the decisions that made things happen.

Finneran gave me his fish-oil smile: See that's how *real* investigative experts do it.

"That should tie him up while the other issues are decided," Wade said. The other issues, rape and homicide, were left unspoken.

Oksanna seemed agitated. Charles noticed it too or was familiar with it.

"My wife doesn't quite approve of all...this." He indicated the manila folder of legal documents.

Her black eyes bore holes into her husband. "I told Charles that we should have just walked out of the hospital with Fyodor." She smiled and caught herself. "That's what we are calling him, Fyodor. Means, *Gift of God* in Russian. Is a good name, no?"

"Yes, it's a good name."

"But the doctors would have tried to stop you," Charles said.

"*Tried!*" Oksanna spat. "Tried. But they would not have succeeded. Who is going to stop a grandmother who has just lost her child from holding her infant grandson? And by the time the police would have acknowledged there was a problem, Fyodor and I would be in Saint Petersberg."

She looked at her husband and then at Wade and me, defying us to contradict her, or deny that she was speaking the truth. Sure, the government could come after her, but after an attempt or two by the American counsel or even the U.S. Ambassador to Russia, they would lose interest.

And as if reading my thoughts, Oksanna said, "And in a few years, after all the legal work is completed, Fyodor and I could return. He would speak Russian as well as English, maybe even French, and he would be safe and protected by his family. His Ivankovo family. "

She was referring to her Russian family, which in this case was, literally, her *Rossiyskaya Mafiya* family. Oksanna, we'd learned, was connected. And while no one could prove any of it, there were rumors. And when it comes to the kind of money the Dillards controlled, believe the rumors.

"So instead," she said, "we are stuck with the legal method."

"He will be with us," Charles said directly to his wife. "Trust me."

Charles then looked directly at Wade and me. "We've run Jordan's prints."

Which I thought was amazing–how'd he get Jordan's prints, how did he get access to the government's data base, how much power did the Dillards really have?

"And?" Wade said.

"They've come back classified."

"He's a Fed?" I said. "No way."

"We can't push any further," Oksanna said, "but perhaps your friend, Detective Ramos can help?" But the way she said it, there wasn't any *perhaps* involved. What she meant was–find out. Now.

Famous and Gonzo were out working their other cases, so we had to track them down. We caught up to them just outside Dodger Stadium where they were investigating a hit and run.

Not for the Dodgers, but for a fan who'd been at last night's game.

"Well, actually," Famous said, "it was a hit and run, then run back, hit again, and again. Son of a bitch ran over the victim, this Tomas Romero, three times before he took off."

"A black SUV," Gonzo said. "So, it's an Escalade. Or it's an Explorer. Or it's an XD-5. Nothing on the plates, and nobody saw the driver through the blacked-out windows. But one witness swears it had triple-chrome Supine twenty-fours. You believe that shit? Can't tell you the car but knows the wheels down to the brand and the size."

"And the price," Famous said. "Fifteen hundred each."

"Expensive ride," Wade said. "So, wheels that size require a special tire."

"Yeah, we got a partial on his jacket." Famous nodded for Wade and me to join him near their unmarked car.

"So, what've you got that's new on Charlene?"

We told him about all the legal documents, but not about Oksanna's illegal dream–to kidnap Fyodor, or as the police records listed him, Baby John Doe.

"Maybe all that lawyer shit will do something, but I doubt it," Famous said. "There's some serious high-ranking heat coming down on this."

First Zak and now Famous.

"What do you mean?" I said.

"We're grilling Jordan," Famous said. "Going at it hard. And Jordan's getting tired. So, I finally say, 'We're going to keep asking until you tell us what we already know.'"

"You know?" Jordan says.

"Yeah, we do know," I say. "We know you're a pedophile and a murderer hiding behind some bullshit cloak of religion. And don't even think of quoting another biblical phrase."

"No quotes, just a question," Jordan says. "Do the stars and stripes still fly over this great country of ours?"

"What the hell's that supposed to mean?"

"It means this is a free country. And my religion is protected. And I am protected. So, all of this is just wasting time. And I need to get back to the Temple."

"You aren't going anywhere."

"Don't be too sure," he says.

"Then he takes one of the yellow tablets and writes down one line and slides it over to me. And I look at it and say, 'Who the hell is Theo Kouros?'"

Famous looked at Wade and me, he's a great storyteller, so he was waiting for us to ask. "And who is Theo Kouros?" I said

"Don't know yet," Famous said. "All I know is that everything's on hold. That came from the top floor. Brother Jordan is not to be questioned. Brother Jordan is to be placed in his own cell, away from the general population. Brother Jordan is going to make bail tomorrow."

30

That night we got more unbelievable news.

And not just when we met Theo Kouros.

Kouros was a burly, no-nonsense FBI agent.

First, he grilled Famous about LAPD procedures, then about us. Then he grilled us. And finally, after he'd vetted us, he said, "I'm not regular Bureau, I am Special Ops. And while it would have saved us all time and frustration, agent Michaels followed protocol by not calling me until all other measures were exhausted."

"Agent Michaels?" Gonzo said.

"Yes. Brother Jordan is Agent Jon Michaels."

"This pervert is an Agent?" snapped Famous. "No way, no fucking way."

Kouros just looked at Famous like he'd said he had photos of J. Edgar in a prom dress.

"Agent Michaels is one of the best and brightest young men the Bureau's had in twenty years. He's put himself at great risk for this assignment."

"You're right," I said. "Pedophiles risk fifteen to twenty."

"This sting operation has been more than three years in the making and we're this close," he held his index and thumb a quarter inch apart, "this close to pay off."

"God damn it!" Famous said. "I don't care if it's fifty years. Your star agent's got a harem of underage girls. All of whom he's raped repeatedly. He's impregnated at least two of them. And one of them, the mother of his child, he hit hard enough to give her brain damage that killed her."

"Those are outrageous and totally false charges."

"The hell they are!"

Kouros took a long, deep breath; as if he was fighting to not explode; or maybe he was suffocating at the news. Or, maybe, he was just a dickhead who took in a lot of air before proving he was a certified asshole.

"The Bureau has no proof of your claims. And while I don't want to appear to be callous, sometimes there's fall-out and collateral damage."

Famous got right in his face.

"Your agent's a sex freak. When did the Bureau add pimping to its service?"

"Detective Ramos, I order you to control yourself and back down."

"You don't order me shit. This is *my* department."

Definite testosterone moment. Two bull elephants about to rumble.

I stepped close to Famous, "C'mon, Juan, I need to talk to you. Outside."

Famous looked at me and I nodded. He stared at me, his eyes gleaming with rage, and then he let out a long breath. "Yeah." He turned to go.

And then Kouros just couldn't let it go.

But then he was F.B.I.–Forever Blowing It.

"I can appreciate your anger, Detective, that this hits close to home. You have a daughter close to the ages of the Sisters?"

Famous spun out of my arm across his shoulders and lunged for Kouros, but Wade blocked his path.

"He's not worth it, Juan. No."

Famous tried to get past Wade, but Jamal moved with him and held out his massive arms.

"Hey, Lieutenant," Gonzo said, and right then showing why he was a rising star by helping to defuse the situation, "Let me buy you a *café con leche*. With a *dolce!*"

Famous looked at his young protégé and while it took a moment, he finally smiled. Then he looked at Kouros, then Wade and me and nodded to Gonzo and they left together.

Wade and I weren't sure what was our next move.

Kouros decided that for us.

"I assume we're done here?" he said. "Unbelievable conduct here in L.A."

And then *I* lost it.

"No, what's unbelievable is you and your total lack of understanding and devastation of what's happened here, to this family, to this young girl."

"Excuse me, Matt," he emphasized *Matt*, "but I know exactly what I am doing."

"Really? I want to be there when you tell Charlene's parents that their daughter, their seventeen-year-old daughter, who became a mother thanks to your rising star, who also killed her, is just 'collateral damage.'"

31

Things were wrecked back in *Paraíso Del Mar* too.

"They arrested Carmen," my dad said. "It's totally bull shit."

"I thought Spanish Carlos had taken care of all that."

"He did for Carmen as an individual, but not for her as the owner."

"How the hell can you be a murder suspect just by owning a company?"

"Assuming you're not Alfred Anastasia and own Murder, Incorporated," Wade said.

"Jamal!" my dad said, "this isn't the time."

Which was one of the few times, if maybe the only time, I'd heard my dad chastise Wade.

"Let me tell you something, Mario," Wade said, a chill in his voice. He looked at my dad and said, "You're absolutely right. My apologies."

"Aw, shit, I'm sorry, Jamal." He threw an arm across Wade's massive shoulders, or at least as far as he could: Wade's shoulders make Dwight Howard's look like Barney Fife's. "I'm just jumpy," my dad said. "Hell, we could use a smartass line or two."

"How the hell did Remington pull this one?" I said. "Or more importantly, why?"

"Spanish Carlos says he'll have her out by tomorrow morning," my dad said. "But she's still spending the night in jail."

I had spent a night in our jail.

Back when I'd just quit the force and Chief Black had extracted his retribution and revenge by having his boys in blue write me tickets for the most trivial infractions; including smashing a taillight on my car and then writing me up and towing my car. The jail wasn't that bad. But then Carmen wasn't a hardened criminal like me, a three- time offender of MB-874–tinted windows: "...*material which alters the color or reduces the light transmittance of the windshield or side or rear windows.*" The fact that the lightly tinted windows of the little Mercedes C-300 I'd had back then were installed at the factory, didn't bother the cops.

"This just doesn't seem like Glenn," I said.

"Maybe Keough's giving him shit," Wade said.

Tony Keough was *Paraíso Del Mar*'s new mayor. A huge surprise to everyone, but especially to Mel Shoemaker, the man who we'd all assumed would be the next mayor.

Mel is a great guy and has the town's best interests at heart. In fact, I think one of the things that made Reed Lockhart so popular was that he'd steal Mel's ideas and make them his own. Before he was murdered, Mayor Lockhart had been running for his seventh consecutive term against his only opponent in each of those elections: Mel Shoemaker. And every four years, Reed would win in a landslide. So, although the circumstances were terrible, after everyone had calmed down over Lockhart's death, it looked like Mel's time had finally come.

And then along came Tony Keough.

Keough had been the city comptroller, dull, buttoned up tight (in his style and personality), So when he made the last-minute announcement that he was running, no one thought he had a chance. But, obviously, or maybe *not* so obviously until it was too late, Keough's campaign–"*TKO Crime with TK*" caught on with the locals and once again poor Mel Shoemaker had lost. Which mean, of course, all the local jokes were trotted out again: "Shoemaker wasn't a shoo-in. "..."The Shoe didn't fit."..."The Shoemaker didn't make it."

Tony Keough was a good mayor. But he was very political. So, he might have been putting pressure on Remington. But Remington had never caved under pressure before.

"Did they even consider motive? I mean why the hell would Carmen kill Steve?"

"Should we give Remington a call?" Wade said.

I considered that for a moment. "It wouldn't do any good, even if he would listen, Carmen's still spending the night. And my guess is we'd just piss him off. And maybe he's not so friendly to us anymore."

I didn't want to think we'd sacrifice Carmen for the friendly insider's track we had with Remington, but there didn't seem to be any win/win in contacting him.

"I agree," my dad said. "You want to keep Remington as a friend. And Carmen will be okay. The jail isn't like a real jail. I mean, other than the occasional drunk, it's usually empty. And if there is someone in a cell, the night watch cop comes down and talks to them make sure they're okay."

"And they did remodel it," Wade said.

"That said, still nobody's breaking *into* it."

32

"Bailiff Conklin! How did so many people get into my Court?"

The Judge, His Honorable Adam Sizemore, waited for an answer.

Bailiff Joe Conklin was a former Marine DI who had maintained order in room C-217 for the last fifteen years. Conklin brooked no bullshit. But he also knew how to ladle out the sugar too:

"Must be your popularity, Judge."

Conklin chuckled, priming the pump. So did Judge Sizemore.

Wade and I were hunkered down in one of the bench seats at the rear, trying to look like we belonged there and trying to not be noticed.

Famous and Gonzo sat up front. So did Finnerman and five guys in thousand-dollar suits -- the Dillards' attorneys. Charles and Oksanna were a few feet away.

Across the aisle Theo Kouros and two other men, who I assumed were also FBI whispered with their heads together. Kouros would occasionally look back at the entrance; obviously waiting for somebody.

Sizemore tapped his gavel and was about to make a pronouncement when the door swung open and two men strode for the front.

"Well, my popularity seems to be growing," the Judge said. "Who are you?"

The older, sleeker of the two men went to open the little gate that would admit them into the hallowed ground in front of the judge's bench, but Conklin took two swift steps and put the ham that he called a hand up in front of their faces.

"Hold it!" he barked.

The sleek man said, "Your Honor, Melvin Turner, Chief Counsel, Federal Bureau of Investigation.

"And Harold Schneider, your Honor, Deputy Counsel, also the Bureau," said the non-sleek FBI.

I glanced at Kouros, he looked damned pleased now.

Finnerman said to one of the Dillards' attorneys, "Did you know about this?"

"Excuse me, Mister Finnerman, were you addressing the Court?"

Finnerman went red. "Uh, no, no sir. No, your Honor! My apologies."

"Sorry, Judge," said the man who looked like the most senior of the Dillard's team. "We…" he indicated the other four members of the firm, the Dillards and Finnerman, ".. all of us, are so surprised to see the FBI in court on a child custody matter that we forgot our manners."

"Yes, Mister Novak," was all that the Judge said.

"Your Honor, I can explain," Turner said. He reached out toward Kouros, and one of the men sitting with Theo, jumped to his feet and handed Turner a stack of documents. Turner didn't even bother to look at them. "We are prepared to show the Court that the Dillards' motions, while understandable, unfortunately, pose a threat to national security."

Oksanna said Something in Russian. I don't think it was 'Have a nice day.'

"That's absurd," Charles said.

Bang! Sizemore slammed his gavel so hard it seemed like a gunshot.

Novak was about to shush his client, but then remembered who his client was and just shrugged towards the Judge.

Turner looked back at Kouros and the other lawyer opened one of those rolling brief cases that could hold a small child and pulled out an armload of documents and dropped them on the table. While Turner talked, the lawyer continued to pull out document after document out of this seemingly bottomless briefcase, almost like one of the cars at the circus where clown after clown after clown keeps getting out–and maybe that's what all those FBI documents were–funny papers.

"If it would please the Court," Turner said, "we have *a précis* of our, the Bureau's, position, and of course, all of the arguments, including black letter case law, a myriad of similar decisions and.." he paused and this time, his partner Schneider handed him a single piece of paper, ".. A letter signed by the Attorney General."

"What?" said the Judge. "Of the State of California?"

"No. Of the United States."

Turner handed the letter to Conklin, who hustled it up to the Judge. Sizemore read it and then appeared to read it again. When he looked up his face was very serious. "Mister Turner and Mister Schneider, in my chambers. You too Mister Novak."

Finnerman rose from the bench.

"Judge didn't call your name," Conklin said and blocked Finnerman's progress.

The named attorneys went through the little gate and back to the left of the court room and disappeared through a side door.

"What the hell you think this is?" Wade said.

"Exactly that," I said, "hell. We're in religious and governmental hell."

Or maybe Purgatory; because we waited for at least a half hour while the attorneys and the Judge did whatever they did behind closed doors.

I couldn't tell who had stuck the better deal by their faces when they all came back into the court room.

Conklin announced that we were now back in session. Then the Judge cleared his throat.

"Well, Mister Novak, I am inclined to agree with *Messrs*. Turner and Schneider."

Turner, to Conklin's and the Judge's surprise, interrupted him.

"Excuse me, your Honor, but it appears that the Court has been unduly swayed by the Attorney General's letter."

"What the...?" Sizemore sputtered, then cleared his throat again.

I saw Conklin reflectively hunch his shoulders, like he knew pain was about to be inflicted.

"Understand this, Mr. Novak, I run my court by the book. I say singular, but in reality, mean plural, in fact, many plurals of the books of Law. And just as our judicial system is founded upon principles of equality, with numerous avenues of recourse for appeal that can eventually, as you know, go to the highest courts in our land, the Supreme Court, there is, also if you will, a hierarchy of legal officers. And the Attorney General of the United States, is, in this Court's opinion, the highest practicing *attorney* in the land. Therefore, when someone of that stature renders an opinion, one would be best served to acknowledge said opinion. Do I make myself clear?"

"I think so" said Novak.

"Think so? What a letter like this means, Mister Novak," and the Judge waved the letter, and because he did it in front of the microphone, there was a harsh rustling sound throughout the room, "is that when the U.S. Attorney General says 'jump', you not only say 'How high?', you ask if you might do a cartwheel too."

Turner and Schneider looked at each other with a slight smirk. I thought Kouros and his attorney buddies were going to do high-fives.

"However," Sizemore continued, "Impressive as the Attorney General's letter is, if it were incorrect, I would *not* admit it. And not to put too fine a point on it, I am also *not* impressed by organizations so big they are known by their initials."

Turner, Schneider and Kouros and his buddies sagged at the rebuff. But Judge Sizemore always showed equality under the law.

"Nor am impressed by law firms whose prestige people think increases by the number of individual names that come after their founder. Right, Mister Novak?"

"Yes, your Honor," was all Novak said.

Novak knows when to speak and when to shut up. He also knows his business card is a baker's dozen–Novak's name, followed by the names of his twelve other partners.

33

"So *compadre*," Wade said as he deftly steered his BMW into the car pool lane on the Harbor Freeway on our way back home,"...it looks like religion trumps the law once again."

"It always does, it always will. Especially when the government buys the uniforms for God's team."

We'd spent five hours in Judge Sizemore's courtroom, listening to the verbal battles as the two opposing batteries of lawyers fired off salvo after salvo against each other. Lots of noise, explosive accusations, brilliant counterattacks, and at the end of the day when Sizemore finally banged down his gavel and adjourned us, the Dillards had lost. Their several billions and legal stars weren't enough to overcome the FBI's trillions and legal geniuses. Plus, the FBI had God on their side.

"How the hell can he walk?" Wade said. "He raped Hope and Felicity, I mean Charlene. And for sure contributed to her death and they can't touch him?"

"There's got to be a way," I said. "Some kind of slip-up."

"And that son of a bitch threatened Famous's daughter." Wade came up fast on a red Chevy Tahoe. Its rear seat had been turned around, so it faced backward at the on-coming traffic. The two kids strapped in there went wide-eyed as Wade swooped in close.

"Shit," Wade said, glanced in the rearview mirror, snapped his head around to check his right, and blipped the BMW across the double yellow lines. As we flew past the Chevy, Wade flashed the two kids the peace sign and they laughed and returned it, with both hands.

We cranked ahead of the Chevy in the lane. There wasn't another car in front of it for a quarter mile. "In for a penny," Wade said and went back across the yellow lines a second time, "in for a grand." We heard the Chevy's horn in protest, but by then we were at a high rate of departure.

"A grand?" I said.

"Yeah, it's three hundred and eleven bucks for that lane violation; so you double that, six hundred and twenty-two. Plus, I'm sure a cop would find some other violations. A grand easy."

"You forgot traffic school."

"Shit, closer to thirteen hundred; plus my time; which ain't suppos'd be cheap, but lately ain't worth shit."

"Yeah, we're definitely small change in this one."

"Time we upped the ante," Wade said. He put his foot into it and the Bimmer rocketed ahead, so that when we changed to the aptly-named 105 Freeway on the long curving ramp that's suspended about a hundred feet in the air, and we were the only car on that interchange, that's how fast we were going.

I took a long hot shower and tried to figure out a way to penetrate the wall that Kouros and the government had put between us and Brother Jordan. After I got dressed, I made some calls. First to my dad, then Leah, then to Zak and Tommie Shea Shoh. None of them answered, so I left four messages and then called Wade. At least he answered, and we agreed to meet in a half hour at Kincaid's. Then everyone else called back. My dad and Leah said they'd join Wade and me. I brought Zak and Tommie up to date, discussed some options and they said they'd get back to me.

Sometimes detective work is just grunt work. Keep plodding along. And, hopefully, something shows up. Sometimes it's picking at a loose thread in the fabric of the case and pulling–which can put a big hole in your theory, or at best, unravels and reveals, if not the solution, at least a direction.

I didn't feel like any of those possibilities were open to us.

We were, all of us, boxed out.

The weight and power of the Dillards was like a b-b against the armor-plated hulk of the FBI. Famous and the LAPD had gotten a righteous bust on Brother Jordan. He was a rapist and child molester who had committed murder. They could prove it, but they couldn't present their case. There would be no justice–not for the Dillards, the Law, and probably not for little baby Johnny Doe, aka Fyodor.

"The Attorney General?" my dad said. "Of the United States? Jesus, what the hell did you guys get into?"

"We're not sure yet. But it feels like we've gone down the rabbit hole."

Wade and I had given my dad and Leah a summary of what had happened So far, but it had taken a lot longer than we'd anticipated because they both had so many questions; for which we didn't have many answers, only explanations. So, it wasn't until we'd finished eating and were having coffee that we'd all come to the same conclusion: This was FUBAR and about all we could do was wait until the smoke cleared.

"Tomorrow we're going to interview the Sisters," I said.

"They'll let you do that?" my dad asked.

"I think as long as we're not involving Brother Jordan, we're okay. Anyway, he was released, but not the Sisters."

"Why's that?" Leah said, I think feeling some sisterly protection for the young Sisters.

"Because the legal beagles for the *Temple*, Brothers Dominic and Victor, are still resting on their collective asses because they think *they* saved Brother Jordan."

Our waiter, Rollie Hagen came by to see if there was anything else and gave us our bill.

"So, how's that beautiful wife of yours?" my dad said.

Wade rolled his eyes and shook his head, but I don't think my dad saw it. Rollie's a good guy, but with Rollie, every silver lining has a cloud.

"Tiffany's...okay," Rollie said.

I was hoping my dad wouldn't follow up. I just wasn't in the mood.

Tiffany was a beautiful woman, part-time model, part-time actress, and according to Rollie, a full-time pain in the ass. Like many beautiful women, she was insecure about her looks; maybe because she felt that was all she had and once those faded, where was she? Tiffany's face had highlighted many internet sponsors websites, telling you she was waiting for your call. And of course, hundreads, maybe thousands, of horny men would call and order a PC cleaner for a computer that worked fine, or a set of "all green" patio furniture that went for a lot of your green ($799.99), or a digital version of *Encyclopædia Britannica*, that you never looked at it; all the while hoping that the woman they were talking to was Tiffany and not some out-sourced order taker in Delhi, India.

I grabbed the bill and threw a credit card on it and told Rollie that'd be all.

"Whew," said Wade, "that was close."

"What?" my dad said.

"Rollie could screw up a wet dream," I said. "He's never happy."

"Really?" my dad said. "He's got a beautiful wife, and a Ferrari. What the hell's he got to complain about?"

"Everything, according to Rollie. His wife's beautiful, but all he does is bitch about all the clothes she needs, the cost of her acting classes. That Ferrari, a 612 *Scaglietti*, Rollie says, is a huge responsibility. He's always worried somebody's going to bang into it. And he says, he's always got to keep it clean. One time he didn't wash it and somebody left him a note saying he was a disgrace to Ferrari owners everywhere."

"He can't be that bad," my dad said.

"Well, you remember how Rollie got that car?"

"Yeah, lucky bastard won almost four hundred thousand in the lottery."

"Right. He missed the twelve-million-dollar jackpot by one number, but he did get runner-up money; which he blew most of on the Ferrari. But you mention the lottery to Rollie, all he does is whine that he was just one number off from the prize of a lifetime."

"Some guys never know when they've got it good."

"Until it ain't so good no more," Wade said. "And then they wish it was like before." He got up, "See you tomorrow. Your turn to drive."

And then just when I thought we had it pretty good because we'd avoided Rollie's complaints, we ran into the Professor.

"Shit, it's Hiram," my dad said, a moment before the Prof looked our way and waved a long, bony hand. My dad did an incredibly fast

U-turn and went back towards the kitchen. That was the long way out of Kincaid's, but for my dad, no distance is too great to avoid the Prof.

"Hi," Leah said as she brushed past the Prof, "off to the loo."

"It would have been cute if Leah had said, 'skip to my lou'," the Prof said as he came up and held out his hand to shake; which I did, reluctantly. Mostly because the Prof's hands are always sweaty and limp.

The Prof used to teach English Lit at Harvard but left the university with his books tucked under his arm and his tail tucked between his legs. Rumor was he used his position to seduce young, willing coeds. The Prof's excuse was that the shit he saw in Vietnam that taught him the meaningless of life and he decided to cram as much fun into however many days he had left. That it meant cramming his dick into as many naïve college girls was just a sidebar to his manifesto.

That would be understandable; given that most men can come up with the most convoluted, self-serving rationalizations for fucking women, but the Prof never got over all those big words he'd learned. So, any conversation with him was usually a pedantic overload that would peg my Shit-o-meter into the red.

"So, it seems like our little beach community is becoming like Honolulu."

"I'm sorry?"

"Oh, you know, on that TV show from the '80s? *Hawaii 5-0*? It's paradise, but every week somebody gets murdered." The Prof laughed his little smug laugh.

"I don't think a man who dies because he inhaled toxic fumes constitutes a crime wave," I said. I wasn't going to let the Prof get into the murder possibilities of Steven Fordham's death.

"No? Then why did our resolute Chief Remington bring in a forensic crime expert? From New York, no less?"

That was news to me. I hated being one-upped, but especially by the Prof.

"Glenn paid to have a guy flown in from New York?" I said.

"Well," the Prof started backpedaling, "he didn't fly him in *per se*. But he's using Robert Mayles on the investigation."

"Oh, I get it. Glenn didn't fly him in, this Mayles lives here. Is that what you're saying?"

The Prof squirmed a little, the air gone out of his gossip balloon. "Uh, yes. He took early retirement from the New York State Police, where he headed up their Forensic Science Laboratory. Quite brilliant, really is Mr. Mayles."

Is that a form of Yoda-speak?

But I didn't say it. The less you say to the Prof, the better. Eventually even he gets tired of hearing himself talk.

But I was wrong.

"I understand," he said, building up steam, "Mr. Mayles holds several scientific degrees from some of the country's highest universities. Well, actually, he doesn't hold them," the Prof chuckled, *(Oh, shit, another of his dumbass jokes)* "they're nicely framed on his wall."

The Prof waits for me to laugh, but when I don't, he frowns slightly, but launches into another discourse. "I might be teaching English in the evening adult education series and I was thinking of trying to make it a little more entertaining."

The Prof doing stand-up? Oh, God.

"So, if you don't mind, let me use you as a guinea pig."

I waited and looked for Leah to return.

"So, is there a word in English that uses all the vowels including 'y'?"

"Unquestionably," I said. And gave him a big smile.

"My, I'm impressed."

I just smiled again. No need to tell the Prof that I'd read that same little word quiz in the local newspaper yesterday. Screw that. Besides, it's terrific to beat him at his own game of linguistic bullshit.

"I've got one you can try," I said. "What kind of word would you invite to a fancy tea party?"

I waited a half-second, deliberately cutting him off before he could come up with the answer. "A proper noun."

"Matt," Leah called out, still several feet away from us, "we need to be going." She came up, linked her arm in mine. "Nice to see you Professor."

"Oh, yes, yes," he mumbled, an actual absent-minded professor because he was still trying to figure out how I knew those answers. "The pleasure is all mine."

When we made the exit, Leah slipped her arm out and said, "Would you mind if I slept at my house tonight?"

She said *I*, not we.

"Sure, everything okay?"

"Why wouldn't it be?"

"Don't know."

She kissed me—fast and efficient. No romance there.

"Sorry, babe. It's just that listening to all of this .. this pain and the bullshit people go through in their lives, I'm just not feeling very romantic."

34

"Do you have sexual urges for me, Matt?"

Sister Chastity looked at me as if she'd asked would I like coffee.

"No," I said.

We had been talking to the Sisters for about a half hour when she dropped that conversation bomb into the group.

"Don't you find me attractive?" she said.

"I have friends with daughters your age."

"That's not an answer."

"It is for me."

"It's okay to have those thoughts Matt. Normal in fact. Because the devil's inside us all."

I nodded, not wanting to go down that road to perdition.

"It's true," Sister Hope said. "The devil isn't some grotesque, yellow-eyed monster."

"So, no pitchfork or pointed tail?"

"Of course not," Sister Chastity said. "Who'd be attracted to that? No, Satan is charming, he's your friend. He wants you to be happy. He wants you to have everything your heart desires. He's that little voice inside of you, inside of us all."

I looked at Wade, who was watching the other Sisters.

"Satan talks to us, too," said Sister Faith, who like Sister Chastity could be a fashion model; probably the Victoria's Secret type, since even through the loose folds of her robe, when it stretched tight, you could tell she had curves.

"Satan talks to you?" Wade said. "What's he saying?"

"He's whispering: Why are they so preoccupied with the carnal side?"

"We're not," Wade said.

"Really?" Sister Serenity said. She had high cheekbones framing warm brown eyes, a wide forehead and a slender aquiline nose. "You haven't asked us any other questions–like are we comfortable here? Do we have good medical care? What do we do for entertainment and fun? No. You've come at us like heat-seeking missiles and your target was our loins."

Loins. Wow, that was getting biblical on us.

"It's true," Sister Chastity said. "Everything's been about our relationship with Brother Jordan: Has he had sex with us? Has he forced us to do anything against our will? Did we…"

"Stop!" I said–loud enough to surprise the Sisters. "We are investigating a murder. The murder of one of your Sisters. The homicide of a young, underage mother, who's left an infant son behind. Obviously, Charlene .."

"Sister Felicity," said Sister Charity, with not much charity in her voice.

I'd said Charlene deliberately; to try and get them to look at her as a person, not as only a member of their sect.

"Yes," I continued. "Sister Felicity had sex with at least one of the Brothers here. We're assuming it was Brother Jordan. She was underage, that means whichever man she had sex with, even if she was willing, even if she was Salome and a temptress, it's against the law. So, when we ask those questions, it's to get more information, and hopefully, to prevent that from happening to you, too."

"So what you're saying is we have no choice in the control of our bodies or our lives?" said Sister Faith.

"You have total control. But the law doesn't take kindly to older men or women who are out of control when it comes to sex with minors."

"Well, thank God, your laws don't apply in the Temple."

"So, 'Thou salt not kill'," doesn't mean anything?" Wade said.

"Now you're twisting our words," said Sister Chastity.

"One of your Sisters is dead!" I snapped. "Probably killed by Brother Jordan. Doesn't that mean anything to you?"

The room was silent for several long, painful moments. Tears welled up in Sisters Faith's and Charity's eyes. And then by some unseen signal, the four Sisters rose as one and walked out of the room. They didn't say a word, they didn't look back.

Brother Thomas came into the room and said, "Thank you, gentlemen." Then he turned around, didn't say a word, and walked out of the room without looking back.

"I guess we've been dismissed," Wade said.

I didn't feel much like waiting around for the triumphant return of Brother Jordan on his release from jail, so Wade and I got into my car, shutting the doors a little extra hard, and I laid a fifteen foot black mark of rubber hauling down the driveway.

"Pretty damn juvenile," I said, before Wade could. "But I don't much give a shit right now."

He shrugged and said, "What the hell do you make of all that?"

"It's clear Jordan's twisted the language and their frame of reference that they're all..."

"Brain-washed," Wade said.

"Pretty much. They're conditioned to *not* see the reality of their situation. They're programmed to believe in the innocence of their leader and not his guilt or his evil."

"Pay no attention to the man behind the curtain," Wade said.

"Yeah. Except the great and mighty Oz turned out to be a pretty nice guy. And Jordan's anything but that."

"And his curtain is more like a twenty-foot high concrete block wall with concertina wire. Funded by the government, tied into religion."

I accelerated down the hill and headed for the Harbor Freeway. "I don't see any yellow brick road showing us the way," I said.

Wade didn't say anything for a few miles. Then he titled his head at me and said, "You remember that group America?"

"America?"

"Yeah, buncha white hippie dudes came out of nowhere."

"I know who they are, I'm just amazed you not only know them, but seem like you're going to make a point about them."

"Well, ain't you the freakin' Scarecrow? Already got your brain workin'."

"Okay, what?"

"They had that Song *Tin Man*? One line of lyrics said, *'But Oz never did give nothing to the Tin Man that he didn't already have.'*"

"Right. So..?"

"So, we already know the answer to bringing Jordan down. We just haven't found it yet."

I thought about what Wade had said for a moment. And realized he was right.

"You still have those ruby red slippers?"

"No. But I have Some size thirteen all red Air Jordan's."

And we said it practically together, "To kick Brother Jordan's ass."

35

"I'm gonna stuff you and your partner's asses so deep in federal prison, you'll be collecting social security in your cell!"

FBI Agent Theo Kouros was apoplectic, screaming into the phone. I was just about to drop Wade off at his house when Kouros had called. I had him on speaker phone.

"What's up, Agent Kouros?" I said in my most smug voice. This guy pissed us off and any chance we could fuck him up was just bonus time for Wade and me.

"You know goddamn good and well what's up!"

I think he was sputtering. He sure as hell was screaming. I turned down the volume.

"Oksanna's kidnapped the baby!"

Wade and I looked at each other and nodded in silent approval.

"What's that mean? Kidnapped?"

"Don't play naïve with me. You two set this up."

"Look, if you're just going to scream and make wild ass accusations without any explanation ..."

"Or facts…" Wade interjected.

"...then I'm just going to hang up," I said.

"Don't you, don't you dare hang up on me."

"Fine. Tell us what happened."

"As of nine-thirty this morning, your client, Oksanna Dillard, went to the hospital and somehow managed to convince the hospital staff that surely the baby could use some affection from its maternal grandmother. And so, under the supervision of the head nurse, she cooed and rocked and held the baby."

"Sounds like a great grandmother."

"Great grandmother my ass! The baby started fussing, the nurse went to get some fresh diapers and when she got back, Oksanna and baby Doe were gone."

"Gone from the room? Gone to the cafeteria?" I said.

Wade gave me a soft high five.

"Gone from the hospital. And as we've just discovered, gone from the United States!"

"Really?" Wade said. And he said it so convincingly I almost believed he was stunned by this news.

"You two fuckers..."

"Agent Kouros; you do *not* talk to us in that tone of voice or manner."

"Yeah? Well, fuck you and try and do something about it. I know you two set this up in advance and are going to pay for it."

"We have no idea nor knowledge of what you might be insinuating," I said. "But more importantly, if the Bureau's screwed up, it's not the first time; nor is it our fault. And I think this conversation's over."

"Wait, don't you..."

And I broke the connection.

He called back immediately, but I sent it to voice mail.

"She told us in advance," Wade said. "And then she did it."

"Good for her," I said.

"Yeah," Wade said. "Gotta like that."

He got out of the car and then his phone rang. "He's calling both of us?"

Then he looked at the caller ID.

"Whoa! It's Andriel!" He clicked on, "Hey baby Sistah! How are you?"

The love and excitement in his voice was so genuine and disarming, coming from such a behemoth, that even after all these years of knowing

Jamal, I'm always surprised at the love between him and his younger sister Andriel.

"Hold on a sec," Wade said, and gave me a thumbs up and a small wave goodbye.

I yelled, "Yo Andriel!"

I drove home, showered, and poured myself a healthy glass of Chianti.

Then I called Charles Dillard. He told me that he was as surprised by his wife's actions as everyone else. And that he had absolutely no idea where Oksanna might be. I took a chance and asked him if he did happen to know where the corporate Gulfstream G550 might be."

"I know exactly where it is: it's flying non-stop to Azerbaijan. The Foundation is hosting a gala party next week and we're out of caviar."

He said it so easily; I could have easily believed him.

"Isn't Azerbaijan near St. Petersburg?" I said.

"Nothing is near anything in Russia. Such a big country."

"And so complicated."

"Yes," he said, and waited.

"And so dangerous too," I said.

36

"Andriel's no longer in-country," Wade said, the excitement in his voice and face obvious. "She's flying out tomorrow morning, a connecting flight in London, then New York. Then a stop-over in Fort Belvoir, Virginia, and she should be here in week to ten days."

"That's terrific news, Jamal," my dad said.

Wade had joined Leah, my dad and me for dinner at *Café Jacque*, managed to contain himself while the waiter poured him a glass of wine and then just exploded with the news.

"Fort Belvoir," I said. "That's the Army's nerve center, right?"

"Yeah," Wade said. "INSCOM." He waited a beat before he showed off: "United States Army Intelligence and Security Command. I'm thinking promotion time."

"Ten-hut," I said. "Maybe baby sister's going to be Lieutenant Colonel Wade."

"Moving up the ranks. But I don't think she's doing Black Ops."

"Give her time," I said.

Andriel was an amazing doctor and had obviously saved more than a few soldiers' lives. Wade had several photos of Andriel from various tours. One showed her in a field hospital, cheek to cheek with a wounded, but highly grateful Green Beret.

Another photo, taken with a soldier's cell phone, had Andriel in close-up, her uniform torn and dusty, her stripes darkened by blood, working on a female Sergeant.

The last photo she'd sent showed Andriel, the entire left side of her uniform arrayed in a shiny formation of awards, decorations and medals snapping off a crisp salute to a two-star general.

But now she was more involved in management and strategy for ensuring that our troops received the absolute best medical care possible. So, a stop-over at in Virginia was significant.

"That's exciting," said Leah. "You must be so proud of her. I always wished that I'd had a sister or brother. That would've helped not being so lonely."

Wade and I looked at each other for a quick moment—the weight of the secret, of Leah not knowing she *did* have a half-brother, but that we did, wasn't pleasant.

We are imprisoned by our secrets. And the regrets of decisions drive us crazy, because we refuse to accept an event that's already happened.

"You were an only child, Matt," Leah said, snapping me back to reality. "How'd you handle it?"

Another family secret.

"I don't know," I said. "I guess I was always doing stuff, you know sports at school, surfing and just having good times. I had it pretty good, thanks to my pops."

"*Grazie,*" my dad said, but he had a funny look on his face.

A look I'm sure I had too.

Because we were both still processing his news about Ali.

My dad that he'd finally told the truth.

And me trying to understand it all.

The waiter came and took our orders and we brought Leah and my dad up to date on everything that had happened.

"Our legal system's gone to shit," my dad said.

"So have the criminals," said Leah. Did you hear the latest on Steve Fordham?"

"They caught his killer?"

"No. And it looks like the list of people who wanted him dead might be getting longer." Leah took a sip of her wine and shook her head. "I only found this out through Jeanie Fairburn, who is Cathy Fordham's attorney. And I don't think it's confidential."

"If it is, your secret remains at this table," I said.

Wade just rolled his eyes at me.

"About ten years ago, Steve was married to a woman named Yvonne, maiden name Jorgensen."

I ran that name through my memory banks but came up empty.

"Yvonne's folks live in Texas and her mom and dad are driving someplace and the father, who was in his seventies, either misjudges the oncoming car, or didn't see it, but he makes a left turn right in front of the car. No chance in hell to avoid the crash."

Leah took another sip of her wine.

"The mother's killed instantly, both people in the other car die in the hospital, but her dad walks away without even a scratch or a bump on the head. Absolutely nothing."

I didn't say anything because I wasn't sure which way to go: Tragedy that the mother died, of course; but a minor miracle that the father's okay.

"Her entire family, she has a younger sister and older brother, is devastated of course."

Leah paused.

I think she's just realized she could be talking about her own life.

"Overwhelming," I said.

She gulped the rest of her wine.

"And in the midst of all this devastation and pain and suffering, Steve checks with the insurance policy and tells Yvonne, 'We could sue your father for negligence. Nothing would happen to him, but I think we'd collect over three hundred thousand.'"

None of us said anything for a long moment.

My dad spoke first. "I'd say you're kidding, but this is a true story, right?"

"Absolutely," Leah said. "Can you believe that?"

"It's hard to believe," Wade said. "But Steve was a real piece of work."

"More like piece of shit," Leah said. "No, a total shit. Her poor father. He has all that guilt and then he's got a lawsuit too?"

"Yvonne didn't go through with it?" I said.

"Hell no," Leah said. "Who does something like that?"

"That was the first crack in their marriage," I said.

"They were divorced four months later," Leah said.

The waiter came with our food.

I waited until he'd left and then said, "Yvonne still live around here?"

"Over on thirty-first," Leah said. "Why?"

"Shitty as that was, I don't see it being a motive for murder. Not after all this time."

"No. But if she's anything like Cathy, with that temper, I don't know. Maybe that fuse was still smoldering."

We finished dinner and another bottle of *pinot noir*, flipped for who paid the bill, my dad won (or lost depending on how you looked at it) and headed for the exit. Leah had to make a stop at the restroom; Wade gave us a nod and went on his way, so it was just my dad and me.

He put his arm around my shoulder.

"I don't know, all that talk about sisters and family, makes me sad," he said.

"Yeah. I'm feeling that way, too."

"And I'm thinking about..." he hesitated; "well, I'm thinking of going to see Ali."

"What?"

"Her gravesite. She's buried at Forest Lawn."

More news to process.

"I know your mother wanted to be cremated and you and I..."

"I remember, Dad, scattering her ashes in the water."

"Yeah. But Ali was so little, so beautiful. We just...we just couldn't bring ourselves to..."

His eyes got bright.

Shit. That never happens to my dad.

I put my arm around him. "It's okay. I'd like to go."

"Yeah?"

"Yeah. It's time I met her."

37

"Hi, Alison," I said so softly I'm sure neither my dad nor Wade heard me. "It's nice to have a baby sister."

My dad had driven over by himself since Wade and I needed to connect with Famous later. Wade and I talked about sisters and family on the drive over and the devastating, emotional impact on my mom and dad.

Naturally, you feel guilty for the dumbass ways you acted as a teenager, selfish and uncaring. Never once even considering their feelings, never trying to understand why they acted and said the things they did except how it negatively impacted your world. I'd like to think that if I had known the burden my mother was carrying, that terrible knowledge and loss of a child, that I might have been more understanding, been a better child. But I wonder.

"I'm sorry, Mario," Wade told my dad when we'd met in the parking lot at the cemetery. Then he gave my dad a huge bear hug. And when Wade hugs you, consider yourself hugged. My dad disappeared in Wade's embrace so all I saw was Wade's huge shoulders and then my dad's arms around Wade's back, but his hands nowhere near touching.

The headstone was small, which seemed appropriate. An engraved angel floated above her name: Alison Leigh Singer. August 10, 1979– November 11, 1979.

"She'd have been forty," my dad said. "A mom by now, so I'd be Grandpa Mario." My dad smiled.

"Alison," I said. "Was she named after anybody?"

"Muhammad Ali."

"What?" I said. Wade and I both looked at my dad.

"It's true. Your mother and I both thought he was the greatest and bravest American of all. To do what he did, and *when* he did it, during what was still a very racist, segregated country, took amazing courage. He said, 'I don't believe in this war and I'm not fighting it.'"

"Right," Wade said. "'*I ain't got no quarrel with them Viet Cong. No Viet Cong ever called me nigger.*'–that's what he said."

I was stunned to hear Wade use that word.

I'm sure so was my dad.

But my dad rallied. "And what did America do? They arrested him! Arrested him. Then stripped him of his title and his boxing license. And he wasn't able to fight for nearly four years."

"Four years in the prime of his life," Wade said.

"They called him '*The Greatest*'. And he was," my dad said quietly.

"And I'm sure Alison would have been too," I said and touched her headstone.

We spent a few more minutes with Ali, and then Wade and I shook hands with my dad and left him to be alone with his little girl.

38

"Fathers and daughters?" Famous said. "Probably the strongest family bond around."

Wade and I had gone straight to a little *tacoqueria* just off Olympic and were having an early lunch of *huevos rancheros* with Famous.

"I made sure Meagan's safe," he said. "She's doing home schooling at her *abuela's*, who lives in Oceanside." He took a big bite of food. "She's not happy about it, but her grandmother spoils her, so she's suffering on satin."

"And hopefully it's just temporary," I said. "There's got to be a way to get Jordan."

"Sonfabitch looks bullet-proof."

"There's a chink in his armor," Wade said. "We've just got to find it."

Gonzo burst through the front door and ran up to our table. He'd been standing outside, watching Famous's ride.

"Don't tell me Somebody's trying to boost my wheels?" Famous said.

"No, it's Kouros," Gonzo said. "He just pulled up in front."

"What the fuck? How'd he know we were here?"

"You checked in with the station, maybe they told him."

"God damn it, head him off."

Gonzo turned for the entrance, but it was too late, Kouros was already through the door. He glanced around quickly and spotted us and torpedoed his way through the other tables.

"Gentlemen," Kouros said. "First, let me apologize to Matt and Jamal..."

"Wade to you, agent Kouros," Wade said.

"Sorry, Wade. And to you Lieutenant Ramos. The Bureau's been. No, let me start over. *I've* been under a lot of pressure." Kouros looked around, snagged a chair from another table, and pushed it next to the end of our table, so he was positioned behind the salsa and hot sauce bottles. "And I had to go through several channels, all above me of course, to get permission to tell you what I'm about to say."

Kouros looked over at Gonzo.

"He's staying," Famous said without taking his eyes from Kouros.

"Sure, sure." Kouros leaned over the bottles. "I know this sticks in your craw, because, believe it or not, this violates everything we each work and stand for."

"This full disclosure?" I said.

"You're going to have to let me be the judge of what I can or can't tell you."

"Screw this," Famous said. "Same old need-to-know bullshit. This is a waste of time." He looked over at the owner and signaled for the check.

"No, wait, wait," Kouros said. "Agent Michaels has been undercover for more than three years; and we feel he's significantly close to busting a high-level *al-Qaeda* cell."

"C'mon," Wade said, "you're gonna blow smoke up our boxers, at least make it aromatic. This stinks, because it insults our intelligence. There's no fucking way what you said is true."

"But it is."

"So how does a religious cult leader connect with terrorists?" Famous said.

"The initial connection," Kouros said, "was... was their views toward women."

I could feel Famous tense from across the table.

"Wait," Kouros said, "don't kill the messenger. I'm giving you the facts, high level facts."

"You're telling us he shares the Sisters with them?" Gonzo said, once again showing another flash of mental brilliance under all that physical shine.

"No. He tells them what they want to hear, gains their confidence. It's all very slow, small, incremental steps."

"So, Brother Victor's *their* man?" I said.

Kouros looked at me like he was surprised I had figured that one out.

"Yes," he said. "Brother Victor came recommended through a man we think is connected to the cell."

"So, Victor's connected to the cell, too?" Wade said.

"Correct," Kouros said.

"So why not *disappear* Victor and sweat him out?"

"We're FBI, not Homeland. That's not our style."

"What do they want?" Famous said. "Women? Drugs? Bombs?"

"They haven't asked or even hinted at anything like that. He gets them airline tickets, rental cars and, twice, false IDs–which we created and control, so we always know where they are."

"Until they lose you and it's too late," I said.

This time Kouros's look was cold and nasty. Doesn't take much to fall out of favor with the FBI.

"When will you have enough information to move in?" Famous said.

"Hard to tell," Kouros said. "This arrest and the media coverage of Agent Michaels has set us back."

"Look," Famous said, bristling, "it's bad enough we've got a slam dunk case against this creep you call a star agent that we can't carry through, but this sonfabitch has threatened me and my family."

"I think you're taking this too personal, Lieutenant."

Famous took a step out of the booth and in one fluid motion got his hands on the back of Kouros's chair and as he rose up, used that momentum and force to fling the chair, with Kouros along for the ride, a good eight feet across the floor where his chair leg hit another chair leg and dumped Kouros on his ass.

It all happened so fast we were still processing the speed and strength and agility of Famous and the sliding chair when we realized he had followed it and pulled his Glock and had it right in Kouros's face who had started to regain his feet, if not his dignity, when he was looking at the Glock's black muzzle hole of eternity.

"Don't give me that *Godfather* horseshit. This isn't business, it isn't the job, it's *my daughter!*"

I'll give Kouros props.

He stared at Famous and quietly said, "Threatening a federal agent with a loaded weapon is a felony. And you're going down; I don't care how personal this gets."

And then Gonzo stepped in and squatted down so he was literally nose-to-nose with Kouros.

"We," he pointed behind him without looking, "Wade, Singer, me and *Senores Gonzales and Morales* and whatever their names are, we *all* saw you draw your weapon first, Agent Kouros. That's why..." and suddenly Gonzo's own Glock was pushing Kouro's chin upward, "...we took defensive, preventative measures."

There was a long moment where *Senores Gonzales and Morales* and none of the other customers, whatever their names, clinked a fork, sipped their *cerveza*, or, I'm sure, took a breath.

"We good Boss?" Gonzo said.

Famous put away his weapon and stood up. "We're good, partner."

Gonzo holstered his weapon and he and Famous turned on their heels, nodded at Wade and me and walked out the door and down Olympic Avenue.

39

Los Tilos was empty.

"I guess Brother Jordan's not the topic *du jour* anymore," Wade said.

"Maybe. Or maybe they were ordered to think that way."

"The press be controlled by dey gov'ment? But we's in the land of dey Free."

I drove up the driveway and parked. Everything looked like it had when we'd first come here. The lazy dogs and cats, the quiet, the eerie feeling that wasn't associated with any religious building I'd ever entered.

Brother Thomas opened the door but didn't invite us inside.

"We would like to talk to Brother Jordan," I said.

"He's not talking to anyone today," Brother Thomas said and moved to close the door.

"No, wait." Brother Jordan's voice came from down the foyer out to us. Brother Thomas looked back and a moment later his mentor and leader stood there in the entrance.

"I will talk to them. *'For by your words you will be justified,'*" Brother Jordan said to us. "Matthew, 12:37. Come in please."

God, I hate Biblical quotes. Well, not so much the quotes, just the self-serving assholes who trot them out to show off and automatically take the supposedly higher moral ground.

Brother Thomas trailed behind as we followed Brother Jordan to the back of the house into a large, hi-tech kitchen. No sign of any of the Sisters.

"Coffee?" Brother Jordan said. Wade and I both declined, but Brother Jordan poured himself a large cup, and then faced us.

"Are you here about the kidnapping of my Son?"

I'm sure I must have flicked my head, as if I'd been slapped. It was hard to imagine someone so callous; someone who slammed in it your face and dared you to do anything about it. It was as if the twin guards of religion and the government had made him untouchable and beyond the constraints of the law, society, and common decency.

"So, you admit that you fathered Charlene's child?" I said.

"Must we really drag out these innuendoes again?"

"Acknowledging you're the father makes you guilty of raping a minor."

Brother Jordan sighed and looked at Brother Thomas as if he'd made a mistake in allowing us into the Temple.

"Psalms 18:32–'*The God who equipped me with strength and made my way blameless.'*" He sipped his coffee and held out a hand before we could say anything. "The age of consent is a moving line. Back in biblical times, when the average age was around forty, it wasn't uncommon for mothers to be fourteen or fifteen years old. In South Carolina, the age of consent is fifteen, New Jersey, Florida and Georgia, sixteen."

"Except, we're in California, where the age is eighteen."

"Under the *Temple's* laws, I am innocent."

"Nothing about you is innocent, Brother Jordan," Wade said.

Brother Jordan smiled at Wade; and none of today's Hollywood leading men, or even the mega stars of the '40s and '50s had the wattage of his smile. It was so bright and seemingly honest that you could almost doubt whether you hadn't misjudged him.

"Innocence?" he said. "That's relative. Guilt? Again relative. Because, surely you see, that Satan is also part of the Almighty, one of his fallen angels. And I believe that He is there just to show us how good we really must be to enter the kingdom of Heaven. It's almost like Satan and Jesus work for the same company."

"Or the Bureau," I said. "Agent Michaels."

Brother Jordan could have been an actor for more than his smile. Because if he was surprised that we knew his cover was blown, it never showed on his face.

"So, you know, then, the seriousness of my work. And the danger."

"What danger?" I said. "Seducing underage girls? Doing favors for some pseudo wannabe terrorists?"

"No!" Brother Jordan snapped and put his fists on the table and rose up and stared at me.

Finally, a reaction.

"You have no idea what evil these men are capable of doing."

40

"What was Charlene doing during the time she left the Temple and showed up at Angels Mercy Center?"

"What do you mean?" Wade said.

We were heading back down the hill after wasting more time with Brother Jordan and getting nowhere.

"According to Sister Chastity, Charlene left the Temple right after dinner. Four, five hours later she shows up at the hospital, carrying the baby."

Which means she went some place, went into labor and then managed to walk to the hospital with her baby."

"Fyodor."

"Yeah, Fyodor. Soon to be a Russian citizen, Fyodor."

"You asking how she did it?"

"Partially. But more of, where she did it? Where did she go into labor?"

I checked the road for traffic and made a tight U-turn. "Let's hope Sister Chastity's out for her morning walk."

She was.

She turned at the sound of my car, then waited for me to pull alongside.

"Back so soon?" she said.

Obviously, she'd heard us talking with Brother Jordan.

"Just trying to learn the truth," I said.

"And will the truth set you free, Matthew?"

"When Sister Felicity left the Temple that last night; do you know where she went?"

Her head turned reflexively back towards the Temple, then stared straight ahead; and she quickened her pace.

"She's gone, your Sister's gone. Hiding the truth can't protect her anymore, she's beyond anyone's protection."

"Except the Lord's."

"Yes. And doesn't the Lord expect, no, *demand*, you tell the truth?"

She stopped and her head hung down. And then she started crying, softly, but deeply and terribly. She pulled her hood over her head and hugged herself, and then loud, convulsive sobs wracked her body.

I stopped, shifted into Park, and turned off the engine.

Wade was out before I had my door open. He gently put a massive arm around Sister Chastity's shoulder, barely touching her. She stood apart, crying for a few moments, and then wheeled into Wade, her sweet face against his chest and bawled. It was heart-wrenching and made me feel helpless and futile.

Wade looked at me and his face reflected my own pain. He placed an arm around her back and held her close, her tears and sobs smothered into his rock-hard body.

Finally, after what seemed like an hour, but was probably only a few minutes, her sobs softened and she eventually looked up at Wade and smiled, and then stepped away.

"I tried to stop her, I did."

"Of course, you did," Wade said. "You're not to blame."

"I warned her, too."

"You warned her, how?" Wade said.

"I told her that leaving the Temple was dangerous."

"You knew she was leaving did you know where she was going?"

Sister Chastity nodded her head.

41

"Don't set foot in that room," Famous commanded.

Samuel Spickard truncated his step, lost his balance and would have fallen into the room if Gonzo hadn't caught him by the arm and held him up and kept him out.

Samuel owned the small apartment building on Milner Street where Sister Chastity had sent us.

"What the hell's wrong with you?" Samuel said.

I had called Famous from the car as we drove down the hill toward Milner. He and Gonzo were heading back from another case, so they met us there. I filled them in on what Sister Chastity had told us and Gonzo knocked on Samuel's door and made him open the apartment.

"This is a crime scene," Famous said.

"Crime scene? What the hell are you talking about?"

"That," Famous said and pointed to a long dark trail that led from the door back into the small living room. A trail that could only be blood.

"Is that blood?"

"Yes, Mister Spickard, and I'll have to ask you to wait outside."

Gonzo moved his bulk in front of Samuel, blocking his view and keyed a button on his hand-held: "Send in the techs and the crew."

"Oh," Samuel said, "this is terrible."

"Didn't you check this room?" Famous said.

"No, she was paid up for a week. And I like to give my guests their privacy." Samuel said that like we should give him points for being such a friggin' enlightened slum lord.

Famous grabbed Samuel by the shirt collar and pushed his head toward the floor. "That's blood, you idiot. A young girl's blood. She died."

"What? No way."

"A pregnant teenager checks in, you don't ask questions, you don't call anybody? Cops, Social services, the Red Cross?"

Samuel couldn't take his eyes off the floor.

"Jesus, this is bad."

"Ya think?" Famous said.

"Hell yes. You know how hard it is to get blood off the floor?"

I think in the old movies from the '40s they called it the Bum's Rush: Gonzo put one hand on Samuel's belt and filled his other hand with Samuel's shirt and whooshed him down the hall and out the door; Samuel's feet barely touching, his mouth flapping but nothing coming out.

Famous handed Wade and me protective gloves and booties. Wade waved off the booties and pulled a pair from his pocket.

"You bring your own?" Famous said.

"Have to. American police department issues only go to size twelve," Wade said; and snapped on his personal set. "Special order from the *Bundesnachrichtendienst*. BND, the top German intelligence agency."

We followed Famous into the room.

The trail of blood went back down a short hall and made a right into the tiny tiled bathroom.

"God damn," Famous said.

Samuel's building was built back in the '20s, when those tiny black & white tiles were all the rage. This bathroom's floor featured them in tidy diamond inset patterns. Only you couldn't see much of them because they were covered in dark blood, with a large globular mess in the middle of the floor.

"This is where she delivered" I said.

"God damn, god damn," said Famous again. "How the hell did she make it to the hospital?"

"CSI squad's here," Gonzo called from the doorway.

There were several smaller splotches of blood leading back to the bedroom that we followed and discovered a lumpy, worn mattress with a large blood stain in the middle of it. On the floor beside it was a thin, grayish sheet with a long dark crimson stain along most of its length.

"It's amazing she didn't collapse from loss of blood," I said.

"Yeah," Famous said quietly. "The more we find out about Charlene, the more admiration I have for her." He stared at the tragedy of the room and what poor Charlene had endured.

Suddenly, he lashed out with a foot and sent the mattress flying.

"Son of a bitch!"

None of us said anything, but Wade and I got on either side of the mattress and lifted it back into place. Two techies came into the room just as it flopped down with a soft whuff.

Famous shouldered his way past the techies and we followed. The CSI squad was snapping photos, taking samples, swabbing, doing their whole routine.

Outside in the hall, the CSI head honcho, Robyn Lucas was quietly giving orders into her cell. Robyn was 6' 3", trim and athletic. She looked like she could still thunder down a volleyball like when she led UCLA to a national championship.

"Hey," Gonzo called out from the building's front door, "what we want to do with Spickard."

"Book him."

Gonzo hurried back to Famous, "On what charges?"

"On being a callous, money-grubbing asshole."

"That's the definition of a slumlord," I said.

That broke the tension, at least for a moment.

"Cuff him and put him in the car," Famous said. "I'll think of something. And keep all the windows closed. Let him contemplate all the fucked-up decisions he's made in his sorry life to get him there." Famous removed his gloves. "When we're done here, cut him loose."

"Lieutenant? Temperature's about 96. People leave their dogs in their cars they crack a window open."

"Yeah, we'd do that. If he was a dog instead of a snake."

Gonzo went off to put Spickard in the squad car and Wade and I pulled off our gloves and booties.

"A rental like this place?" Robyn said, "We could have fifty different sets of prints."

"I know," said Famous. "But we only have to match two. The victim. And the killer." Famous tapped on his Samsung GIII and held it out so Robyn could see. There were three file folder icons. "Give me your phone," he said. They touched phones and Famous downloaded the files.

Famous put his phone back in his suit pocket and nodded to Wade and me. "There's a great little coffee shop a couple blocks up near Las Palmas. I could use an iced tea."

As we went out the entrance, Famous signaled for Gonzo to join us.

"What about Spickard?" Gonzo said.

"You locked the doors?"

"Sure."

"Windows rolled up?"

"Absolutely."

"Then what about Spickard? He's not going anywhere."

It was hot enough that by the time we'd walked the two short blocks to the coffee shop, I'd wished we had driven.

We took a booth, and everyone ordered an iced drink–tea, coffee and an Arnold Palmer for Gonzo.

"Shit like this happens," Famous said, "and you can see why citizens take the law into their own hands."

Our drinks came. Famous drained most of his iced tea by the time the waitress had set down the last glass. "I'll be needing a refill, please," he said.

"Man, you weren't lying when you said you were thirsty," the waitress said. "I'll be right back. With a pitcher."

"Let's say they find Jordan's prints. He's still protected until the Bureau and the Department work out something. And I don't see a deal being made."

"That's 'cause shit only rolls downhill," Gonzo said. "If this case was the opposite? That an undercover cop had gone rogue and the FBI was involved? They'd have his ass out of here and on a plane to some remote prison and we wouldn't hear about it ever again."

He took a big gulp of his drink.

"At least not officially."

42

"Officially? We are pursuing all possible avenues of investigation," Alan Harbaugh said. "Unofficially? We're fucked."

Alan was one of *Paraíso Del Mar*'s three detectives. Why we even had one detective was something I'd never understood since so little seemed to happen. But then there was last year–and Chief Black and Mayor Lockhart and Miguel Santiago who had died forty years earlier– the three men whose lives *and deaths* would forever be linked to our town.

And now there was Steve Fordham.

So, things were changing in paradise.

It was unusual for any cop to tell the truth when it came to progress on a case.

But then it had been that kind of day.

Because when we had gone to the little café for iced teas, Famous had said things I'd never heard before from him. Strange, dark talk about "what if" scenarios and rogue gangbangers and "hits" and getting away across the border and it not costing a lot of money.

And Famous was a cop who bled blue and held the law sacred.

Wade and I didn't know what to say. What could we say? It was understandable. Hell, it was probably even expected and for sure a course of action we'd all thought about.

But then Famous rubbed both his hands across his face. "Shit," he said, "lots of talk, but it's not me." He rattled the ice in his empty glass. "But that's what happens, your family gets threatened. You lose your perspective, begin thinking it's *okay* just for you, *just this one time.* But there's never a *one time.* From then on, it's always there, what you did. And then you start lowering your standards, your reasons for just this one time, and bang, you're onto your second." He signaled the waitress for the check. "And one more tea to go," he said to her. "A large."

"Man, you're thirsty, Lieutenant," Gonzo said.

"It's not for me. It's for Spickard."

On the drive home, Wade and I talked about what Famous had said and how satisfying it would be to have Jon Michaels or Brother Jordan, however you wanted to describe your target, taken out.

"But that's not us," Wade said. "Just like it's not Famous."

"And what I'm about to say isn't like us either."

Wade looked at me and raised an eyebrow, waiting.

"I'm thinking of giving the Dillards their money back."

Wade blinked a couple of times and then looked out the window.

"Do it," he said. "We put in a lot of time, but we got squat for results."

I called Charles Dillard from the car and put him on speaker so Wade and I could both talk and listen.

It was a short conversation.

"Absolutely." Charles said. "Not."

He then went on to express his gratitude, his sorrow, everything a bereaved father does when his entire life has changed and will never, ever be the same.

After I hung up, Wade said. "That was good for two reasons. One - that you called Charles and he was right about all the hard work we did. And just because we weren't bigger than the FBI, isn't a reason to think we failed."

"I agree. What's the second reason?"

"Good thing you didn't call Finneran."

"That's for sure. Mister supply and demand."

"Yeah, he'd demand we return the supply."

So, as we sat at Kincaid's with Alan Harbaugh, I was in a weird mood. Because while I knew we *hadn't* failed, I didn't think we'd succeeded.

Yes, we'd found Charlene and yes, the Dillards had to take responsibility for waiting so long to call us, but there's never a perfect time to start a case. You're *always* behind the curve, *always* running to catch up.

And yes, we had caught Charlene's killer. Or, to be technical, we'd caught the suspect. And from there the natural progression of the Law should have kicked in and justice served. But that hadn't happened. We'd done a face plant into the wall of government–just like Wile E. Coyote when he's racing after the roadrunner on a high rate of over-take, zooms around a corner and runs smack into an Acme safe that's right in the middle of the desert; or the safe, falls out of the sky and flattens him to pancake status.

That was us: flat-lined spirits.

So, we'd decided that the only thing that could revive us would be the liquid spirits that Kincaid serves.

We were nursing our third round when Alan joined us at the bar. It took him two fast rounds of doubles to catch up and loosen up.

"Yeah," he said, "unofficially, but irrevocably *fucked.*" He held up his glass to Kincaid for a refill. "Hey, Pat," he said, "another glass of 'Loudmouth Soup." He turned to me, "that's what I call Absolut on the rocks, Loudmouth Soup. Because, well, after a couple, you're..." He smiled and shook his head. "You know how many real estate agents there are in town?" And before we could even hazard a guess, he said, "More than eight hundred."

"But not every one of them can be a suspect," I said.

"No, but our DP guys can retire pretty soon just on the over-time they're racking up in analyzing the data. First, we had to get a subpoena to access the real estate board's records. Jesus, you'd have thought we were asking for secrets to the Vatican. Then it's been non-stop computer crunch time."

Kincaid put a fresh drink in front of Alan. "Here ya go, a Loudmouth, ya Loudmouth." Kincaid checked to see if we got his bad joke about a double.

I gave him an obligatory smile; then shook my head and he got the hint and went to see what other customers might need cheering up.

"So, you're tracking which houses Steve accessed with his electronic lockbox key, right?" I said.

"Steve got around, that's for sure. We had to check every single house. Ask the owners, see if they might have a connection to him; maybe he screwed them on a real estate deal, something."

"Anything there?"

"Nada. Most of the owners didn't even know he'd been in their house. Not that they would. Agent goes to check out a house, maybe he's previewing it before his client sees it, maybe his client is with him. Most owners don't know."

"Unless their agent gives them a report."

Alan thought about that for a moment. "Yeah, I suppose that could happen."

"Only *if* there were a lot of showings," Wade said. "Making brownie points with the owners–'Hey, Mr. and Mrs. Jones, look at the action I'm getting for you.'"

"But if the house isn't getting much action, maybe because the agent's not doing any marketing, or maybe it's just priced way too high and people don't bother, then he's not going to give them a report."

"Roger that," Alan said.

"So, you went through the owners," Wade said, "and then it was on to the agents?"

"Yeah, all eight hundred and forty-nine of them," Alan said. "We cross-referenced agents who'd ever done a deal with him. Then it was agents whose IDs showed up as going into any houses were Fordham had gone."

"How far back did you go?"

"Two years."

"And you obviously talked to Lo-Lo," I said.

"Of course. And Marcella Turner and Joleene McCane and Anne Bingham and Chloe Tibideaux. I tell ya, freakin' Fordham not only got around, he got around with some smokin' hot women." Alan gulped down his drink. "But if I never see another goddamn real estate agent, no matter how good looking, it will be okay with me."

Then he realized Wade and I were real estate agents.

"Uh, 'ceptin' you guys, of course."

Alan stood up and reached for his wallet.

"No," I said, "I've got this."

"You sure?"

"Ab-so-lute...ly," I said.

He smiled at my weak joke and patted me on the back.

Then, as he turned to go, I thought of something. "Hey, Alan, what about the agents who went into the house on Spinnaker just before Steve?"

"First thing we checked."

"And...?"

"Dead end. Fourteen agents saw the property. And they all check out."

"One of them was Laura DeSantis," I said, "because it was her listing."

"And she double-popped it the second day it came on the market," Alan said. "And since she knew her buyers were good for the deal, she removed the lockbox on day three of the listing. And until the day they put on the tent, Laura had the only key which she said was always in her possession."

"She unlocked the door for the termite guys?" Wade said.

"Yes. She let them in at eight o'clock; then around noon when they've got the tent up, she goes back, locks the deadbolt and leaves.

"So, after the lockbox was gone," I said, "none of the agents had access."

"Right."

"And fourteen agents saw it on the first day?" I said.

"No, just twelve."

"When did the other two see it?" Wade said.

"According to the log, 11:23 AM. Laura removed the lockbox at 5:30 PM."

"One of those two agents must have made a copy of the key," I said.

"That's what the Chief said. But then we found out who they were."

We waited. Alan has a flair for the dramatic.

"Marge and Alice Dayton," he said with a big smile.

"The twins?" I said. "*They* were the other two agents? Hell, they started selling when a lot on the Strand was only three hundred thousand. How old are they now?"

"Seventy-four. And they weigh maybe two hundred pounds. Combined."

"So, forget whacking Steve and carrying his body," Wade said.

I thought about all this for a moment.

"And forget accident, this is definitely a homicide," I said.

"That's the premise we're working on," Alan said.

"And are you only looking at women?"

"No."

"Well you should. Because a woman killed him."

"Oh, really?" Alan was a little pissy now. Maybe it was the loudmouth Soup kicking in. "And what's your theory on that?"

And maybe it was my own reaction to the drinks.

But, damn, this felt exactly right.

"It's not a theory. The fact is if Steve Fordham never used his electronic key on the lockbox, whoever killed him brought him there."

"Okay," Alan snapped. Definitely the loudmouth Soup talking. He was belligerent.

I could see Wade's brow was a little furrowed too—like: Where you going with this, partner?

"Terminator mode," I said.

"*Dit-dit-dit?*" Wade said.

"Loud and clear."

Wade put a hand on Alan's arm.

"You should listen to this."

"Think about it," I said. "What man would sneak into a house that's about to be fumigated?"

"A guy who wanted to steal," Alan said.

"Nothing to steal. House was empty."

"Okay," Alan said.

"Only man would do that was a guy with some kinky, wild ass reason. Like getting laid."

Alan's eyes widened.

"Steve Fordham fucked a lot of women. I'm sure he was jaded by his success. So, the only possible reason that I can see that he'd sneak into a house that's about to be fumigated would be because he thought he was about to have the best fuck of his life."

I looked at Alan and Wade and finished my drink.

"He just didn't know it was going to be the last fuck of his life."

"Oh, man," Wade said, "the political shit just hit the fan."

Alan looked at him, still a little behind the curve because he'd been pounding down the drinks.

"You're going to have to ask all those women for a DNA sample," Wade said.

"Not all of them," I said. "Steve just went after the beautiful ones."

Alan looked at me and then at Wade; and a big smile creased his face.

Loudmouth was the Soup *du jour*.

"Well," Alan said, "I guess we can cross the Dayton twins off the list."

43

The Dayton twins weren't the only ones who didn't make the list.

No one made it.

Because in a case of clear sexual bias, the *Paraíso Del Mar* coroner's department hadn't checked for any kind of sexual activity on Steve Fordham's body.

"How the hell did that happen?" I asked Hal Bartkowski.

"You're gonna bust my balls, too?" he said. "First, I had to endure all those questions from Jeanne Nichols, that bitchy reporter from *The Gold Rush*. Then the Chief ripped me a new one. Jesus, we were looking at a guy who we thought, at the time, had died from inhaling sulfurye fluoride."

"Except you told me you thought it might be a homicide; since he'd been hit at the base of his neck."

"Yeah. Homicide."

"Exactly. And if it had been a woman's body, you would have automatically checked for vaginal bruising, penetration, all of it."

"We fucked up on the fucking, okay? Happy now?"

"I'm not trying to roast your ass. I'm just trying to figure out what's my next move."

Hal looked at me for a long moment. "What the hell's this got to do with you?"

"Nothing, really. But Carmen Rosales, the woman who owns the termite company? She was a suspect for a while."

"And I heard she'd been cleared."

"Yes, but it's always better if you can wipe the slate clean instead of just white-washing it."

"So, what do you need?"

"Any chance Steve's clothing would have traces of a sexual encounter?"

"Maybe, but even if his clothes hadn't been cremated with him, that's a long shot. I doubt if there'd have been enough on it." Hal moved the mouse on his desk and his computer screen came to life. He tapped keys on the board. "Well, wait, here's something."

I moved around to look at the screen.

"Mary Guilletei, she's the new assistant. The new old me, so to speak."

I hadn't known they'd hired Hal's replacement, but then why wouldn't they? He'd moved up, somebody had to fill his former spot.

"We did do his fingernails and his limbs." Hal tapped more keys. "But...not much. Some rug fibers and...well, maybe, appears to be some kind of cotton fiber. Black."

"Maybe it's from the woman's skirt or dress."

"Or maybe it's from the tablecloth where he had lunch, or the shirt Steve was wearing that day. Do you know how many thousands of possibilities there could be? If you thought the Department was in shit city trying to get DNA swabs from a couple hundred women, this is exponentially worse."

"But you'll do it, I know."

"Hell no," Hal said.

"NO?"

"Why the hell do you think I got an assistant?"

Hal and I talked for a little longer and then I was heading for my car when Joe Bryant saw me and came over.

"Hey, Matt, how ya doing?"

Joe is eighty-two and could pass for a couple of decades younger. Joe was a former "Mr. California" back in the late forties, early fifties and he's always pumped iron.

"Joe," I said, and we shook hands. Joe's grip is damn strong. "Still looking good."

He smiled. "Ah, you know, no matter how hard you work out, you get to be my age, the meat just doesn't hang close to the bone anymore."

"C'mon, I'll bet all the sixty-year-old women hit on you all the time."

"Sixty? I don't date older women. They can't keep up." He laughed. "Naw, you know I'm just kiddin' ya. Only girl for me was my wife Betty-Jean. And once she passed, God rest her Soul," he crossed himself, "I didn't think any other woman could compare and didn't see any sense in trying."

"Yes, I agree."

Joe looked a little wistful for a moment. "Yeah, I miss Betty-Jean. So even though I'm still going to the gym, I'm just waiting for God to take me."

"Hell, Joe, God's the only one who could."

Joe laughed again. "Where are you heading?"

"Going to pick up my partner, then we're going downtown LA."

"Keeping the streets safe are ya?"

"Trying, Joe, trying."

He slapped me on the shoulder and there was a definite whack to it.

"Trying's all you can do, Matt. Just don't let the sons of bitches see ya feeling pain."

44

Stoic was the only way to describe Famous when Wade and I saw him down at the new Parker Center. The LAPD's state-of-the-art building dominates the city block it occupies at 100 West First Street in one of the older, seedier sections of east Los Angeles.

The new building sparkles and is a beautiful, angular architectural creation that's home to about twenty-three-hundred of the ten thousand dedicated officers that are the country's third largest police force.

We were meeting with one of them, Sergeant Antoine Galatian, who was out of the LAPD's newest department, Counter Terrorism and Special Operations Bureau.

Galatian was a tall, prematurely grey black man who looked like he could bench press the Dodge Charger he drove up in and waited while the three of us climbed in–Famous in the front seat, Wade and I in the back.

Famous introduced us and Galatian said, "I'll shake hands when we park."

Then he accelerated and headed South down San Pedro Street.

"So, Agent Kouros is crying red alert?" he said. "More like red horseshit. Unless he's got better, deeper connections than we do, and I seriously doubt that," Galatian looked in the rearview and caught my eyes, then shifted to Wade, "Sounds like CYA time."

Cover Your Ass time. Sounded familiar when you got politicos and problems. "They're stone-walling us," Famous said.

"Yeah," Galatian said, "but why?"

The Bureau that Antoine worked for had been created back in 2010 when the Counter Terrorism and Criminal Intelligence Bureau had merged. It provided specialized tactical resources in support of field operations for the LAPD; especially during elevated terrorism threat conditions. So far, nothing had made a blip on their radar screen. And for sure, nothing like the crisis that Kouros wanted us to believe superhero Agent Michaels was working to prevent.

"We were able to download the transcripts from all the telephone calls made from the Temple. And unless you count ordering Domino's Pizza as a national security emergency..."

"Only if they're more than thirty minutes," Wade said.

Galatian smiled and didn't seem to mind being interrupted, "Right. So, we're not buying any of it." He made a tight turn and glanced at Famous. "Anything come from Milner?"

"It was definitely Charlene's blood, but nobody else's. Lots of prints, I'm sure from other desperate people that rented the place. Jesus, I wonder if Spickard *ever* cleaned. Anyway, lots of prints, but none from Michaels. A couple of the prints we lifted turned out to be dudes with records. One of them was a guy who'd violated his parole, left a forwarding address with Spickard; so he had a surprise when he went to pick up his mail–like two cops in uniform. The other guy was clean and moved to Florida a year ago."

"A year?" I said. "You weren't kidding about not cleaning."

"Yeah, well he'll have to do it now. If only to get rid of..." Famous faltered a little, ".. the blood."

Galatian pulled up in front of a small store front and shut the engine. "I think you guys will like this," he said. But before we went inside, he made good his promise and shook my hand and then Wade's. "Good to meet you," he said to both of us.

It wasn't until I went through the door that I saw the small name plate, *Thai Thani* that I realized it was a restaurant. The owner seemed overjoyed to see Galatian, and not just because he greeted him in Thai. A slim, beautiful waitress whose name tag said Tak in cursive writing, showed us to a large red leatherette booth in the back. We'd barely sat down when two more highly attractive waitresses served us water and Singha beers.

"The usual, Tak." Galatian told our waitress.

"Certainly, Mister Antoine," Tak said in a high, but sultry voice.

The "usual" was mostly appetizers, but incredibly delicious. We started with *Chiengmai Treat*, which was ground pork mixed with green onion, ginger, peanut, and lemon juice. Then came *MeeKrob*–crispy fried noodles with shrimp and chicken sautéed in a delightful sauce, served with bean sprouts and green onions. Next came a few *Thani Spring Rolls* filled with ground chicken, sliced bamboo shoot, and glass noodles. We finished with what *Mister Antoine* said was the specialty of the house: *Pineapple Rice*, which were several large, scooped-out pineapples filled with shrimp, chicken, pork, crab claw, and rice. We each had another Singha beer and by then we'd learned everything Galatian was allowed to tell us.

None of the cells his Bureau had under surveillance had any connection or contact with Brother Jordan aka Agent Michaels. Of course, it was possible that a new secret black ops cell had been formed, but if so, they were extremely clandestine and had made no contact with Brother Jordan of any kind.

"Somebody is shoveling shit," Galatian said. "Either Kouros, or Michaels."

"Is there a way to leverage this knowledge against him?" I said.

Galatian shook his head. "I don't think so. Or at least not very soon. Because if we come at him now, there's only a small chance we get him, and a big chance we blow our links to the cells. And we're back in shit city."

"You think there's any chance he *is* on to some radical groups?" Famous asked.

Galatian shrugged. "I had to lay money on it? No. Hundred-to-one odds. But there's always that one long shot that comes from out of nowhere."

"I agree. I think he's a lit fuse," I said. "There's some serious messianic shit going on behind his blond pretty boy facade."

"Yeah," said Famous. "Serious shit. Because if something doesn't blow with the *spies*," he spit out the word like he'd bit into a foul-tasting piece of fruit, "then I worry about those young girls up there. They're in danger and they don't know it."

"Maybe that's what we work on," Wade said. "Getting the Sisters out on being underage minors."

"How the hell we do that?" Famous said, "Kidnap them?"

"Yes," Antoine Galatian said. "Only we call it Asset Extraction."

45

"Then I guess you'd call me an Asset Addition," Andriel Wade said.

"You got that right," Wade said, laughing.

Andriel's surprise visit turned out to be even more of a surprise when Wade and I pulled up to my office and there she was, waiting.

After Wade jumped out of the car and bounded up the stairs, Andriel meeting him halfway, they hugged and kissed and laughed and looked at each other in wonder and love.

I noticed the silver oak leaf clusters on her uniform and saluted. "Ten-hut. Officer on the stairs."

"Come here, private," Andriel said, her big smile so warm and welcoming.

Like her brother, Andriel is big, but you really don't notice it until she gives you one of her tight bear hugs and you not only feel yourself enveloped in her loving arms, but realize those arms are damn strong.

"Congratulations," I said.

"For sure," Wade said. "I am so damn proud of you."

Andriel pretended it wasn't any big deal to be one of the youngest and fastest-rising officers in the US Army, but she beamed under all our attention and lavish praise.

Her stay at Fort Belvoir, was briefer than she'd thought: they'd fast-tracked her for her promotion, had a couple of pow wows as she called them, with the top brass and they'd given her an extra three days of leave.

"And here I am," she said. "Just another girl down at the beach, hoping to hang out with two cool dudes."

"I'm not so sure about two," Wade said.

"Oh, c'mon, Jamal, I said, "you don't need to put yourself down like that. I'm sure we could go one-and-a-half on the cool."

We had a terrific dinner at Kincaid's; my dad and Carmen and Leah all joining us. Kincaid gave us an outstanding bottle of *Veuve Clicquot* on the house, to celebrate Andriel's promotion, several people stopped by because they were attracted to these six people having a party, bought us more drinks, and we pretty much closed the place.

My dad and Carmen went home, probably to his place. Leah understood we three had things to talk about, so she went home alone with my promise to come by and see her for breakfast.

When we went back to my office to collect Andriel's bag, we brought her up to date on what had happened. We started local and went through everything that had happened on Steve Fordham's murder.

"*Cherez la femme*," Andriel said, repeating what Francois had said back at *Chef Fritz*. "I think you're right, Matt. Look to the woman."

"It's got to be one of the women he slept with."

"And maybe jilted," she said. "'Hell, hath no fury…?'"

"That's a long list," Wade said. "I mean every time he had a new one, usually meant he'd dumped an old one. Although he was seeing three or four at the same time."

"Don't discount a woman he dismissed," Andriel said.

"What do you mean?" Wade said.

"Maybe someone who wanted to join the party and didn't get an invitation."

"The *Zaggat Guide to Great Lovers*," Wade said. "Hmmm, Steve Fordham. Okay, I'm gonna try me some of that. And when she tries to book it, he says, 'Sorry, I'm full. Dat what you be sayin', sistah?'"

Andriel's eyes flared a little, then she shook her head slowly at Wade.

"Andriel doesn't like when I's talks like dey folks in dem ol' blackie and whites movies."

"It's funny between us, but others may not understand them."

"Fuck 'em dey cain't take a joke."

"So, what's the other case?" she said.

"This one is pure evil," Wade said, shifting immediately back to his normal tone.

We ran down everything about Brother Jordan, Charlene, and the Sisters to Andriel. And probably one of the reasons she's risen so quickly, through it all, she listened very closely, asked a few questions that were spot on, and then after Wade said Galatian's line of "Asset Extraction" is when she called herself an "Asset Addition."

"It's not my field," she said, "but I'm a good sounding board."

"It's total Black Op," Wade said. "There isn't any kind of legal justification for doing it."

"And in doing it," I said, "we're guilty of kidnapping, probably aggravated assault and I'm sure a train wreck of other crimes."

"And there's no guarantee it will work, even if the raid is successful. And that's what you're got–a Commando Raid," Andriel said.

"What'd you mean, if it's successful it still might not work?" Wade said.

"You're going to have to do an intervention. Meaning brain wash them *back* to where they were or as close to it as they can get. And there's still no guarantee their families will understand or deep down, forgive them."

Wade and I thought about that for a long moment.

"Well, there's always the high ground of morally it's right."

"And how many wars been fought over *that*?" she said. "And since it's off the grid, it has to be secretly funded. And that takes money. Big money."

"Which we don't have," I said. "But we do have Charles Dillard."

Wade looked at me like I'd stayed up past my bedtime and was talking nonsense.

"I think I can convince him."

Andriel shifted on the small sofa that sometimes has doubled as my bed on long nights. "You have any photos of this Agent Michaels?"

I pulled the file and handed it to her.

She studied the photos of Brother Jordan; the mug shots from when he was booked, and some secret ones Wade had snapped with his cell phone.

"So handsome," Andriel said. "And what's this?" she held out the police photo of the close-up of Jordan's tattoo.

"Supposed to be the *Janus* of religion," Wade said.

"That's one positive ID mark," Andriel said. "No way is somebody else mistaken for him." Andriel frowned, "What a waste. A man like that has to pull shit like that? On young innocent girls no less?"

"Like I told you, he's evil," Wade said. "Pure evil and needs to be erased."

"Yes," his sister said, nodding her head. "Too bad he's here and not over there with the Afghanis, there's a young soldier I took care of who could take care of that little problem for you."

Wade and I looked at each other: Wow, not like the Andriel we knew.

She studied Jordan's picture without looking up and kept talking. "Rhett Riley. Georgia boy, what else with a name like that? Ole Rhett caught a ricocheting bullet in his calf, had to be ordered by his commanding officer to come in for medical treatment."

"Was it that bad?"

"His calf was hanging down by his ankle. I'm still amazed that he could even walk. But Rhett was anxious to get back to work."

"What division was he in?" Wade said.

"Infantry. Part of EXACTO. Expert with an M107 LFSR."

"What do the initials mean?" I said.

"The EXACTO stands for EXtreme ACcuracy Tasked Ordnance."

"What the hell's that even mean?"

"Means the bullets are like little guided missiles. Fin-stabilized or spin-stabilized. Might have external aero-actuation controls."

"Wow," was all I could say. Then I asked, "What about the other initials?"

"LFSR? Long Range Sniper Rifle. Delivers a .50 caliber bullet, which is a machine gun bullet, at over a thousand-yards."

"A thousand yards? That's ten football fields."

"It is. The record's over twenty-five hundred yards. A Canadian shot a Taliban combatant back in 2002. I think it's been broken since then. But Rhett's the best they've *ever* seen. Don't know if he's officially on the record books."

Then Andriel looked at her brother and me and shrugged. "Aw, I'm just wishful thinking here. You know, when somebody's done something and they're untouchable and you can't do anything to change it? So, you fantasize?"

She stood up, hoisted her bag and said, "Hey, bro, I hope you kept that guest bed made, because if not, I'm just flopping on top in my uniform. I am wasted."

46

"I thought you'd be too tired," Leah said.

"Any man says he's too tired to make love to a beautiful woman, isn't tired, he's dead."

"You have more bullshit lines, Matt Singer," she said, as she put her arms around me.

God, she felt good.

"They're working though, right?"

She kissed me. "Yeah, they are."

The next morning after breakfast, Leah and I went our separate ways.

I went north to my office to meet with Wade to get ready for our meeting with Antoine Galatian and Famous.

Leah went South to Seaview Real Estate.

For the first few weeks after her father's death, Leah was reluctant to go to the office, since she didn't feel like she belonged there among all those pros. And she told everyone she really didn't know enough about the business to tell anybody anything.

Pure Lockhart spin doctoring.

Because all those years that her father had acquired real estate, he'd also talked to Leah about them. Just sounding off, telling her his ideas, his theories, and absolute rules. And Leah didn't miss a beat on any of it. She may have acted like she wasn't listening or that she didn't care, but she *knew* the business.

At first. she just went in one day a week for a few hours to get an overview. But then as she dug into the information and reviewed her agents' portfolios and how they were going after business, her hours increased.

She didn't want Seaview to lose business, she wanted it to grow.

"Learn from your own mistakes, but profit from others' errors," she said. "That was one of my father's rules."

She had her own rules, too.

And several top-notch agents balked at them.

And after a few weeks, they were no longer at Seaview.

Leah's increased interest in Seaview helped me and Wade too.

Because it gave us a direct line to the latest news and scuttlebutt on Steve Fordham's murder. The Seaview agents were more connected in town than any others. So, if there was a new bit of information, if there was a new theory or idea, they usually heard about it first.

Chief Remington still hadn't officially declared it a homicide, but he was probably the only one in town who hadn't.

I got to the office, made a pot of coffee, and opened the door to Wade and Andriel. Wade was dressed in his usual casual but professional style, but Andriel came in with a snug aqua-marine shift that hit her in the middle of some spectacular cocoa-colored legs. She wore color-matching flops on her long, thin feet.

She held up a large rainbow-hued bag. "Beach day," she said and then laughed. "Jeez, all that time over there and I go right back to the sand. But at least there's some cool, blue water at the end of this patch."

"I made coffee," I said.

"Oh, thanks, but I need to see the ocean." She turned and opened the door to leave and...there was...Antoine.

"Oh," said Andriel softly.

"Uh..." was all that Antoine managed.

For a long, long moment, they just stared at each other.

The scene in *The Godfather, Part II*, when Michael and Apollonia first lay eyes on each other, sprung to my mind.

They'd been hit by *un fulmine:* Thunderbolt in Italian.

And are *reso ammutolito.* Rendered speechless.

"Beep, beep," Famous said. He was behind Antoine on the narrow stairs.

"Andriel and Antoine both laughed nervously; and then Andriel moved back into my office, never really taking her eyes off Antoine.

Antoine and Famous followed her in and Andriel recovered first and said, "Hello, Famous. It's been a while."

"Yeah," he said and gave Andriel a big, warm hug.

Then she turned to Antoine, "Andriel Wade." And her smile could have lit up Broadway.

"Antoine. Antoine Galatian." And his smile was a quick flash of white teeth.

"This beautiful woman here," Famous said, "is one of the youngest and brightest Majors in the US Army."

"Lieutenant Colonel," I said.

It took Famous a second to process and understand the significance of that. "Damn, girl, congratulations." He and Andriel slapped a low five, several times. "Hell, make that the *fastest* and youngest *Lieu-ten-ant Col-nel*."

Everybody laughed.

Then Wade said, "All right, who wants java?"

Being big brother, despite himself.

We all placed our orders, everybody black except Antoine who wanted sugar and cream.

To which Andriel said, "Oh, here, I know where Matt keeps it." And opened the small refrigerator where I kept the sugar and cream. And an emergency supply of *Pacifico* beer.

She carefully added cream to Antoine's cup.

"Thank you," Antoine said.

"No problem. Sugar." She waited just enough So even the dullest of us could understand what she was really saying, and then handed Antoine the sugar bowl.

Then, for a while we sipped our coffee, talked about anything but the reason we were here. Antoine tried to be casual, but as much as he wanted to hide his fascination, or make that infatuation, with Andriel, he ended up asking about her career in the Army, how long she was here on leave, what was it like taking care of wounded men and women during battle?

I could see Famous fidget, so I said, "Uh, guys? We can start anytime. We told Andriel about our mission."

There was a long, frozen moment when I wasn't sure how Famous or Antoine would take the news.

Then Antoine said, "Okay. We could use a woman's perspective, given that we are rescuing women."

"Right," Andriel said. "Asset Extraction, good term. Just make sure you don't use Asshole Extractors."

From out of the mouth of babes.

"You're spot on," Antoine said. "The team members need to be cool and contained." He smiled at Andriel and looked at the rest of us. "I have a couple of guys in mind."

We then spent a good twenty minutes discussing candidates; because Famous knew a guy who knew a guy. And Wade had a guy in college who'd been a cop, and like so many before him, quit the force and opened a security firm.

Andriel listened and never said a word.

Finally, Famous, and not Antoine, said, "Andriel, what do you think about all of this?"

"I'm just a sawbones." She smiled and adjusted those magnificent legs. "But there was a Sergeant I treated the first week I was in country. Guy named Bryan Olliphant. Got a Purple Heart, Go-Home wound and came back to the states. He got honorably discharged and opened a private security firm OPS: Olliphant Protection Services. And I hear he's damn good."

Andriel punched Some numbers on her cell phone and then looked at Wade, "I just texted you two of his numbers. The company. And his private cell number. The cell might have changed, since he's very security conscious, but I'd try that first."

She pulled her shift down over her thighs and stood up. "And I'm off to the beach." She gave Wade and me a small wave, then hugged Famous and gave Antoine a handshake that turned into a quick hug and another huge smile.

"You want to have lunch?" Wade asked.

"I'll be straight down by the 26th street lifeguard tower."

Antoine watched her go out the door then quickly consulted his cell. I looked at Wade. I wasn't sure what he was thinking exactly, but I was pretty sure that when he and Andriel walked into my office this morning, the last thing either of them expected was that Cupid would be here too.

And would fire all the arrows in her quiver.

47

"Everything the Foundation has is at your disposal," Charles Dillard said.

I'd been prepared to cajole, argue, even beg, but I had barely gotten started with "Operation Angel" as Antoine decided to call the plan before Charles agreed to fund it."If we can save those other young girls, I don't care how much it costs," Charles said. "I made the mistake of my life with Charlene and no matter what I do there's no forgiving myself for that. But..." and he took a long breath while I waited for him to go on, "...but if we can help those other parents and those young women– Goddamnit they're just *kids!* get away from that monster, it's something good."

He didn't really want to know the details, just that any requests I made were directly through him and not Finneran. Of course.

We had outlined our game plan and then everyone left to do their job.

Antoine got the numbers from Wade and was going to call Bryan Olliphant.

Famous left to go see his friend.

Wade picked up a couple of sandwiches and iced teas and went down to the beach to have lunch with Andriel.

And I'd called Dillard.

Then my dad called and wanted to know if I had heard anything else about Steve Fordham. Despite no longer being a suspect, Carmen was still bothered by the events; especially because while everyone knew she was innocent, she'd still been considered a suspect. "Don't worry," I'd told her before, "for the police, *everyone* is a suspect." It keeps them busy. And gets them overtime pay.

I met my dad for lunch at Giovanni's and over a large Mediterranean pizza, house salads and beers, I told him about Operation Angel.

"That's like a private SWAT team, going in there and taking those girls," he said.

"But this has *got* to be secret, something that never happened."

"You and Wade aren't going to be part of the team, are you?"

"If they'll let us. You know, another adventure for the Caped Crusader."

He looked at me and sipped his beer.

"More like Crusader Rabbit."

"Who?"

"Crusader Rabbit."

I guess my face didn't register any recognition because he said, "Oh, c'mon, all those Saturday mornings we used to watch together? You don't remember?"

"Uh, no. Sorry."

"Crusader Rabbit and his pal a tiger named Rags? That was the very first cartoon ever made just for television. Way back in '49."

"Dad, I'm only forty-two, remember?"

"Don't be a smart ass. We watched them in re-runs. Your mother liked to take Saturday mornings off, so I'd babysit you and we'd watch Crusader Rabbit and other cartoons. You used to giggle your ass off."

"I'll check them out on YouTube. And this rabbit reminds you of me?"

"No. It just popped up when you said Crusader."

We finished lunch and I promised him I'd see if I could learn anything else about Steve Fordham's murder.

Back at the office I checked out Crusader Rabbit on YouTube. It definitely looked like the first cartoon made for television. The animation was simplistic and roughly-drawn; the characters jerky in their movements and every one of them had a weird voice. Disney it was not. But it did have its own innocent charm. The fact that Crusader sometimes wore a knight's armor and carried a lance to tilt at windmills wasn't lost on me, although that might have been putting too much of a Raymond Chandler spin on the idea. Then I wondered: How would Wade feel about being a tiger?

I went to the refrigerator and opened one of the emergency-only *Pacifico* beers.

It *was* a damn emergency in my mind. Here we were putting together a commando raid, using goddamn mercenaries, to supposedly rescue several young girls who had made conscious choices, had left families where there must have been some kind of trouble, and yet, now, seemed happy, and we were doing it under the banner of "saving them."

Like Andriel had reminded us it was *exactly* that kind of thinking that started just about every war: My God is better than your God. My beliefs and ideas of Society are the *only* ones that matter damnit, and if you don't think so I'll make sure you do; even if I have to kill you doing it.

And yet, everyone that knew of the plan, approved the plan. So, there was *some* justice to it.

Of course, the people that didn't know about the plan and wouldn't know until it was too late, meaning Agent Michaels and Kouros and the FBI, would probably go ballistic.

Which is why secrecy was so vital to our success–before, during and after the raid.

Which is why when Antoine called me at the end of the day and said that after talking to Bryan Olliphant, Wade and I were out, I understood. I didn't like it, but I understood.

Wade didn't like it or understand it. But Andriel convinced him. It took an hour, but she was persuasive.

"So, let me understand this," Wade said after he'd finally agreed we weren't going to be part of the rendition, "we've gotten Charles Dillard to pony up a lot of money for an operation which we'll never see except from a distance?"

"Yes."

"You comfortable with that?"

"No. But what the hell choice do we have? If the FBI finds out we were part of it, in fact if they even think we're part of it, we're in for a shitload of trouble. Not to mention the possibility of prison."

"That's why," Andriel said, "when it goes down, you guys are on a plane flying to Hawaii, or sitting in the third base dugout seats at a Dodgers game, so maybe your mugs will be on television; something that establishes your innocence."

"An alibi?" Wade said.

"Bullet-proof, iron-clad and irrefutable."

"Gimme another of those beers," Wade said. "Shit, I really wanted to put Brother Thomas on his percale-covered ass."

"Who says you still can't do that?" I said.

Wade took two long swallows and looked very hard out the window where the sun was dipping into the ocean.

"Sheet-wearing KKK mutha."

Then he burped very loudly.

48

"Why do men always lean over to fart?" Carmen said.

We were all at dinner: me, Leah, Wade, my dad, Carmen, Andriel and her surprise date–at least a surprise to me and Wade–Antoine.

Andriel had asked me for his number and I'd reflectively looked at Wade.

"You don't need to be looking at my brother for permission," Andriel said.

"You're absolutely right. I hereby apologize for my innate male chauvinism, which reared its ancient atavistic head."

Wade looked at me.

"When you make a mistake, dazzle them with bullshit as a cover-up."

I'd given her Antoine's cell number she'd called and invited him down to dinner and here we all were at Kincaid's.

"No, I'm serious," Carmen said. "Why do men always lean to fart?"

What had brought on the question was that at a nearby table an older man, who looked to be in his eighties, had leaned over, almost precipitously, and I'm sure, cut one. Because the women sitting at his table, immediately turned their heads away from him and started fanning the air.

"Oh, Jacob," a small woman next to him said, probably his wife.

"That was an SBD, Grandpa," a little boy of around nine or ten laughed.

The other men and Grandpa all snickered a little, but loud enough for everyone at our table to notice.

"Well?" Carmen said.

"I can answer that," my dad said. "Men lean because if you don't you could get seriously injured."

Heh-heh.

Wade knew this was going to be funny.

"It's true," my dad said, trying to hold back his laughter. "One time I was lying in bed, half-asleep and had to fart and was just too tired to roll one way or the other, so just let loose."

"And?" I said, the sidekick son.

"And the blast hit against the mattress and exploded up and fluttered my balls."

"Oh, Mario," Carmen said, and slugged him hard in his shoulder. "You're disgusting."

"It's true. My right nut hurt all day."

The men all laughed, the women chuckled, politely.

"See," my dad said, "secretly women like farts."

This was met with an indignant crescendo from Carmen, Leah and even Andriel.

"Well, every time a man says the word 'fart' women always smile."

And despite themselves, Carmen, Leah, and Andriel couldn't hide their smiles.

"But that's not the right kind of smile," Carmen said.

Fortunately, the waiter and several other staff members arrived with our food and the subject was closed. But as he took his plate, my dad looked at me, smiled and gave me a big wink.

That's my dad. You're never sure if he's telling the truth with his stories or just trying to entertain everyone.

We couldn't talk about Operation Angel, so after we covered the national news, some sports, the weather, we finally got to what everyone *really* wanted to talk about: Steve Fordham.

Owning the most successful real estate company in town gave Leah the insider's track on the latest non-legal news which was rumors, wild ideas and just plain gossip. The legal news was still stonewalling: No new suspects, the case was still under investigation.

At least Leah's news was juicy.

"About a week before Steve died, he almost got his head handed to him by some guy named Kyle Larent."

"Let me guess, Kyle's wife and Steve?" I said.

"Too easy, huh?"

"Steve was too laid back to cause trouble, so trouble had to find him. It had to be a pissed-off husband."

"That's putting it mildly. This Kyle's an Aussie and was some crazy cage fighter back in Sydney. So, when he found out about them, he goes berserk and comes after Steve."

"What happened?"

"Kyle comes storming into Julian's Bar, and somehow Steve sees him, throws a full plate of salsa and chips at him, and while Kyle's ducking the mess, Steve manages to sprint for the side door. Kyle goes after him, but slips on the salsa, and he's already got a bad knee–in fact, that's why he had to quit cage fighting, his knee kept getting blown out by opponents–and he goes down. In fact, his knee was so bad he couldn't walk and a few days later he went into the hospital for a total knee replacement.

"Steve's lucky," Andriel said. "Cage fighters are psychotics."

"I'm assuming," Wade said, "that Kyle was in the hospital when Steve died?"

"Yes," Leah said. "But when the cops came to talk to him, he tells them he's glad the wife-stealing bastard had died."

"Oh, that was smart," Wade said. "What an idiot."

"Jamal," Andriel said, "you're expecting a cage fighter to be intelligent?"

"So, we're back to Matt Singer's Crime Fighter's Rule 32: 'The beauty did it.' That being a variation on 'The butler did it.'"

Andriel turned to Leah and with the very slightest shaking of her head, rolled her eyes.

As if Leah must be a long-suffering heroine to put up with me. Jeez.

Antoine had been quiet during all of this since he didn't really know what was going on, so when he asked to be updated, we all kind of joined in, giving him little bits and pieces and our opinions.

When we were through, he said, "And the cops have ruled out the husbands of the other women? Marcella? And...I forget the others."

"Joleene McCane, Anne Bingham and Chloe Tibideaux," Leah said. "And, yes, they're all clear."

"Joe Tibideaux's decided doesn't want to be married anymore," my dad said. "He's filed for divorce."

We all kind of shook our heads in agreement, or at least, acknowledgment.

Trusting your spouse after something like that was damn hard; not impossible, since many marriages navigated the rocks of infidelity and maintained their course, albeit sometimes in a new direction.

"Man," said Antoine, "I'm glad I only have to deal with wackos who want to take down the United States. These romantic affairs can drive you crazy."

Andriel said, "But if it's not driving you crazy, it's not true romance."

49

Things got hot and heavy real fast.

The next day we were in my office going through the proposed team members for Operation Angel with Bryan Olliphant.

Bryan looked just like what you thought the head of OPS, his private security firm, would look like.

And then he didn't.

You expected him to be an uber-wide, maybe steroid enhanced physical machine with no neck, enormous chest and arms that stretched his custom-tailored suit to the limits. But what you didn't expect was his choirboy face and a thin, reedy voice that sounded like puberty was still ahead of him.

"I like this guy," Antoine said. "Blake Austin."

"I agree," Bryan said, "Blake would be an excellent choice."

"I like that he's former SEALS, that most of his work's been in Europe and the Middle East, and that he's been with your company from the start," Antoine said.

"He was the second man I hired," Bryan said. "Dave Higgins was the first; and you've already picked him."

"Any reservations about Blake," Wade said.

"Reservations?" Bryan's voice went up a notch, which I thought was impossible. "I've personally vetted everyone that I hire. If *I* had *any* reservations, they wouldn't work for OPS."

"I'm sure of that," Wade said. "But what I meant was: if you could only take three people, would he be one of them or would you choose someone else?"

Bryan thought about this for a moment. "No. Dave and Blake would still be my numbers one and two."

"Okay," I said, "we have four candidates left. Who's your favorite?"

"Not my favorite," Bryan said, "but vital to this mission, given that we're dealing with young women, actually still girls; Leslie Kent."

Wade and I looked at Leslie's photo and her resume. She had a narrow, angular face with piercing dark eyes that stared defiantly at the camera. Her black spiky hair went in a lot of different directions but seemed planned that way. She was 5'6", 120 lbs. and had served two tours in Afghanistan before getting honorably discharged and joining OPS.

She didn't seem like the sisterly type, but I didn't say anything. Being the only female in an outfit like OPS couldn't have been easy; and probably required psychic armor plating.

We passed her info to Antoine who checked it out very quickly and nodded his approval.

Sam Reiker was our fourth choice and we all pretty much agreed on him right away. His photo showed a calm, rugged face; and his background included being an instructor at the U.S. Army's Ranger school in Fort Benning, Georgia.

"So, who's the fifth?" Famous said.

"Me," said Bryan.

"What?" Antoine said immediately. "No way. Not that you can't handle it, but I need you as coordinator."

"My company, my rules. Besides, I've got six guys who can coordinate things better than me. I'll pick one. But *I'm* doing this."

Antoine held out his hands in a WTF moment and looked at Bryan for an explanation.

"This so-called agent Michaels? A freakin' detriment to the Bureau. Not that I love the FBI, but this guy's a menace. And the fact that he's hiding behind this bullshit terrorist story and preying on underage girls makes this personal."

"But he's not going to be there," Antoine said.

"He does his show *every* Sunday?" Bryan said.

"So far," Famous said. "Goes to this little television studio on Gower, just off Sunset and he records his sermon. Then he goes electronic and broadcasts it over the internet, YouTube, and any and every form of streaming media platform around." "Just like every other evangelical con man," said Wade.

"He's looking for converts," Antoine said. "Preferably young and beautiful."

"And vulnerable," I said.

"So that gives us six days to perfect this," said Bryan.

By *us* he meant *his* team.

Wade and I were just going along as back up. Which meant, *way* back up the road, don't get anywhere near *their* action.

"First strike, we immobilize, or if necessary, subdue Brother Thomas and Brother Jonas," Bryan said. "Then we get the girls. Four girls, five team members, should be a piece of cake."

"The van will be where?" Antoine said.

"Halfway down the hill when we go in, then it's stormin' up the driveway, right to the front door. We'll have four members in the van, ready to go."

"Gonna be a lot of screaming and yelling and crying," Wade said.

"No shit," Famous said. "I don't see them coming along at all, much less without kicking up a fuss."

"That's what Leslie Kent is for," Bryan said; and said it a little too hard I thought. Like he was trying to make a point.

So of course, I had to say, "She's adding that feminine touch. Even if that touch could knock you on your ass."

Before anyone could smile, Bryan was pissed off.

"Hey, *Goddamnit*, everyone on my crew is a trained professional, they don't rattle, and they don't get pissed off."

"Just like you right now?" I said. And stared him right in the eyes.

Yeah, I was pissed off too. So was Wade. We didn't like being backup.

Bryan immediately shut back down. Weird Jekyll and Hyde side to the man.

He held out his hands. "Sorry. My crew's better-trained than I am. But trust me, she's hard, no doubt about it, but she's still a woman and she'll be able to relate to the girls."

"No problem," I said. "My bad. Just being a wiseass."

"Okay," Antoine said. "We get them in the van and the van boogies over Mulholland, catches the Hollywood Freeway and hauls ass to Burbank Airport, where..." he looked at me.

"Where Charles Dillard has one of his Lear Jets ready with a flight plan cleared for Santa Fe. They land there, get into another van and head for the mansion, where, hopefully the transition back begins."

"That's gonna be a bumpy flight," Wade said.

He shook his head. The audacity of what we were going to do was staggering. And the risk factor was off the charts. Not so much in being discovered, although that was high enough; it was in the long odds that the Sisters could ever be the same again. Or that their families could ever be the same again. The forging of new bonds and trust and empathy, on both sides, was fragile and precious, and going to take a long time; if it ever truly worked.

"Anybody have any idea of the Sisters real identities?" Bryan asked.

"Not yet," Famous said. "Once we get them away from the Temple, we can take their fingerprints; for whatever that's worth."

"Which probably won't be much," Antoine said. "We've got to find out their real names; otherwise there's no way to contact their families. And no way to try and bring them back to Society."

"Assuming they want that," I said.

"This could take a year in mending things," Wade said. "And maybe it'll never hold."

"I know," I said. "But no matter how long it takes or how much it costs Dillard has pledged his assets. Which are bottomless."

50

"I'm in over my head," Detective Alan Harbaugh said.

We were having early drinks at Jimmy's Outrigger Bar. Early because it wasn't even 3:30, but we'd used the tired excuse that the sun must be over the yardarm some place, so it was clearly time for a drink. Alan and I weren't sailors in any sense of the word, but if you need to justify having a drink, that one worked as good as any.

I had come to Jimmy's because it was one of the quieter places in town. Locals came here because it was dark and quiet. And while its picture window didn't look out at the Pacific Ocean, it did have a great view of the town's recent 2-storey parking structure. Tourists stayed away for the very same reasons.

We were into our second round.

"This should be the easiest goddamn case," he said, "and we're all lookin' like freakin' assholes. The Chief is spittin' bullets and wouldn't mind shootin' a few."

"I don't think I've ever seen Glenn pissed off," I said.

"He went to the Mayor and requisitioned an emergency budget increase for overtime for every staff member. *Every* member, including the receptionist."

"Ah, gentlemen," Someone said from behind my shoulder.

I turned. Shit, the ProfesSor.

"Late lunch or early start to Happy Hour?" the Prof said.

"One for over the yardarm," Alan smiled and saluted him with his glass.

No, no I wanted to say. But too late.

"You know where that expression comes from?" the Prof said.

Alan looked at me: Shit, my bad.

"It's an old nautical term. At certain times of the year, particularly here in North America, it will appear from the deck that the sun's risen far enough up in the sky that it's above the highest yardarm, which is the horizontal spar from where they hang the square sails."

"Which was after 11 am," I said, trying to torpedo the Prof's sailing yarns.

Not a chance. He continued, "This was by custom and rule, the time when they would issue the first rum tot of the day to officers and the men."

"I'll drink to that," Alan said, and threw back his entire gin and tonic. Listening to the Prof will drive you to drink or drive you from the bar. I wasn't sure which one Alan was doing.

"Of course," the Prof said, "the officers had their tots neat, while the crews were diluted."

"Privileges of rank," I said.

The owner, Jimmy Peersell, came over with another drink for Alan. "Hey, Prof," he said, "get you anything?"

"No, no, I'm just heading for the head." The Prof chuckled at his own joke and gave us a last pedantic shot, "So that custom was transferred from the sea to the land, which meant there's always *some* place on the planet where the sun is indeed over somebody's yardarm and, hence, time to drink. A custom which our very own James Peersell acknowledges is a boon to this fine establishment."

The Prof went back towards the restrooms.

"I think the Prof's got a yardarm up his ass," Alan said. "What a fuckin' stiff. And so boring." Alan took a big hit from his new drink. "Where the hell was I?"

"Chief Remington on the warpath."

"Oh, right. So, the Chief says how this is a blemish on the sterling record of *Paraíso Del Mar's* police force. And that we must continue the tradition of honesty and integrity, that we must prove to the town, and more importantly, to ourselves, that we are among the best crime fighters in the nation."

"Wow," was all I could say.

"Pretty heavy shit," Alan said.

"Not to mention, political spin, considering what happened less than a year ago."

"Yeah. If that shit didn't happen, Glenn doesn't become chief." Alan took another hit on his drink. "Glenn was a damn good cop before he became a politician."

"Glenn was always a politician; even when he was riding in a patrol car."

"So that's why I'm meeting Lo-Lo here; to ask her the same damn questions we've already asked her a half-dozen times. But what the hell. She's sure easy on the eyes."

"That she is."

A few minutes later, the door opened and the late afternoon silhouetted Lo-Lo standing in the entrance, hip cocked, checking things out like some irresistibly magnetic *femme fatale* on the cover of a '50s hard-boiled detective novel, her silk teal-colored dress hugging her every curve like a Ferrari racing in the *Mille Miglia*.

"Easy on the eyes," Alan repeated himself, "and hard in the pants." He waved at Lo-Lo and she started our way.

"I'll go sit over there and just ogle," I said.

"No, don't bother. Nothing's gonna happen."

Before I could decide, Lo-Lo was with us.

"Hello, Matt. Detective Harbaugh."

"Come on, call me Alan. This won't take long. What're you drinking?"

I moved over and Lo-Lo perched on the stool between us.

Jimmy appeared as if summoned by invisible forces, which was probably Lo-Lo's sex appeal sending out a force field to all points of the compass.

"I'll have a Ruby Red Slippertini," Lo-Lo said.

Jimmy nodded and went off to work his magic.

"What's that?" Alan said.

"Ruby Red Absolut, Triple Sec, grapefruit juice and a splash of cranberry juice. Jimmy makes the very best." She looked at me, a bright shine to her blue-grey eyes, "Definitely a girl's drink." Then she turned to Alan, "But after a couple, I'm betting that even a police detective would be slightly woozy."

"Is that a challenge?" Alan said.

Lo-Lo just smiled again.

"Hey, Jimmy," Alan called out, "make that two. In fact, make that two rounds."

"You want four drinks?" Jimmy said.

"Yeah. Two for me and two for Lo-Lo."

"You better ask me your questions fast," Lo-Lo said, "because you may forget them later; and I'm sure you won't remember my answers."

"No worries. Matt's the designated listener."

And I didn't say 'I'm all ears.'

"Wait, before you start," Lo-Lo said, "are you going to ask me anything *new?*"

Alan looked at her for a moment, pulled a folded sheet of paper from his inside jacket pocket. "No, why?"

And now it was Lo-Lo's turn to pull a folded sheet of paper; actually several of them. "These are the questions you asked me before. And my answers, written in full, by my attorney's legal secretary. You remember she was there during our last session?"

Jimmy placed two drinks in front of him and then two in front of Lo-Lo.

"Yeah, I remember," Alan said. He took the pages from Lo-Lo and scanned through them. "Okay, are any of your answers different from before?"

"No."

"Do you want to augment or delete anything from or to them?"

"No."

He handed the papers back to her.

"See, that was easy."

"No, wait," Lo-Lo said, "I *would* like to add something."

Alan looked a little disappointed at this as if it meant he couldn't get to his drink as fast as he wanted.

"Well, it's not really anything to add to those questions," Lo-Lo said, "more like, an explanation or just a perspective."

Alan decided that was reason enough to take a drink, which he did.

So, did Lo-Lo.

And while I wasn't having a Ruby Red Slipertini, I drank my vodka and tonic.

"I've been doing real estate for over fifteen years," Lo-Lo said. "I've got more than a thousand personal sales. I've been the *L.A. Business Journal's* Broker of the Year two times. Reporters from every TV channel, the *L.A. Times* and just about every newspaper in L.A. County have interviewed me on one part of real estate or another. Christ, I was even included in a long article in *The New Yorker*."

Lo-Lo was building up steam. She took a long hit from her Slipertini.

"My record with the Department of Real Estate is perfect. *Perfect!* Every major servicer, from banks to financial analysts, hell, even to damn termite companies and carpenters and plumbers think of me as one of, if not their *preferred* broker."

She picked up her glass and drained her drink. She set it down with a loud clink.

"So, while I was upset at being dumped by Steve, I've got too much going for me to let a little setback like that lead me to kill the handsome son of a bitch."

She reached for her second drink.

"Like I read somewhere, to put it crudely, 'No piece of tail is worth going to jail.'"

"A teeny bit crude, but definitely heart-felt," Alan said.

He clinked his glass against hers.

"Duly noted and it will be put in my report. Except for the crude part."

51

"This is highly refined, very expensive," Hal Bartkowski said.

He was looking under a microscope at the fiber found on Steve Fordham.

I had gone over to see him after my designated listening to Lo-Lo and Alan indicated that those Ruby Red Slipertinis tended to make you see things through rose-colored glasses.

After two of the drinks, both of which Lo-Lo and Alan pounded down, their conversation had nothing to do with a police interview, and everything to do with sex crimes of the consenting nature.

I left as they were ordering their fourth round and was pretty sure neither heard me say goodbye.

Hopefully, Lo-Lo *was* innocent So that Alan's reputation, if not his badge and career, wouldn't be at risk when her attorney began defending her.

As I was walking out of Jimmy's, I bumped into Hal. Literally. I couldn't see going from the dark cave-like atmosphere of the bar into the bright sunlight; and Hal's glasses have the thickest lenses I've ever seen.

After we apologized and then laughed about the collision, he invited me back to his offices and showed me the fabric.

"How rare?" I said.

"Like, if the tests prove accurate, and I'm sure they will, not even from the twenty-first or twentieth centuries."

"What's that mean, Hal?"

"This fabric dates from the mid-1850s to the late 1890s from feudal Japan."

"So, a ghost samurai killed Steve."

The door to Hal's office opened and Mary Guilletei, his assistant walked in carrying several folders.

Hal introduced us and said, "Mary did all the hard work on this, I'll let her tell you.

Mary was an assistant straight out of central casting.

If you were casting a Tim Burton movie.

Her long black hair was shaved on the sides; so, she had a horse's mane that went from her high forehead back and down to her shoulder blades. Her full lips gleamed with shiny blood red lipstick. And when she looked at me with her pale blue eyes, it was hard not to notice the double sets of false eyelashes and kohl eyeliner.

"Hello, Matt," she said, smiling. "Hal's told me a lot about you."

"Nothing I can't live down, I hope."

"No, it's all good."

She turned to Hal, "It's hot in here, do you mind if I take off my lab coat?"

She didn't wait for his approval and ripped down the zipper and shrugged off the white garment in two quick shakes. Mary exercised. Because her arms were toned with high definition. And a rainbow of riotous colors from the array of tattoos that went from her deltoids all the way down to her wrists.

"Nice guns," I said, pointing to an intricately detailed set of crossed six-shooter revolvers.

She caught my joke and held up both arms and rotated wrists back and forth, saying, "Ta-ta-ta-tuffff."

Then with the last dragged-out 'f" she flexed and popped some impressive biceps–both in color and size. She had a beautiful Stargazer Lilly on her right arm, the Millennium Falcon from Star Wars on her left.

Mary had a sense of humor.

"Boom, boom," I said.

Then she got right to business.

"The hottest trend in fashion today, like so many companies and people going 'Green', is to *reclaim* fabrics. Some designers do it from cutting room floors; others raid the fashion industry's trash cans. And some *avant-garde* boutiques or small designers are reclaiming garments and fabrics from the past."

I saw Hal beam, like the professor showing off his prize pupil.

"I have two more tests to run, but I'm pretty sure this came from Japan, probably closer to the end of the century rather than in the middle."

"You mean like a kimono or ceremonial robe?" I said.

"Maybe. The silk thread count is high enough, but more importantly, the construction and way it was woven, suggest samurai, but I don't think shogun status. Hard to tell. This was about the time when Japan went through a social earthquake; they had a tectonic shift from the conservative, isolationist policies of the *Edo period*, which was the last *real* shogun-dominated period, to try and modernize and engage with the rest of the world."

Whoa, that was some research.

"Back then, the military class was number one, then the common peasant farmers, followed by the craftsmen and artisans, and finally, the despised commercial class. Someone of their so-called lower orders could have gotten access to this kind of quality."

"So, this could have originally been the robe of a master swordsman," Hal said, "or maybe just a businessman who exported tea."

Mary went to the microscope and looked at the sample. She talked without looking up. "We need to run some more dye lot sample tests. If we can pinpoint the dyes a little closer, that will tighten our search parameters."

"I called Alan Harbaugh," Hal said, "but he's not picking up."

"Actually," I said, "he is."

52

"My business is going crazy," Carmen said. "We're suddenly booming."

Nothing like a little notoriety to get you in the spotlight.

"That's great," I said.

"No. It's disappointing."

That threw the rest of us at the table—me, Leah and my dad—for a moment.

"It's true," Carmen said. "Everybody thinks I have secrets about what really happened just because Steve died in a house we were tenting."

"I'm sure," my dad said, "there might some people like that, but your business is doing better is because your company does a great job."

We were all having dinner at the newest and hottest restaurant in town, *Partners*, which was booked at least three weeks in advance, but somehow my dad had made a call earlier today and there we were, sitting at the best table in the house.

"I want to see if their swordfish platter really is the best in town," he'd said when he called me. But my guess was that the invitation came with an attachment: Carmen. Just like the customers who had disappointed her, she was looking for *anything* on Steve Fordham. And between Leah's links to the real estate community and my links to being nosey, we were probably a good bet.

It was hard to understand why Carmen was so affected by what was just routine police procedure. As the owner of the termite company, she would have automatically been on the list of people to be questioned. It was routine, and probably nothing more than due diligence and something they could check off their list.

She didn't see it that way.

When her husband Ricardo had been alive, his company had an exemplary record for honesty and a high standard of ethics and business policies. Carmen had continued the tradition. That, for Carmen, should have been enough.

"Her pride's been hurt," my dad said to me on the phone. "You know the story of how her family came across the border thirty years ago and she had to endure all that prejudice and how her father and Ricardo's father busted their butts to make it in America. So, she's a little defensive."

"The police should just *know*," she'd said. "There is no reason to question my values. I take care of people, not harm them."

She held the police, and probably society, in too high a place: lofty goals and a professed love for mankind don't translate to innocence.

In fact, usually the most heinous crimes against mankind are committed under those very banners.

Rodrigo Borgia was the Pope and disposed of countless enemies with a holy vengeance. A vengeance ordered he said by the Creator Himself to protect the Church. Not *my* church, but *the* church; so there could be no confusion as to what the Almighty asked.

But you didn't need papal finery to display your desire for carnage and victory.

Wearing a crown worked wonders too.

And while being King may have made your own head lie heavy, it did give you the power to relieve so many of your loyal subjects of that same burdensome cranial weight–be it by guillotine or the headsman's ax.

So, if being connected to heavenly powers or having earthly powers didn't excuse you from being capable of chicanery and foul deeds, a perfect record of killing termites and doing it for the quoted estimate with a two-year guarantee, was small potatoes indeed.

But I was determined to avoid talking about it, if possible.

"When do you think Jesus is coming back?" I said.

Jesus Zapoteca was our waiter. He'd gotten us drinks and appetizers very quickly, taken our dinner orders and then disappeared. I hadn't even seen him waiting on other tables.

"You mean Jesus our waiter, or the Messiah?" my dad said. "Because if it's our Savior, it's not happening. Not tomorrow, not next year, not never. Never."

"Now, Mario," Carmen said, "you know that for sure, how?"

"Let's say Jesus shows up? You think people in today's society would believe him? Hell no. 'Prove it!' they'd say. 'Show us.' I mean you have entire organizations who say the Moon Landing never happened. Despite all those thousands of people who were there at the Cape to watch it take off back in 'sixty-nine, me included. You got all those people who saw it in person, and yet, you have these dumbasses who insist, even today, that it was all a fake, all done in a studio."

I smiled because I knew my dad was just stirring up the pot, adding a little sidebar of entertainment to the evening.

"They doubt man landed on the moon, you think they're gonna believe some guy shows up says he's Jesus Christ, Son of God? He could change water into wine, raise people from the dead, walk on water–you name a miracle and all those damn fools would say, 'Prove it. I know it's a trick.'"

"Oh, surely, God would show them the Way," Carmen said. "Just like it says in the Bible."

"I would like to think that's true, but that's not the way it would happen. Let's say, just to show his doubters, Jesus took a fish and a loaf of bread and fed all the homeless people downtown. All of them. They all came shuffling by and there's Jesus, just smiling with his long hippie hair and beard and that glowing white robe, puts his hand in a basket, and *bling!* here's a little trout for you. And for you, a loaf of whole grain."

My dad demonstrated by putting his right hand under the table and brought it up with a pretend fish and handed it to me and then gave Leah the virtual loaf of bread with his left hand.

"*'Here you are, my child. Go forth and hunger no more. And for you..and for you.'* Fast as those people would come up, that's how fast Jesus would give them a fish and bread. And you know what would happen?"

"They'd ask Him if he could cook it too?" I said.

"You got it," my dad smiled and nodded his thanks for my joining in.

Then, fortunately, our waiter Jesus saved things by coming to take our orders.

"People kid you about your name?" my dad said.

Jesus frowned as if he had no idea what my dad was saying.

"You know? Jesus, food, breaking bread?"

"I recommend either the *scallops Provencal* or the *swordfish menuire*," Jesus said.

And then Jesus didn't say another word when we ordered. No *"excellent choice"* or *"that's our most popular item."* Just gave us a curt nod and went back towards the kitchen.

"After dinner," my dad said, "I'm going to give Jesus a big tip: get a fucking sense of humor."

And he pushed his chair back and stomped off for the restroom.

That was a big surprise. My dad doesn't curse, especially around women. I'm sure he was embarrassed that his joke had gone over so badly. My cell buzzed. I checked the caller ID. "Sorry, I have to take this. I'll only be a minute or two.

I went towards the bar to take the call.

"Zak. Thanks for calling back."

"Yeah. Sorry I haven't been able to find out anything else about Brother Jordan."

"Not a problem. This isn't about him."

"Oh? So, what am I going to be doing?"

"What men always do: chase a skirt."

53

"Antoine be sniffin' in the wrong places," Wade said.

"I'm sure if he gets too curious, Andriel will smack him on the nose," I said. "She's a more than capable woman. And a Lieutenant Colonel. She can take care of herself, Jamal. And make decisions for herself."

"So, you think I'm overplaying the Big Brother role?"

"Yes. And so do you."

We were in my office having coffee. I'd briefed Wade on having put Zak on the hunt for the only possible clue about Steve Fordham, the expensive fabric of the skirt. But Wade's attention seemed to be elsewhere, so I'd asked him what was bothering him and he'd skirted the issue for a while until I'd asked him about Andriel and Antoine.

"Is it because he's a cop?" I said.

"I don't know, just something about him, rubs me the wrong way."

"You sure it wouldn't be any man who dates her?"

He sipped his coffee and stared at me for a moment. "Might be some truth to that. Not entirely, but some."

"So, let it be. I mean, Andriel's got what, another week?"

"Yeah, then back to Afghanistan." He looked away.

"That's what's really bothering you; her going back there."

He sipped his coffee before he said anything.

"Yeah. And I know she's a doctor and pretty much away from the bad stuff, but damn, you know her unit's taken losses before."

"And that she sometimes goes out to give aid to troops who're close to the action," I said. "American fighting men and women sacrifice a lot more than most Americans realize. The toll of just being there has got to be enormous. And most often, not recognized."

"Or understood," Wade said.

"I worry about her too," I said. "So, if she's having some good times with Antoine, she deserves it. And if by some magical reason, they've got something that lasts through this deployment, that's terrific."

I wasn't so sure Wade agreed with the lasting and terrific parts, but he nodded.

"So, how's the 'Asset Extraction' going?"

"Nothing from Bryan. He doesn't want us around, even as Chris Berman would say, *"back-back-back-back"* up. But Famous says they look damn slick. They've got everything mapped out, timed to the second and are ready to roll."

"Including a contingency plan?"

"I'm assuming."

There was a creaking sound on the stairs to my office, then a quick knock and Andriel peered around the corner. "Ah, I was hoping I'd find you here."

"Hey," Wade said and got up and gave Andriel a big hug. "I didn't see you last night."

Shit, Big Brother line.

But Andriel played it straight out.

"That's because Antoine and I were out dancing at The Falcon in downtown L.A."

"That like The Exchange?" Wade said.

"Yes. Only the music's louder, the strobe lights are wilder, and Antoine knows the DJ, Trance-X."

"Sounds like a fun package."

"This girl hasn't partied in a long, long time. So, I kicked it last night. And today, my butt's kicked. Hate to think I'm getting too old for rock 'n roll."

"You? Nevah, Sistah," Wade said, and slapped palms with Andriel.

"You probably need coffee," I said.

"Intravenous would be good."

She moved for the coffee maker, but I waved her off, took the biggest mug I have in the cabinet and poured it almost to the brim.

She inhaled the aroma, then took a good swallow.

"So, I have some news," she said.

By the look on her face, it didn't sound like it was going to be good news.

"I'm being called back early."

"What?" said Wade. "They can't do that."

"Come on, Jamal," Andriel said, "you know they can do anything they want. But it's not quite as bad."

"What's that mean?"

"I'll only be deployed for three months and then…" she paused a moment and a big smile lit up her face, "..and then I'll be stationed in the U.S. They want me at Fort Belvoir."

It took a second for that to register, then Wade got up again and gave his sister another hug. He stood back, his hands still on her shoulders, looking her right in the eyes. "Damn, damn, Andriel. Wow, I am So proud of you."

She beamed.

"Yes," I joined in, "that's terrific. Congratulations."

"So, when do you go back?" Wade said.

"0:1800. Today." She tried to make light of it. "That's six o'clock for you civilians."

"No. You…shit," Wade said. "Shit."

"Wow," I said, "when the military moves, they *move*."

Then Wade proved he really was a brother in a big way.

And before Andriel could say a word, he said, "I'll get Antoine on the phone. You get packing."

I locked the door behind me, but as we reached the bottom of the stairs, Andriel said, "Matt, let me have your keys. I left my cell in your office."

She took them from my hand and bounded up the stairs.

"Damn," Wade said. "Talk about good news, bad news."

"Good news is she'll be in Fort Belvoir."

"I was thinking that's the *bad* news. All that cloak and dagger secret crap."

"I don't think Andriel's going to be planning dark ops."

"No, that's for her big brother."

We laughed. I looked up towards my office; she was taking a long time.

Then she came out the door, locked it and jogged down to us and handed me back the keys.

She didn't have her cell.

"I must have left it back at Wade's house."

54

"I'll be back home before you'll even have time to miss me," Andriel said.

Her eyes were bright with tears as she gave Wade a fierce hug.

She'd already hugged my dad and Leah; hugged me and kissed my cheek and whispered, "He'll worry, but tell him not to; that everything will work out."

She and Antoine had said their goodbyes privately at Wade's house when Antoine had bolted from a special meeting of everyone in the Counter Terrorism and Special Operations Bureau and made it down to the beach in record time.

Two very precise and rugged-looking Army Sergeants waited at the boarding gate, both looking straight ahead, at parade rest. As Andriel approached, they snapped their boots together with a click that carried to us and fired off twin crisp salutes. Andriel returned their salutes and led them down the corridor. She stopped just before it turned from our sight and gave us a big smile and wave. And then, being Andriel and all-girl, even under all that military bearing, blew us a kiss.

Antoine passed on dinner. No big surprise. He had some explaining to do; none of which would be the real reason he blew off the meeting.

So, we all went down to *Paraíso Del Mar*'s very first restaurant, established before the city became incorporated, *Jose's Tacos*.

We're talking five generations of the Riveras family owning and running the best Mexican food in town. And always with at least one Jose Riveras in charge. At least one because the first borne male in every new branch of the family tree–and the Riveras had a lot of sons and daughters - was named Jose.

Sometimes that meant there were four Jose Riveras working at the restaurant at the same time: grandfather, father, and two cousins named Jose.

But more than continuing the name, along with the other Miguels and Carlos and Gracielas and Marias of the Riveras who made sure the restaurant carried on the tradition of the first Jose of having fresh chips and salsa, and clean tables and spotless glasses, they preserved what I think was the real reason for the restaurant's longevity and popularity: their ancient grandmother Inez's secret recipe for *Molé sauce*.

The margaritas weren't bad either. If having two rounds of them is any indication. We then ordered the *enchiladas especiales,* finished with Mexican coffee and several shared *Boca Negra Mini Cakes*.

I was paying the bill when my cell rang. I checked the caller ID and said, "Zak, hold on." I told Leah, "Give them a good tip and sign my name. I've got to take this."

Wade looked at me, but I shook my head: I would tell him everything later.

"So, what do we have?" I said after I'd walked out on the sidewalk.

Jose's Tacos is two doors up from the Strand, but tonight the moon was blocked by clouds, so the dark waters were formless until they broke on the shore in small waves.

"Man," Zak said, "I now know more shit about exotic and rare fabrics than any straight man should. Not that I'm saying that the knowledge is a gay thing, I'm just saying."

"So, say it. What?"

"Your guy, Hal? He was right. This sample *was* from Japan. Right around 1890. And there are several cutting edges, Ha-ha, no pun intended, but, hey that was funny.."

"Zak."

"Okay. I mean I've been busting my hump and it's almost midnight and.."

"My bad. I'm Sorry."

Jesus, sometimes coddling genius is a pain.

"So...there must be a boatload of *avant-garde* designer firms specialize in taking these kinds of materials from the past, reconfiguring them and then selling them for like a five thousand percent mark-up. These companies are all over the planet, but your boy Zak knows how to sift through the data.."

"Zak...."

"Okay-okay. Geez and I'm the one working late. So, the material, which I'm pretty sure is a skirt, but let's just say garment just in case, was made by a company called *Le Chat de Paris.*"

55

"*The Cat of Paris*. Yes, they're one of our more celebrated suppliers."

Wade and I were talking to Helene DuChamps, the owner of easily the most exclusive, and, therefore, most expensive shop in town: *Rara Avis*.

Zak had called too late for Wade and me to go into the store, so we'd waited until the next morning when the shop opened at ten. I should have called Hal to give him some props, as well as called Alan Harbaugh to give him a heads-up, but we'd decided to spearhead this one for now and see what developed. Being relegated to the bench for Operation Angel had definitely pissed us off.

Helene DuChamps was a former runway model who had parlayed her high cheekbones into a high net worth status. *Rara Avis*, like its name, was unique to *Paraíso Del Mar* because it had very limited hours open to the public and conducted most of its business by appointments and private showings.

Her single assistant, Aubrey Harte, went wide-eyed when Wade and I walked through the door. "Oh, I'm So Sorry," she said, "but we're not open to the public today."

"Perfect," I said. "I think Helene would prefer it that way."

Aubrey was clearly confused and stood there.

"Maybe you should go get her," Wade said. "Like now."

Aubrey spun on her elegant high heels and clattered to the back of the shop where she disappeared behind a curtain. We could hear the murmur of hushed voices and then Helene swung her hips into the room and came up to us with an extended hand and big commercial smile.

"Good morning," she said. "I think you've frightened my assistant."

"Sorry," I said.

"Probably my fault," said Wade. "Not everybody appreciates dreads."

He waited and, fortunately, Helene smiled.

"How may I help you?"

Which is when we explained about Zak's findings and *Le Chat de Paris*.

"Come into zee back room," she said, deliberately over-doing the bad French accent. We followed her into a tidy office just off the storage room, passing Aubrey in the hall. I almost said "Boo!" but decided since we wanted Helene's cooperation, that might be a better exit line.

She sat down at her desk and spun her computer monitor around So we could all see it, tapped her keyboard, and up came *Le Chat's* website. "Marnie Marineau is the talent behind *Le Chat*. She's amazing. She started out by reclaiming fabric remnants and, what were really waste products, from various designer houses' trash cans all over Paris."

"She could do that?" I said.

"It was considered trash by the companies, so until she started getting noticed, nobody cared, or even knew. Marnie and her staff, which was two of her classmates from design school, also went directly to several designers and asked for their strike-offs, production ends, and swatches and whatever they could get their hands on."

"Resourceful," Wade said.

"To say the least," Helena said. She scrolled through various examples. "Her style is really, no-style. It's neither *haute couture* nor ready-to-wear. I mean look at this," as she showed us a very distinctive tri-paneled dress. "It's edgy, with an unusual silhouette. Then as her designs caught on, she was able to go directly to the really big houses and work out Some exclusive arrangements."

Helena tapped several more keys and a parade of models in a highly stylized collection of flowing dresses, tops and skirts appeared. "But she was one of the first to, essentially go back in time, like she did for the Japanese materials. She created an amazing collection, what you're seeing here, the *Shogunate Series*. Sold out in record time. For record prices."

"So, this skirt you bought from her…"

"Actually, two skirts. Unfortunately, we still have one in stock."

"So, what does something like that cost?"

"Twenty-three hundred dollars."

I didn't say anything. I'm sure my open mouth said enough for me.

"Could you look up who bought the one skirt?"

"I don't need to look it up. An item like that, you don't forget the customer." Helena smiled at us, "Lo-Lo Martin."

56

"Louisa May Martin, you're under the arrest for the murder of Steve Fordham."

I didn't hear Alan Harbaugh say those words or the rest of the Miranda statement that every cop in town carries on a plastic-coated card and reads from so there can never be a question of someone not being advised in full of their rights.

But he was telling me because he owed me one for getting the news to him about what Wade and I had learned about the *tres*-expensive skirt.

I had called Hal first.

"You hit a home run on that one," I said.

"Thanks, but it was really Mary. I'll tell her."

"So, you'll call Harbaugh?"

"Okay, but I'll make sure he knows you and Wade tracked it down."

"Once you point us in the right direction, we just follow our noses."

So, after Alan got the news and got a warrant together in record time, he'd arrested Lo-Lo, filed more paperwork and then had stopped by my office.

"So, you know what she says then?" Alan said. He hesitated because he realized he'd just hung himself out to dry, "First you fucked me and now you fuck me. Nice."

"Not much stops Lo-Lo."

"So, all that hype about her perfect record and having no reason to kill Steve that was just what real estate agents do: Bullshit you right to your face."

"Not every real estate agent does that. And she wasn't bullshitting. Lo-Lo is one of the best in the business. And I don't think she did it."

"That fabric links her directly to Steve."

"Assuming she was wearing it."

"What's that mean?"

"Helene DuChamps said that only ten skirts were made."

"Yeah, I know. We contacted that company that you said, the Paris Cat."

"*Le Chat de Paris* means The Cat *of* Paris."

"Whatever. Of that ten, six got shipped to the U.S. New York got two, Chicago and Dallas each got one. Then the two that came here."

"You're going to have to track down the other four and check their alibis."

"You kidding me? We're not doing that. It's a waste of time. Lo-Lo did it."

"But what if one of those other skirts made it out here and…"

"Bullshit," Alan interrupted me, "that's something a lawyer would say."

It was obvious Alan's mind was made up.

"What did her lawyer say?"

"Miscarriage of justice, rush to judgment, all of it. And that they will prove Lo-Lo has an alibi." His cell buzzed and he read the text message. "They got the search warrant ready." He gulped the rest of his coffee and stood up. "I'm heading over to Lo-Lo's place. Search her closets."

57

"Search warrant? Hell, we needed a search party."

It was four hours later and Wade and I were having dinner at Kincaid's when Alan Harbaugh blew in like a nor'easter.

He saw us, came over and sat down and ordered a drink and then told us what had happened after he'd left my office.

"Her closet is as big as my living room. And she has two of them. And they're both jammed with clothes. Guess how many black skirts we brought back as evidence?"

"Ten?" I said.

He didn't wait for Wade to guess, "Twenty-six. Can you believe it? And that's just the black ones. I'm sure she's got half that many in every damn color you can think of. When the hell does she wear them?"

"One at a time," Wade said, smiling. "And probably only once. Lo-Lo is definitely fashion-forward."

Alan downed his drink and waved to Kincaid for a refill. "And here's the kicker. The skirt that matches the fabric? Not there. We had Hal and his assistant, what the hell's her name…?"

"Mary."

"Right, Mary. Man, you see her hair? She's definitely freaky. And those tats? Rainbow city."

"I hope you don't say that out loud outside the station," Wade said.

"What?" Alan said, slightly offended. "I said tats, not tits. Although she's got a nice set of those too. Looks like she works out."

Wade and I just looked at each other. If anyone but a cop in town said those kinds of things in the workplace, they'd be looking at a discriminatory lawsuit.

"So, Hal and Mary checked all twenty-six skirts and the Japanese fabric one isn't there"" I asked.

"Why would it be? That'd make this case too freakin' easy."

"Looks like you're going to have to call New York, Chicago and Dallas," Wade said. "Just to be sure."

"Chief says we may have to buy one of them, for positive identification. Can you imagine all that crap?"

"Those aren't phone calls I'd like to make," I said. "You've got to contact the cops in those cities, get their cooperation. Then contact the store, then the women who bought the skirts."

"That could take three months." Alan took a hit on his drink. "I guess it could be worse; it could've been panties." He looked off for a moment, "But Lo-Lo doesn't always wear panties."

"Jesus, Alan." I said.

"Sorry. The Chief's on my ass and if he finds out Lo-Lo and I were...friendly."

"Lo-Lo's smart enough to keep a secret."

"Yeah, but if it saves his client, her lawyer won't just be dropping the dime on me, it'll be a manhole cover."

"But that's only if she doesn't have an alibi. And you said her lawyer was going to prove she was innocent."

"He's coming in tomorrow and meeting with the Chief. That'll be interesting."

"Lo-Lo's not looking so much like the number one suspect," I said.

"I know," Alan said. "I'm thinking the same thing. Her lawyer's too cocky. And Lo-Lo, I gotta say, maybe she had a lonely night or two staring out the window after Steve dumped her, but she's too resilient for that kind of revenge. I think her armor's too strong. Fordham may have dented it, but no way he pierced it and got to her heart."

"And it took a lot of planning and perfect timing. Not to mention being able to sell a real kinky and dangerous tryst."

"You don't think Lo-Lo could do that?" Alan said. And the way he said it, made me think those Slippertinis had been more potent than expected.

Alan's career was on the precipice because like so many men, as the old adage goes, had let his lower brain overpower his upper brain.

As comedian Robin Williams said, 'God gives men a brain and a penis. But only enough blood to run one at a time.'

So, constrict the blow flow to the brain with three or more strong drinks, add a woman like Lo-Lo and the mixture was as volatile as a Molotov cocktail: It had blown out any inhibitors, governors or whatever kind of restraints or warning devices Alan had possessed, including those as a police officer sworn to uphold justice.

"I've got to break this case," Alan said.

He stood up and got ready to go solve the murder, and, hopefully his life. "Hey, Matt, this goes in the toilet, you ever think about adding a third partner?"

"Not a chance," Wade said. "He can't handle the one he already has."

58

"Singer, Wade and Harbaugh," I said. "I don't think so."

"What makes you think your name would still be first?" Wade said.

"Now that really tears it."

"We be a two-man team," Wade said.

"Always."

Wade held out his massive fist and we bumped.

My cell rang, but the caller ID was blocked. "Hello, this is Matt."

"And this is Agent Kouros."

I mouthed who it was to Wade as the first thing I thought was that Operation Angel was grounded, that, somehow, Kouros had figured something was up. Maybe he'd stumbled on Bryan's surveillance and was running down possibilities. Only one way to find out.

"Agent Kouros, what's happening?"

I heard him take a deep breath, like he was about to plunge into a cold lake. "I'd like to start over," he said quickly. Then took another breath, "Wipe the slate clean."

"Okay."

"I mean I understand that the Bureau can be..." And then he stopped; because he'd realized I had said "Okay" and wasn't resisting and he didn't have to lay out his bureaucratic bullshit. "Oh.. So, good, good."

"Anything else?"

"Uh, perhaps you'd let me buy you and Wade a beer, I have some information that you will find interesting. In fact, I guarantee it."

"Sure. What's Sunday morning look like for you?"

"Hold on a sec." I could hear little beeps from his cell as I'm sure he was scrolling through his calendar. "Sunday's good. What time?"

"Eleven. And let's meet down here at Kincaid's. Nothing like seeing the ocean on a nice, quiet Sunday morning."

"Sounds good. See you then."

I hung up and looked at Wade. "One less asshole to worry about."

"You remember the movie poster from 'The Godfather'" Wade said.

"Black and white with some guy on a string?"

"Implying the Don was the Master Puppeteer."

"Yes, great iconic image."

"You just pulled the string on Agent Kouros."

"With this finger too," I said.

And raised the appropriate digit.

59

"The iron fist in the velvet glove." Hal Bartkowski said. "The Chief and poor Alan Harbaugh never saw it coming."

Hal had called me and offered to buy me and Wade lunch, so I knew there had been a dramatic outcome from the meeting with Lo-Lo and her attorney. We hadn't even ordered when Hal burst forth with all the news.

"Jason Waterman, that's Lo-Lo's lawyer," Hal said. "He comes in and says 'Would you mind waiting for the Mayor?' And the Chief says, 'What does Mayor Keough have to do with this?'"

"I'd ask the same thing," I said.

"Apparently everything. Keough comes in, you know how he has that real quiet way of talking, never raises his voice? And he tells the Chief, 'I have had a private conference with Mr. Waterman and Ms. Martin, and I am sufficiently informed that she is innocent of any of these charges.'"

"Damn," Wade said.

The waitress came and we gave her our orders as quickly as possible so we could get back to the story.

"The Chief says, 'but, sir, this is a criminal investigation.' And the Mayor says, '"And it shall continue to be that. Just not with Ms. Martin as a suspect.'"

"So, what the hell happened?" I said.

Hal smiled. For a very precise, intellectual and highly educated forensics expert and a city official, he flat-out *loves* political intrigue.

"Waterman slides a series of documents over to the Chief, says, 'Everything you need to know is in those files.' And he and Lo-Lo, who didn't say one freakin' word all this time, and you know Lo-Lo loves to talk, and they just get up and walk out."

"And the Chief let them? That's not the Glenn Remington I know," I said. "What the hell was in those documents?"

"Photos. Very compromising photos. Photos that wouldn't look good for Keough."

"No way. The Mayor was banging Lo-Lo?"

"The rumor is no. But apparently, he spent a wild afternoon with Lo-Lo and a couple of her friends. I think one of them was Fiona O'Hallaran."

"The Irish actress?" Wade said.

"Yes. Apparently, she and Lo-Lo go way back. So, Fiona and Lo-Lo and two other women, I can't remember their names, they'd had some afternoon party and, somehow, Tony got involved. I think Lo-Lo was showing him a house, they ran into Fiona and the other women and pretty soon they were all in Lo-Lo's hot tub, naked, drinking, smoking weed and.." He stopped talking and shrugged. And then couldn't stop the smile that crossed his face.

Wade and I didn't know what to say.

"The freakin' Mayor! Can you believe it?"

No, I couldn't. Lo-Lo and Harbaugh, yes; because they'd gotten drunk together. But Tony Keough and her?

"For a so-called sleepy little beach town, more shit goes on in *Paraíso Del Mar*. It blows me away," Hal said. "Mary and I are in our chambers with all our scientific shit and every once in a while, we get to examine a dead body. But outside? Outside it's a *Bacchanalia.*"

"So, rendering unto Caesar," I said, "Mayor Tony Keough shuts down any investigation of Lo-Lo."

"You gonna have an alibi, that's the man to have," Wade said.

"The Chief was handcuffed in his own investigation," Hal said. "He read through the file and threw it across the room and stomped out."

"And Alan picks it up, reads it and knows he's…"

I stopped and drank my iced tea.

"Know he's what?" Hal said.

Oops. Full flaps, Matt.

"Knows he's still got to solve the case," I said.

Which was true, but was really my way of deflecting any further conversation along those lines–because I'd almost said that Alan had dodged a bullet because now he didn't have to add his name to Lo-Lo's list of guilty men that proved her innocence.

"The other thing is," Hal said, "Lo-Lo said that the skirt should have been in her closet."

"I'm assuming she checked the cleaners and other places."

"Yes. And since she's got an alibi, I doubt if she made up that story."

"Unless she lost it someplace," Wade said.

"I don't think so" I said. "For all of her wild abandon, Lo-Lo's always in control."

I thought about what I'd just said for a moment.

"Maybe somebody stole the skirt."

Wade and Hal looked at me like that was the dumbest idea they'd heard in a long time.

"Somebody gonna break into Lo-Los, they ain't just taking one skirt," Wade said.

"She should take inventory; see if anything else is missing."

"What're you talking about?" Hal said. "An accessorized thief?"

"No. A stylish killer."

60

"We think it's a close friend of yours, Lo-Lo" I said.

She looked at me for a long moment; I'm sure her brain whirling through possible suspects. Then she shook her head. "I don't think so. The women who are my *close* friends don't need to steal from me; they know they're welcome to borrow anything I have. Hell, they like it enough, they can keep it."

"And you checked with them about the skirt?"

"Of course."

"You fire anyone lately?"

"I never fire anyone. I just suggest that they might be happier with another agent and then I set up interviews for them."

"Kind of *de*-hiring them."

"It avoids emotional earthquakes." She smiled, then said, "You really think someone that worked for me stole my skirt?"

"Anyone you, ah, *helped* with their career?"

"Diane Norris left about two years ago, but that was because she was having a baby and there's no way Diane would have fit into one of my skirts, even before the baby. Then there was Lorenzo, Italian exchange student from SC, smart as hell, but then he discovered beach volleyball and girls in bikinis and then…"

Lo-Lo snapped her fingers.

"Patrice Fowler. Shit. Patrice Fowler. She came on board right after Lorenzo. And she was terrific for about eight, nine months. Then just like that, her work went into the toilet. She'd forget to list appointments on my calendar, didn't return calls to clients. I gave her a couple of warnings, but she just kept messing up. I'm sure she was having boyfriend trouble."

"Who was the guy?"

"That was the trouble. She didn't have a boyfriend. She was cute enough, natural redhead, a set of blue eyes that a husky would've envied. And she was bright, too. But it just wasn't clicking for her."

"Who were the agents you sent her to see?"

"Just one. Laura DeSantis."

We got Patrice's cell phone number, her address and anything else that Lo-Lo thought was important. But when I called Patrice's cell, I got a no longer working message. We drove by her address, but nobody answered, and a neighbor said she'd moved away just last week.

I called Alan Harbaugh and he immediately went to tell the Chief.

Then Wade and I went to see Laura at the company where she worked–Van Dyke & Partners Real Estate.

Laura was less than enthusiastic about answering questions and wasn't about to give out any personal information about Patrice.

"Shouldn't this be a police matter? I mean, why isn't Detective Harbaugh asking these questions?"

"We're just trying to clear Carmen Rosales' name," I said.

"But I thought she wasn't a suspect anymore."

"She wants the slate wiped clean," I said, echoing the lines I'd said before to Hal Bartkowski. "She wants justice, as I'm sure you do."

"And just how does Patrice Fowler connect to this?"

"She probably doesn't, but we're just running down every lead we have, no matter how far out it might seem."

My cell rang, and it seemed like a good moment to break, maybe re-group and see if we could crack Laura.

"Hey, Leah." I walked to an empty desk away from Laura, leaving Wade to charm her. Or scare her. I didn't care which tactic he used, just so long as we made progress.

I told Leah what we'd learned, and she was as surprised as any of us.

"You think it's true?" she said.

"We won't know until Laura tells us where to find Patrice."

"Let me talk to her."

"What? Why?"

"Just put her on."

I walked back to Laura's desk and said, "Uh, Leah Lockhart? Wants to say hello."

Laura looked slightly pissed and yet took the call.

Wade and I walked back to the empty desk.

"What's that all about?" Wade said.

"Don't know. Leah insisted she talk to Laura."

I looked back. Laura had turned her back to us and was nodding her head vigorously. Then she laughed a little, said," Yes, absolutely." Nodded again and said, "I'm looking forward to it."

Laura turned around and waved us back over and handed the phone to me.

"You owe me big-time Matty-boy," Leah said.

Laura handed Wade a sheet of paper and we got out of there. I hadn't said a word to Leah until we were out of earshot.

"What the hell did you do?" I said.

"Told her I thought she was under appreciated at Van Dyke & Partners and that Seaview was always looking for great agents."

"No way."

"Absolutely. Agents *love* to work here. You know that during the twenty-six years my dad had the company, not one agent left? Some retired, but no one ever went to another real estate firm. And we don't just take on anybody."

"Would you really hire her?"

"Depends if she can deliver the goods."

Wade held up the piece of paper.

On it was Patrice's name, her new cell number, and her address.

61

"Hi, this is Patrice. You know what to do at the beep."

I did, but I didn't do it and just hung up the phone.

Wade was driving us over to Patrice's, a little one-bedroom apartment in Culver City, in the 900 block of Krueger Street.

"That's right near the studios," Wade said.

"Actually, *the* studio - Culver Studios. Some of the biggest movies Hollywood ever made, they made right there."

"You have a summer job as a tour guide in high school?"

"No, one of our neighbors when I was growing up, Huge Clayton, used to work there and he was always telling my dad the latest gossip. Who was banging who, how they had to pay off some cops and reporters to hide some big star's sexual inclinations or an attraction to uppers. So, I picked up a lot of stuff just hanging around."

"See you were in early training as a gumshoe."

"Gumshoe?"

"We're talking 1940s movies, I'z jest be usin' de vernacular. Boss."

I decided to ignore that. "Three of the biggest films right there– *Citizen Kane, King Kong* and…"

"*Gone With The Wind,*" Wade said. "Don't need no neighbor to know that."

"Okay, smartass. Did you also know that Lucille Ball got turned down for the role of Scarlett O'Hara?"

"So, did just about every actress in Hollywood at that time."

"Yeah, but Lucille was the only one that got even. Years later she bought the studio, turned it into her own *Desilu Studios*, and took David O. Selznick's office as her own."

"Don't screw with a redhead," Wade said. "Maybe including Patrice Fowler."

He turned off Culver Boulevard to Ince Boulevard and then made a left on Krueger Street.

"There it is," he said and pointed to a two-story yellow building that could only have been built in the 1950s when the California draftsmen that called themselves "architects" created the *moderne* style.

"So, what if *our* redhead's not home?" I said. "We wait?"

Wade looked at his watch. "I figure we give it an hour. By then Harbaugh and friends of the *Paraíso Del Mar* po-leece department be here. And we can go to one of those trendy restaurants on Washington and hope we be discovered."

"That was *Schwabs* Drugstore, which was on Sunset where Lana Turner was supposedly discovered by some hotshot talent scout. But that was just another Hollywood hype bullshit story."

"They didn't call it tinsel town for nothing. '*Such stuff as dreams are made on.*'"

"That was Shakespeare, not David O. Selznick."

"I know that. And I also know it's from *The Tempest*. And dey Bard be talking 'bout actors. So mah point be right on."

I dialed my cell.

"Now who you calling?"

"Laura."

She picked up and I said, "Hey, Laura, Matt Singer. Sorry to bother you, but we had one question .."

"Just one?"

"Just one, promise. You had the only key to Spinnaker. Did you have one made or was it an extra from the owner?"

"I had Patrice get a copy made at 1A Lock & Key–that's what assistants do."

"Thanks." And I hung up.

"When Harbaugh gets here, we're going to 1A Lock & Key."

"And why are we doing that?"

"Because I don't think Patrice had just one key made to Spinnaker. I'm betting she had them make two."

62

"Oh, yeah, she had two keys made. Paid cash."

John Lindsey, the owner of 1A Lock & Key remembered Patrice Fowler. "She blew in here like Katrina, 'Oh, my boss is going to kill me, please can you help me.' It only takes a minute to make a key, so I couldn't understand what the problem was."

"And you're sure this is her?" I said, having him look at the photo of Patrice again.

"Can't miss that red hair. And she came in wearing these dark sunglasses and kept them on. Then when it comes time to pay, she can't see in her purse so has to take them off. Then she just stares at me with those incredible blue eyes and gives me this kinda *poor me* 'smile."

John looked at the photo again.

"Patrice Fowler? Didn't know her name, but woman looks like that? You don't forget that face. I'm sure she's got men after her all the time."

"John was right," Wade said, as he drove us away from the locksmith shop. "Patrice does have men after her. Only not the way he meant it."

"You mean half the town's police force?"

"And us."

I looked at Patrice's picture. "Makes you wonder why she's gone down this road. She's extremely attractive."

"And Lo-Lo and Laura both said she was bright and had a great personality."

"But they both said after a while, she started making mistakes."

"Maybe she got a bug up her ass. And I don't mean termites."

"That was terrible," I said.

"You're a harsh judge."

"Maybe it was like Lo-Lo said, boyfriend troubles."

"Hard to see that being the first step down the road to murder."

"And to bring Shakespeare in again, *And thereby hangs a tale.*"

"More like that saying, 'When you're up to your ass in alligators..' " Wade said. "Because how the hell do you go from stealing a skirt.."

"Which may or may not be connected," I said, interrupting Wade.

"...to deciding that having sex in a house that's about to be fumigated is a smart idea," he said.

"Maybe she was into kinky."

He slowed down, checked the traffic both ways and did a quick U-turn.

"Where we going?"

"Scene of the crime. That's what we gumshoes do when we be on the trail for clues."

A few minutes later we parked a few doors up from the house on Spinnaker. We just watched the place for a minute with the sound of the BMW engine ticking as it cooled down.

"We are in a weird place," I said. "And I don't mean just because we're by the place."

"Go on."

"Well, so far, all we've got is maybe she stole Lo-Lo's skirt. Maybe. And maybe she made two keys. So what? Maybe she's just a smart assistant, planning ahead just in case one of the agents forgets to return the key to the lockbox."

"So why are we doing this? Despite all the maybes?"

"Why else?"

"Because we be gumshoes?"

"'Dere you go."

63

"Here she comes," Leah said to me on the phone. "Almost there."

We'd left Spinnaker and gone back to my office when Leah called and said, "In about thirty seconds you're going to have a surprise visitor. Actually, two."

My office door opened and the last person we were expecting to see was the most wanted woman in *Paraíso Del Mar*. Followed by Leah Lockhart.

"Thank you," Patrice said so softly I could barely hear her, "for doing this."

I wasn't sure what "this" was and looked at Leah.

"Patrice feels trapped and is afraid." Leah said. "She called Laura, who told her to call the police."

"Which I refuse to do," Patrice interjected. "So, then I called Leah."

"And here we are," Leah said.

I wasn't sure what Wade and I could do for Patrice.

"How can we help?"

"Just listen for now," Patrice said.

Listening sometimes was the worst thing you could do; because if someone said something incriminating, it raised so many ethical issues.

"Maybe you should hire us," Wade said.

"Great idea," I said. "Don't say anything, Patrice. Not yet." I went to my keyboard, hit the keys and then hit print.

Patrice looked at me, not understanding; and then looked at Leah.

"If you hire them, then anything you say is privileged and confidential."

"I can't afford a detective service."

"Sure, you can," I said; and handed her our standard form contract. I had filled in the payment amount for ten dollars."

Patrice scanned it quickly. "This is generous, but I don't need charity."

"I can make it a dollar."

"No, make it Something realistic."

"Just sign that for now, and we'll work out the amount later."

She took a pen from her purse, signed, and handed back the contract.

"Okay, first," I said, "do you have an attorney?"

"Marty Corran. But I haven't talked to him except when Steve...when this all happened."

"Tell me what happened," I said.

"First, let me start by saying that I didn't kill Steve Fordham. And second that

Steve is .. was .. a kinky guy. And that–being kinky–is why he died."

"Okay." That's about all I could say to that kind of an opening.

"For all of his smooth and good looks," Patrice said, "Steve had a twisted, dark side. It was his idea to do.." she gestured, somewhat perplexed as to having to put a name on it, "...to do...what we did."

"His idea? How'd that come about? I mean because I've got to admit, having..." And then I stopped, because I really didn't know what had happened inside Spinnaker, hidden by the red tents. I shrugged and waited for Patrice to continue.

"It started a couple months back. He hit on me while I was working for Lo-Lo. And I told him I couldn't betray her that way. And Steve says, *'But you would if you weren't working for her?'* And I didn't answer right away because I had to think about that for a moment. And then he says, *'Well, don't let that worry your pretty little face because Lo-Lo and I aren't long-term.'* But I still didn't...you know."

"But at some point, you did."

"A few weeks later. He came by the office when Lo-Lo was out of town, and one thing led to another and..." Patrice smiled.

"And you did it right there in the office?"

"On top of the fax machine. Which got a couple of interesting images while we were doing it."

I wasn't sure how detailed I needed this just listening part to be but didn't say anything.

"Then Lo-Lo came back and of course I was nervous and feeling guilty, but everything seemed fine. At least with Lo-Lo. But Steve? He didn't call, didn't return emails. Nothing. And finally, when he did come into the office to pick up Lo-Lo because they were going to dinner, it was like I wasn't even there."

I looked at Wade. Patrice's claim that she didn't kill Steve was looking a little shaky: she sounded like a jilted lover. And an angry one, too.

"A couple of days later he stops by, drops something off for Lo-Lo and just leaves. I ran out after him and caught him at his car and he says, *that* was our cover, total non-acknowledgement, so Lo-Lo wouldn't know."

Patrice shifted on the couch.

"I mean, I'm not Lo-Lo, but men *notice* me."

Wade and I made a quick eye contact: Roger *that*.

John Lindsey had spent maybe five minutes with her making a set of keys and couldn't forget her.

"So that non-acknowledgement was just a total bullshit story. He'd jumped my bones and had moved on."

Patrice didn't say anything for a few moments. I thought she might cry, she certainly looked sad enough.

"I don't know," she said, "then I started feeling really bad, so guilty."

"About the sex or about the skirt?"

Wade and Leah both looked at me: Asshole.

But it didn't bother Patrice.

"Both," she said. "And it obviously showed in my work. I was so distracted. I missed putting appointments in her calendar. And one time I completely forgot to meet a client at a showing. So, after about six or seven weeks of that, and Lo-Lo was so nice about it, gave me so many chances, talked to me, but I was a goner, she set up the interview with Laura."

"How long after you started working for Laura did she get the Spinnaker listing?"

"A month. Because a week or so before we got it, Steve called and said that he had broken up with Lo-Lo. And then we started seeing each other again. Not really *seeing* each other, like a couple, you know, going to dinner or to a movie. It was a friends with benefits arrangement. He'd come by at night. Late, usually after ten."

Patrice stared down at the floor and didn't look up when she said, "And I wasn't always sure where he'd been because a couple of times, he had this...this scent on him. From a woman. And I don't mean her perfume."

Patrice slammed the Sofa. "Jesus, what an idiot I am, such a loser."

She looked up at Leah, maybe for confirmation or to show the depths she'd sunk and the levels of abuse she'd acquiesced to: "I'm pretty sure one time I even smelled it on his fingers. But I didn't say anything."

"Would you like some water?" Leah said. "Or coffee?"

Patrice shook her head.

"And one of those nights I mentioned Spinnaker. And that it was a fast sale with just one code issue–the upstairs railing was too low and that was going to be an easy fix. And then I told him we were doing termite the next week. And that's when he came up with the.." Patrice made air quotation marks with her fingers, "..The Adventure."

"Just like that?" Wade said.

"Pretty much. Steve was always spinning out these crazy, wild ideas."

"Yes, but didn't you think it was weird?" I asked.

"Yeah, but the way he explained it, it seemed like it would be a hoot. A kick. And I was hurting. He hadn't come by for four days. I missed him."

"So, what happened?"

"We were like two kids watching from up the street while they put the tent up. Then when we saw them leave and go to lunch, we stuck inside. He wanted to do it upstairs on the balcony landing, because it has that upstairs picture window where you can just see the ocean. And..." she stopped.

"And what happened then?"

Patrice started crying. Not hard, just her eyes grew shiny and glistening, and several tears leaked out and down her cheeks.

"So, we...had sex. And I mean *sex*. Probably the most violent, passionate sex of my life. It was over pretty fast because, you know, we were both so excited for it. And then as we're catching our breath, he goes over to this bag that he'd brought with him. I'd asked him about it when he carried it inside and he said, '*Oh, that's a big surprise.*'"

"A bag?" I said. There was nothing about a bag in the police report.

"Yes, he had this sports bag with his name on it. I have it at my house."

That explained why it wasn't in the report.

"You know what was in the bag? Two gas masks."

That stopped everyone.

"Gas masks. He wanted to wait until they started pumping the poison and do it again."

"Holy shit," Leah said.

"I said no way, that's crazy. And then he went nuts. Started calling me a whore and a cheap slut. And I started crying because he'd humiliated me. And I moved to get past him, and he grabbed me, and I twisted away and then he slapped me. Hard and it hurt. And I just reacted and kicked out and caught him right in...the balls and he doubled over, yelling and I was so scared and angry, I pushed him. And he staggered back and I still don't know how it happened, but he hit the railing,..."

Patrice took a deep breath. "That railing, like I said, *was* in violation for the building code. That was one of the items for repair and part of the sales contract. You can look it up."

"So, he hit the railing," I said, already knowing what had happened.

"The *too-low* railing. And he...just went over...and it was like some slow-motion movie...he went down and his head hit the top of the banister...you know the..."

"The newel," I said.

Wade looked at me like: How do you know that?

"Right, the newel," Patrice said. "He hit it so hard. And his body just flopped to the floor, and even as I was running down the stairs. I knew he was dead. I felt for a pulse, but he wasn't breathing. I did CPR. I beat on his chest so hard. But nothing worked. And I was getting dizzy. So,

I ran back upstairs, got the bag with the gas masks and got the hell out of there. I re-clipped the tent and ran down the side yard."

"So. you're saying it was an accident?"

"Of course. Why would I kill him? I *loved* him."

"So why didn't you come forward and tell the police?"

"I was too scared." Patrice looked down at the floor, then back at me. "And I was too ashamed. I mean, who would do something like what we did? My God when this comes out."

We spent another hour grilling Patrice, asking details, trying to find the one lie in her story, the telltale linchpin that would pull everything apart.

But, in the end, we had to believe her.

The courts would come at her with all they had, which, in the end, wasn't much.

Because they'd try to prove that since Steve *was* breathing when Patrice ran away, she'd killed him. They'd cite all of Hal Bartkowski's forensic evidence–that his brain was swollen close to fifteen percent; and that his lungs were filled with fluid, his kidneys were congested. They'd trot out all that nasty data.

But it wouldn't stick.

Marty Corran was an excellent attorney. He'd blow the prosecution's case out of the water with a self-defense argument.

An argument that he couldn't really prove.

Nor the prosecution disprove.

Marty would point out that she had risked her own life to try and save Steve. He might even get some doctor to file a report stating that Patrice had slight scarring on her lungs and other respiratory tissues from her heroic actions. He'd bury them with paperwork.

Then they'd try to cut a deal, reduce the charge to involuntary manslaughter. But I didn't see that working out either.

The only hard evidence, unless there was another surprise waiting, was Steve's personal gym bag and the gas masks. And if his fingerprints were on the masks, she was home free.

Her testimony would be circumstantial and hearsay.

But it would be the *only* testimony.

The *only* suspect was the *only* witness.

And she would walk.

64

"I'm running the light," Wade yelled. "Hold on!"

I did.

And he did–jamming his BMW through the intersection of Highland and Wilshire, his hand on the horn, his foot on the gas. We shot through, Wade swerving around an old Ford Torino, its driver's startled face frozen in disbelief.

A crescendo of angry horns bleated behind us, but we were already fifty yards away, blasting towards the Hollywood Hills and the Temple.

And it wasn't Sunday.

We had been going downtown to meet with Famous and Antoine for our final Friday run-through for Operation Angel when my phone rang. The caller ID was blocked, but I answered and said, "Hello."

"Matt? Oh, Matt…"

"Sister Chastity? What happened? Are you okay?"

"He…hit…me." Her words were slurred, like she had difficulty talking with swollen lips, or maybe a concussion.

"I'm .. so…dizzy."

"Where are you?"

"Upstairs .. in the media room. I've…locked the door…but I don't…he left with Brother Victor."

"Wade and I are on our way. Where are the other Sisters?"

"Sister Felicity's here with me and Micah. He's so frightened. Please, Matt...hurry."

"Get the other Sisters. All of them and lock yourselves in that room."

"Okay."

"Call me if anything happens. *Anything*."

Wade had already taken the off-ramp and turned east for the Temple when I called Famous and told him.

"Goddamnit," Famous said. "Antoine and I will get there as fast as we can."

I think he put the phone to his chest, so when I heard him yell at Gonzo, it was a deep, rumbling bass. "Gonzo! Get the Angel gear. And call Bryan."

He came back to me, "Fifteen minutes, outside."

"We'll be there in ten."

"Matt, wait for back-up."

"Right," I said and hung up. I looked at Wade. "I think Brother Thomas and Brother Jonas are the only ones up there. You think we need back-up?"

Wade answered by putting the BMW into a tire-screaming turn and accelerated up *Los Tilos*.

Wade's car wasn't fully stopped, but we were sprinting for the front door. This time both the white dog and the cats got the hell out of our way. Wade slammed the door with his fist a couple of times. Nothing. He hit it again and I kicked it.

"Whoever's doing that, stop it." A voice came from inside, and then Brother Thomas flung open the door. I don't think he registered that it was Wade and me before Wade's fist hit him. He was going down when we ran past him.

"Sister Chastity," I yelled and took the stairs two at a time.

Brother Jonas came roaring around the corner. He had faster reactions than Brother Thomas and threw a fist at Wade.

That never landed.

Wade slipped the punch and elbowed Brother Thomas in the throat and the big man hit the floor like a beached whale, flopping around, gasping for air.

"Matt," I heard Famous yell from outside. "Matt."

But I was already at the top of the stairs.

"Sister Chastity. It's Matt."

A door opened at the end of the hall and Sister Chastity's swollen and bruised face looked out at me.

It was worse than I had thought. That son of a bitch had *beaten* her. The left side of her face had ballooned, and her eye was closed shut. She tried to smile through her battered lips, and I saw blood-stained teeth.

"Oh, Matt, thank you."

She collapsed in my arms and I held her close. Wade ran up and I could hear Famous coming up the stairs.

"Jesus," Wade said.

He eased past us and went into the room. I half-held, half-carried Sister Chastity and we followed.

Famous stopped behind us.

"God damn it, God damn it," he said.

"Please do not take Our Lord's name in vain," Sister Faith said.

"I didn't, Sister," said Famous. "I believe the Lord would damn *any* man who laid a hand on a young woman. Much less do *that.*"

Famous was enraged, but I could tell he was determined to maintain control.

"Sister," I said to Chastity, "we need to get you and the others out of here."

"What?"

"To someplace safe. And we need to do it now."

"But...but I can't leave. This is my...and Micah's...home."

"So, Micah *is* your child?"

"We are all his mother," said Sister Serenity.

Damnit, not now.

"Everything's secured," I heard Antoine say from the doorway. His automatic was holstered, but he looked ready to use it.

"I had to give the one guy CPR," Antoine said. "Whoever hit him ruptured several vertebrae in his neck. We need to call an ambulance."

"Brother Thomas," Wade said. "I'll go down and look at him."

Antoine held out a hand. "Gonzo's covering him. And the other Brother."

From outside we all heard the screech of brakes, car doors slamming open and a few moments later the pounding of footsteps up the stairs.

All of the Sisters were shocked to see Leslie Kent and Bryan Olliphant, wearing black body armor, armed and sure as hell dangerous, in their doorway.

"The van is right behind us," Bryan said, his reedy voice piercing, but filled with authority. "We need to go now."

He and Leslie moved into the room like black shadows.

"If you...Sisters will just follow me," Bryan said. He motioned toward the door, but none of the Sisters moved.

"We are not leaving the Temple," Sister Charity said. "This is our home."

Leslie went to Sister Charity, took her by the arm and moved her towards the back of the room. She stood very close to her and started talking in a whisper that none of us could hear.

"Sister Chastity," I said. "Brother Jordan is going to jail. The Temple is going to be closed. You and your son, and your Sisters need to be taken to safety." She started to protest through her bruised lips, but I held up a finger. "Listen to me, just listen." I raised my voice a little so the other Sisters could hear me too. "Brother Jordan is a charlatan. This Temple, this religion that he spouts, is just a cover for his real mission in life. That of a spy."

The Sisters gasped and Hope actually laughed.

"It's true," Wade said. "Brother Jordan's real name is Jon Michaels. He is an undercover agent for the FBI."

"Stop," Sister Hope shouted. "Stop this nonsense right now. Brother Jordan is a vessel for Our Lord and Savior Jesus Christ. His mission is to help us, to save us. And for all of us to help save as many others here on earth as possible."

Sister Chastity stared at me with her one good eye.

"Are you telling the truth, Matt?"

"I have no reason to lie. Your life and Micah's and all the Sisters are in danger. He works for the government. But I think he also works for another government."

"But he's always telling us how bad the government is."

"And he also preaches non-violence. And look at you."

I hated saying that, but this was time for the truth.

She tried to blink back the tears, but they flowed from her good eye and just kind of leaked out of her swollen one.

"What's next?" I said. "You end up like Sister Felicity?"

She took a deep breath and started to say something, but never made it.

There was heavy pounding down the hall and the rest of Bryan's crew arrived, plus the crew from the van. They swooped in, each man going straight for a specific sister.

Then Sister Charity turned from Jan and said very loudly, "Sisters! Do not resist. It's time for us to go. Now. We must follow these people. Hurry, please."

I looked at Leslie, whose face was impassive, but had the slightest glow of triumph.

Sister Chastity looked at me for confirmation and I nodded.

"Yes, please, go with them."

Then she reached up and kissed my cheek. "Goodbye, Brother Matthew. Thank you." She reached down and told Micah's hand and started for the door. Then she turned back and leaned close to me and whispered, "Anne Browne."

It took me a moment. "Anne Browne?"

She nodded.

"Nice to meet you Anne. I won't forget."

Then she followed Bryan and her Sisters out to the van.

Their future was lying open and waiting for them.

All they had to do was leave their past behind.

A journey that could take a lifetime.

65

"This guy's secret life had a secret life," Famous said. "Look at this shit."

We were in Brother Jordan's personal room.

After the black van had taken away the Sisters and the white ambulance had driven off with Brother Thomas, Antoine had marched a woozy Brother Jonas upstairs.

"Here, this is Brother's Jordan's room," Jonas said. The room was a mess. The bed was rumpled and looked like it hadn't been made up for a week. There were empty food cartons, several robes and clothing on the floor.

Famous checked the closets and Wade went into the bathroom. I tried a door that I thought was another closet, but it was locked.

"What's in here?" I said.

"That is Brother Jordan's personal sanctuary. No one is allowed inside. It is always locked."

Dave Higgins ran down to the van and returned with a battering ram. He and Blake swung it once and the door to Jordan's room went flying inside, taking the door jamb and part of the wall with it.

This room was the direct opposite of his bedroom. It was tidy, nothing out of place. But the most startling thing, and why Famous had said that Brother Jordan, aka Agent Jon Michaels, had a doubly secret life—was that this was the room of a *traitor*.

A huge poster of Satan dominated the room–a Satan whose face was the map of the United States. A poster of *Bin Laden* was on one side and on the other side, a blown-up photo of *Abu Jafar Al-Mufid*, an underground *Shia* leader who'd dedicated his life to annihilating America.

"Jesus," Bryan said, "This isn't part of his cover. This fucker is sick."

Leslie sat down at the computer and inserted a slick-looking thumb drive. She tapped a couple of keys and the monitor immediately started flashing and rows of numbers and symbols cascaded down in a blur of data.

Bryan picked up a bulky land-line phone and hit redial. An explosion of rapid-fire beeps burst from the receiver and he held it away from his ear. This was followed by a different series of whoops .. blips and then a voice came on and spoke rapidly in a foreign language.

Bryan thrust the phone to David Higgins, who spoke in what seemed like the same language. David listened, spoke again, listened, spoke, and listened again, said something final and hung up the phone.

"That call was to the city of Mashad, the second largest city in Iran. And we were speaking Pashto."

"About what?" Antoine said.

"He wanted to know where *Nouri Javeed* was and who I was. I told him my name was Brother *Yousef Habid*. I took a chance that *Nouri* was Jordan and told him that our good Brother was at the studio. He wanted to know why since it wasn't Sunday and I said that Brother Jordan didn't share that with us. He got a little nasty then, so I asked him who was talking to me in such a disrespectful manner. And he hung up."

"We've got to hustle," Famous said. "I'm sure the guy that called is dialing Jordan right now. And he'll be on his way back."

"Good," said Blake. "I'll wait."

"No," Bryan said, "we're shadows here. Leslie, you got what you need?"

"Thirty seconds," she said.

I picked up the phone and hit the menu. "Shit," I said.

"What?" Wade said.

"This phone should store at least forty numbers. There's not one on here."

"So...?"

"Clear," Leslie said. She popped the thumb drive and moved away from the machine.

"So…" I said, "I'll bet that Brother Jordan was lazy and didn't want to scroll through the numbers and…" I slid out the computer tray and bent down and looked under it. "And here they are." I carefully removed the adhesive tape from a sheet of paper and handed it to Famous.

"Gonzo, get tech support on the phone, scan that with your phone and send it to them."

Gonzo took a shot of it.

Then while Gonzo was dialing tech support, Famous said, "If we can get an address on those numbers, we might find out the other members of the cell."

"Should we call Kouros?" Bryan said.

"Absolutely," said Antoine. "In three days."

"I don't think you'll have to," I said. "Right after Jordan gets his call from Mashad, he's raising the alarm to Kouros."

"Okay," Bryan said, "If you touched anything, wipe it down and let's boogie."

I swabbed the underside of the shelf while Leslie did the keyboard and we pounded down the stairs and headed for Wade's BMW.

We got in and as he started the engine, Wade said, "Not like agent Kouros and Brother Jordan ain't gonna know somebody was in that room."

"You mean because of the door they destroyed?"

Wade accelerated out the driveway and shot down *Los Tilos*.

"Yeah. They be coverin' up mouse tracks when a damn rhinoceros done tramp through the room."

66

"We're ready to charge," Famous said.

He was crouched down behind his squad car, with Wade and me next to him. We were up the street from an old warehouse in the Chinatown section of L.A.

The street was sealed off at both ends by squad cars. Just at the perimeter of the loading docks, two S.W.A.T. teams were ready to swarm the place. The warehouse was where the first telephone number on the sheet was registered.

I saw the S.W.A.T. team leader hand signal the countdown...three .. two.. one.. GO! They exploded out of their positions and hit a small side door so hard with their battering ram that the door flew apart like matchsticks. They were right behind the door, screaming in attack mode.

Famous and Antoine sprinted out from behind their cars and ran into the warehouse. Wade and I kept our positions because, officially, we weren't supposed to be anywhere near this event.

Two minutes later, Famous appeared at the former door and whistled for us.

We ran as fast as we could and stopped when I saw his face.

"Fuck," he snarled. "Just fuck-fuck-fuck."

And a moment later I saw why he was so angry.

The S.W.A.T. team stomped back out, giving Famous angry looks of contempt.

Then out came the terrorists of Brother Jordan's deadly cell: Five tiny Chinese ladies who were at least fifty or sixty years old, all the poor dears scared to death, none of them able to speak a word of English. Along with them was an Amerasian man in his late thirties, and a thin Chinese woman holding a small infant.

"Please," the man said, "please do not shoot. We have our papers, yes."

About five teams of L.A. cops came up and took the group.

"That list was bullshit," Famous said. His cell rang. He took the call and walked away. But even from a few yards I could hear him say, "Fuck. God damn it."

He stomped back to us. "They're all bogus. Every one of them. The place in Burbank? The man that lives there's a German refugee, needs a walker to get around. West Hollywood? A Domino's Pizza."

"What's the point of doing that?" Gonzo said. "I mean to send us out on a wild goose chase?"

"To make us look like assholes. And to buy time."

Famous was right.

Brother Jordan and Brother Victor weren't coming back to the Temple.

They were in the wind.

67

When Brother Jordan landed, it was with claws out, striking right at the heart.

Famous's heart.

A week later, Famous called me, his voice strained with emotion. "Matt, how soon can you and Wade get here?"

"We're on our way now," I said as I grabbed my keys and Wade and I headed for my office door.

Thirty-five minutes later we were in a private room downtown with Famous and Gonzo. Famous had set up a monitor and held the remote in his hand.

"This morning, I go by my mother's house to pick up Meagan. And she's all happy to be coming back home, all that good stuff. And as we're driving back, she says, 'Oh, daddy, a man said to give you this.' And she hands me an envelope."

Famous shook his head, swallowed hard.

"So, I asked her, 'A man? What'd he look like?' My heart's already pounding. And she says, 'Oh, he was sooo cute. Had this beautiful long blond hair…'"

"Shit," I said.

"I asked her, 'He do anything? Touch you?' And she looks at me like I'm psychotic. 'No, of course not. He was just a very nice guy. And then, just before he walks off, he says, *'God bless your father.'* I thought that was so nice.'"

Famous pointed to the screen. "There was a thumb drive in the envelope. And this is what was on it."

There were several flashes and then there was Brother Jordan. He was wearing his white robe, his long blond hair flowing and shiny.

"Hello Detective Amos. And I'm sure your *compadres* Matt Singer and Jamal Wade. And your *Pancho*, Hey, Gonzo, how're they hanging?"

Jordan grabbed his crotch for the camera and then sat back down.

"I'll make this short since I have a plane to catch. The Lord sure works in mysterious ways, doesn't He? I know you won't bother trying to track this since it'd be a waste of time."

Jordan leaned closer to the camera, his voice dropped to a sinister whisper: "It's scary isn't it, Famous? There's your beautiful little daughter Meagan...and she *is* a beauty, maybe a little dark for my taste...hmmmm."

Jordan licked his lips, slowly, sensually, rubbing it in.

"So, where was I? Oh, yes, the lovely Meagan. And just like that, "Jordan snapped his fingers, "she'd have been mine."

"Fucker," Famous said, but didn't take his eyes from the screen.

"But that's behind me," Jordan said. "I leave with some sadness of course. All the muses–Hope, Faith, Serenity, Charity and Chastity, although she really didn't have much of that. And of course, the beautiful Felicity, mother of my son. Felicity screwed up my plans, going to the hospital."

Jordan sighed, flipped back his hair–very feminine, I thought.

"And believe me, I didn't mean for her to fall down the stairs. But as it's said in the second book of Timothy 4:17, *'I have finished my course.'* I know you hate those Biblical quotes, Matt, but they're great for so many things."

I gave a finger to the monitor.

"I assume you'll give this to agent Kouros. What a piece of work he is. *'Don't sleep Soundly America, if that's who's guarding your shores.'* By the time you view this, I'll be touching down in the New Land. It's been a real slice of heaven. Peace be with you."

Jordan moved to get up, but then sat down again.

"But just so you know, *Juan Amos*, I let Meagan go because of you. Yes, sentimental isn't it? Because beneath all that tough guy armor and your compulsion to control, you're really just a family guy. A Dad, for crying out loud. A Father who'd put his life on the line for his daughter in a heartbeat. So, I gave you a pass."

Then the tape went black.

Nobody said anything for a long, quiet, suffocating time.

"We already checked the airport tapes," Famous said. "And we got this." He tapped some keys on the keyboard near the monitor and security videotape came on the screen. There was a long line of people ready to board at the Lufthansa gate. "There, about five people from the gate."

He pointed with a laser at a man wearing a navy Yankees baseball cap, his long blond hair pulled into a ponytail that went out the back of the adjustable cap. We watched the man get closer. It was hard to tell if it was Jordan or not. Then, just as the man got his ticket and boarding pass cleared and was motioned to move forward by the airline attendant, the man looked up to the security camera and whipped off his cap and smiled right into the camera.

It was Jordan.

Famous hit pause, and Jordan's face loomed at us. Then Famous hit several keys and the picture zoomed into a close-up of the man's hand as he pulled the hat. "Son of a bitch, covered it up," Famous said. "See, he's got a big bandage over his hand, right across and over the palm."

"When did that flight leave?" I said.

"Flight 5770, left 12:30 A.M., two days ago. Two stops. One in Heathrow, the other in Frankfurt. We've asked for surveillance tapes from both places to see if he stayed on board, but nothing back to us yet."

Famous clicked off the monitor.

"Doesn't matter, he's gone," I said.

Again, none of us had anything to say right now. We all had to absorb this.

Finally, I said, "What's the game plan?"

"I checked with Kouros but didn't tell him about this. And the guy's worthless. He tells me that, *Agent Michaels has been reassigned. His location is classified.*"

"Classified, all right," Wade said. "As in we don't know where the hell he is or what happened, so we're going to bullshit everyone for as long as we can."

"Yeah," I said. "A day after we hit the Temple, Kouros called me. I'd set him up for a meeting on that Sunday, to get him out of the way, just in case..."

Famous and Antoine nodded: way to go.

"So, he calls," I continued, "and begs off. I missed the call, damn it, because I'd have loved to grind him. Kouros is history."

"And so is Brother Jordan," Wade said.

"I sure as hell hope so" said Famous. His face was tense, worried.

"He's not coming back, *Juan*." I said. "He doesn't have a reason. And he hates America."

68

"I absolutely *love* this." Leah said. "The coastland is so rugged and beautiful."

We were driving along the fabled seventeen-mile drive in Carmel.

After the shit storm of Brother Jordan and the Sisters, and Patrice Fowler and Steve Fordham's murder, Leah and I went north. We took advantage of the room service at the Pine Inn; and in a decades-later echo of Timothy Leary, dropped out of society for six days.

As we were leaving for home, we decided to go the *tourista* route and take the tour along some of the most majestic ocean scenery in America as the last part of putting the past events behind us.

But the past is never far away.

And when I got back to work, I was cleaning up and was about to close out the Dillards' file when Wade walked in and plopped down on one of the chairs in front of my desk. He'd brought coffees and blueberry muffins. Good man.

As we brought each other up to date, I looked through the file. Everything was in order except I couldn't find the photos of Brother Jordan. I pulled open drawers, looked on the floor, checked everywhere, Sometimes in the same place twice.

Finally, Wade said, "What the hell are you looking for?"

"Jordan's pictures, they're not in the file."

"You put them in another file?"

"When have I ever done that?"

"Always a first time for everything."

"No. And it was our only case, remember?"

Neither of us spoke for moment or so and then Wade said, "And no one would come in and steal them."

"No." I looked at him and didn't want to say the thought that had bubbled up.

"And the only other person that saw the file was…" he didn't finish his sentence and looked at me and shook his head slightly. "Andriel. Shit."

And just like that, there was an 800-lb gorilla in the room.

"Why the hell would she take them?" Wade said.

"I don't think she took them," I said. "Besides when could she have taken them? I think I'd know if someone broke in here."

But then maybe no one had to *break* in if they could just *let* themselves in–and I remembered the day Andriel told us she'd been called back to duty and was leaving that night. And I remembered that she'd said she'd left her phone back in my office and took my keys and ran back upstairs. I also remembered that she was gone for three or four minutes and then said she couldn't find her phone and had probably left it at Wade's house.

But that line of thinking could drive you nuts. And my own frank heart, unlike King Lear's, didn't want to go down that dark road where madness lies.

"It doesn't make sense," Wade said, echoing my thoughts. "And I'm not just saying that to protect my sister. It doesn't compute."

"Screw it," I said. "He's gone, good riddance."

"Yeah," Wade said. "That fucker dropped off the face of the earth; he can drop out of our files too."

And that was pretty much it for Brother Jordan.

Until…

Nine months later Wade and I were sitting in my office, having coffee and muffins when the mail came. There were some promotional flyers, a couple of bills, and standing out from the rest, both from its size and its origins, was a large, cushioned manila envelope.

It had been sent from Switzerland and didn't have a return address.

"You think some Swiss sent you a mail bomb?" Wade said. "Or anthrax?"

"Don't know, but considering I've never been there and they're pretty much neutral about everything except money, I think it's okay to open it."

I sliced open the envelope and out slid a record album.

Beggar's Banquet, one of the Stones' earlier albums. The cover was pristine. And still sealed in cellophane. I looked inside the mailing envelope but that's all it contained.

"This is an oldie but a goodie." I put it down on the desk and picked up my coffee cup.

"Aren't you going to open it," Wade said.

"Why? I don't have a record player, so why let it dust get on it? My dad loves the Stones; I'll give it to him."

Wade grabbed the album and slit open the edge with a thumbnail and shook out the record and held it by its edges. He hefted it. "A little heavier than the usual American product. Must be an original pressing done in Japan. That's where the top- quality records were made."

He handed the vinyl disc to me by the edges. It really looked brand new, but in today's digital and micro times, it seemed like some quaint artifact from an earlier, simpler era.

I put two fingers into the album's opening and was going to slip the record back inside when I noticed there was something else inside the record jacket.

How could that be? The album had been sealed in cellophane.

I carefully placed the record on my desk, then tilted the album cover and held it open:

Four objects slid out—one of them clattering brassily on the desk.

"What the hell?" said Wade.

I picked up a spent brass cartridge almost four inches long. I looked at the empty hole where the bullet had been: It was damn big.

Then I looked at the other three things.

They were color photos of a man. Or of what once *was* a man.

In the first photograph, there was a huge bloody hole where his left eye used to be. It was a grisly, gruesome sight. The rest of the facial features seemed so distorted, as if his skin and other organs had been pulled into the hole of his eye socket.

The second photo was the back of the man's head. Or what was left of it. If the bullet had left a big hole penetrating the eye socket, it had left a gaping maw on its exit, taking most of his skull and brains with it. The gore and mass made your stomach clench.

The third photo was of a man's right hand.

In the webbing between the thumb and index finger was a tattoo–a highly detailed *Janus* face: Jesus facing left, Mohammed facing right.

No denying it.

This was positive confirmed death of Brother Jordan/Agent Jon Michaels.

Neither Wade nor I said anything.

I picked up the cartridge again and looked at the back end. In the center was a deeply cut ring with the indentation from the firing pin in the center. Stamped along the edge of the ring were the letters "E" and "X"; and the numbers "9" and "2."

"Damn," Wade said. "Damn, damn, damn."

There was a long moment when he didn't raise his eyes to look at me.

Then when he did, he said, "Rhett Riley that sharpshooter from Georgia."

"Shit. Really?"

"You're thinking the same thing. You can say it."

And so I did.

"This 'E' and 'X' has to be for Exacto. The '9' and '2' must be factory stampings."

"No, I meant you can say Andriel."

There was a long, long silence while a hundred thoughts flew through both of our heads.

And then Wade and I spent a long time going through every kind of theory, explanation, or idea. But there was no way we could ever really find out because this wasn't anything Wade could ask Andriel. Or would even want to: "I'm just a sawbones," she'd said.

Not a dark ops agent.

I had Zak find out what he could–if the FBI had anything, if there were any reports of enemy dead or, since special agent Adams was, technically an American, any reports of Americans killed in Afghanistan, Iraq, Iran or any damn place on the globe.

Nothing.

We left it like that–nothing. No news, no reports.

I didn't say anything to Leah of course.

Wade and I told Charles Dillard but didn't show him the photos. Or tell him any of the details. Just that the man who'd killed his daughter was dead.

We knew he would get word to Oksana.

He told us that the adoption process had finally cleared two of the highest hurdles and that Oksanna and Fyodor would be home by Christmas. "I'll probably have to make a little donation to speed that process up, but it's worth it."

We told Famous and Gonzo and Antoine and showed them the pictures.

Famous didn't ask how or why, just said thanks. And while it might have been the sunlight shining through the windows of the restaurant, I thought his eyes were very bright and shiny.

Antoine didn't say anything. Just stared at the photos and rolled the discharged .50 caliber cartridge in his hand. It was hard to tell if his connection to Andriel had gotten stronger; or was shattered. He didn't ask any questions either, but he was too sharp to not know.

But...

...who can ever know the heart's darkest secrets?

If our own heart is a mystery to ourselves, how can we ever fathom the black depths of someone else's?

Did Andriel just get word to Rhett? Or make direct contact? How was it set up? Who sent the album? The photos? The discharged cartridge? And if Rhett took the shot, who took the other shots–the photos that confirmed the "kill."? One of them had been a long distance from Jordan, the other up close and personal.

Andriel was now full-time at Fort Belvoir, so maybe her trip from Afghanistan had included a detour in Switzerland.

You only had to meet Andriel once to know she was one of the best and brightest people, of either gender. And the bravest too. And she believed so fiercely and purely that an individual should be allowed to reach his or her fullest potential no matter what, that for Jordan to murder Charlene, and then assassinate the other Sister's Souls with his brain-washing deviltry, was a crime against not just women, but humanity. A crime that she took very personally.

That she took it to another level can't be justified.

Except to say that, sometimes, justice is its own reward.

And vindication.

And solace.

Because if revenge is best served cold, then retribution is best served hot and fast and silent from ten football fields away.

Yes, it was murder.

But war is murder, just done under the banner of your country's flag.

And I couldn't think of one person who was sorry that it had happened.

Not even Theo Kourous, whose career had vanished for his mishandling of Agent Jon Michaels, would be sorry. I wouldn't tell Kouros; not because he turned out to be such an asshole, so blind and proud, but because once he learned about Jordan, he'd try and find out how it happened and who did it and wouldn't be able to leave it in the past.

The people who knew were the people that *needed* to know. The circle was complete and closed. And we were all moving on.

And then, totally unexpectedly, I expanded the circle to include my dad.

We were finishing dinner when he said, "I'm thinking of going out to Forest Lawn tomorrow, see Ali."

"You want some company?"

He looked at me and then smiled. "You don't have to go, Matt."

"I know, but I'd like to."

"Good." He sipped his coffee, sighed, and said, "I read something the other day that Charles Dillard donated fifty million dollars to create a fund for runaways."

That was some 'little' donation I thought.

"That figures," I said. "Hopefully, that will help."

"I think it'll help the Dillards," my dad said. "Which is really the point. They went through a lot. That bastard Jordan. What a crap load of humanity. He raped Charlene, killed her. And got away with it. And then turned out to be a traitor to his country, too. Somebody ought to track down that son of a bitch and kill him."

"Yeah," I said. I took a sip of my coffee and thought, what the hell; especially given all the pain my dad still felt, and would always feel, about Ali and his empathy with the Dillards.

"You know, pops, somebody did."

"What?"

"Killed him."

He looked at me; both surprise and hope flickering across his face.

So, I told him.

He didn't say anything after I was done talking, just nodded his head.

"And so now the Dillards and Famous can finally have some peace," I said.

"A little," my dad said.

"A little? Jordan's gone, So, is the threat."

"Yes. And each day they'll get a little better. But the problem is that when someone like Jordan can get that close to your family and you know, deep down, you can't stop him, it stays with you for the rest of your life. You realize you were powerless in protecting your child. And as a parent, that's almost as bad as losing your child. It happened on your watch."

He drank some more coffee and said, "I'm thinking of going up in the late afternoon to see Ali, so maybe we should take two cars."

"Why? I can drive you back."

"I've got to go to my meeting."

"What meeting?"

"It's the first Wednesday of the month. And that's when I go to the Compassionate Friends meeting."

"Compassionate Friends?"

"It's parents who've lost a child of any age from any cause." He looked at me for a moment. "I've been going for years. You never noticed?"

"I don't think you've ever mentioned it."

"It's an amazing group of parents. We all come there and we...just talk. Some parents, and those are the ones you really feel for, have *just* lost their child and are so shattered. Not that any parent who's lost a child doesn't always have a crack in their heart, but those first few months and..."

His voice broke a little, not something I usually hear from my dad.

He took a sip of coffee.

"Mothers and fathers share their experiences, tell stories about what their kid was like, how they died, what they're feeling. Some parents have lost two children, sometimes very close together and.... God, I don't know how they do that. But we all share our stories and talk about our journeys. It helps, it really helps."

"It sounds great, Dad."

"It is Matt. Wonderful people. You should tell Charles and Oksanna about it."

"I will."

"Doesn't matter how much money, hell all the money in the world can't take away that pain. But if they go, I know it will help them. And I'm pretty sure there's a group near where they live."

I nodded.

"Then not too long ago I discovered this great website, *grievingdads.com*. This guy Kelly Farley started it, wrote a terrific book about it. Really wonderful. It's called *Grieving Dads*, but I'm sure moms read it too. Biggest point he makes is that we're all trained to be macho. '*Men don't cry.*' You know, like we're all goddamn Marines. But, sometimes, that pain is so incredible and deep, it consumes your life. The site helps because I can read about how other fathers feel." He sighed deeply. "We're all the same. Me, Charles, Oksanna."

I thought about that and agreed with my dad.

"You're right, pops."

And then I did something I don't usually do, but should, I put my hand on top of his and squeezed.

"I'm glad it helps you, Dad."

"*I morti Sono sempre con noi.*" he said.

It took a moment, but I translated, "*The dead are always with us. For all of our lives.*"

"Until we join them."

-The End-

About the Author

As an award-winning screenwriter, Jack Polo is a verbal camera, bringing the reader into the story with strong emotional "hooks" – family, love, honor and most of all, truth. *Paraiso Lost* is the second book in his "sunshine noir" series – where dark things happen in the bright sunlight of a rich beach town.

About the Author

NOTE FROM THE AUTHOR

Word-of-mouth is crucial for any author to succeed. If you enjoyed
Paraíso Lost, please leave a review online—anywhere you are able.
Even if it's just a sentence or two. It would make all the difference and
would be very much appreciated.

Thanks!
Jack

Thank you so much for reading one of **Jack Polo's** novels.

If you enjoyed our book, please check out the first book in the
Sunshine Noir series!

Death in Paraíso by Jack Polo

"...an entertaining, tense ride into a world
of lavish criminals and intrigue."
–*INDIEREADER*

View other Black Rose Writing titles at
www.blackrosewriting.com/books and use promo code
PRINT to receive a **20% discount** when purchasing.

www.ingramcontent.com/pod-product-compliance
Lightning Source LLC
Chambersburg PA
CBHW011130100726
47898CB00009B/2924

* 9 781684 335930 *